CW01506874

The Honey Trap

Rebecca Ambrose

HEADLINE
Liaison

First published in 1996 by
HEADLINE BOOK PUBLISHING

A HEADLINE LIAISON paperback

10 9 8 7 6 5 4 3 2 1

ISBN 0 7472 5169 X

Typeset by Avon Dataset Ltd, Bidford-on-Avon, Warks

Printed and bound in Great Britain by
Cox & Wyman Ltd, Reading, Berks

HEADLINE BOOK PUBLISHING
A division of Hodder Headline PLC
338 Euston Road
London NW1 3BH

The Honey Trap

Chapter One

Gayle Webster stood in front of her extensive wardrobe wondering what to wear for her meeting with Donna Lewis. It was always more difficult with the wives and girlfriends. If she'd been on an assignment it would have been something slinky, but the image she wanted to portray tonight was efficient, professional. Yet she also had to convince her prospective client that she was up to the job.

In the end she settled for a pink suit with a short skirt, a low-necked navy chiffon blouse and navy high-heeled pumps. Classic, but still sexy. She surveyed herself in the mirror: shoulder-length blonde hair brushed to a high gloss; subtle make-up that nevertheless accentuated the size of her dark blue eyes and full lips; curvy figure only partially disguised by the boxy lines of her suit; legs that owed their well-defined shape to twice-weekly sessions at the gym. Gayle sighed. It was so long since she'd had to dress up for a man. A man of her own, that is.

Donna was already waiting for her at a corner table in the restaurant. She was a pretty brunette but her face was ridden with anxiety, her brown eyes darting nervously about the place as Gayle walked up, pretending to greet her like an old friend.

'I hope this is all right for you,' Gayle said, lowering her voice. 'It's pretty quiet tonight.'

'Yes, it's fine. I'm awfully grateful, Miss Webster . . .'

'Gayle, please.'

'I've never done anything like this before, you see.'

Gayle smiled. 'Not many people have. I'd never dreamed of consulting an investigator myself until I found myself in the middle of a rather messy divorce. Shall we order?'

Until the food came Gayle continued with small talk, trying all the while to gain an impression of the woman's personality. She noted the edgy way Donna toyed with the cutlery, kept looking around the room as if she expected someone she knew to walk in any minute. Yet Gayle had the impression that, beyond her nervousness, there was a sweet and loving woman. She was clearly feeling insecure, tortured by doubts about her husband, Brad, but whether she had real grounds for suspicion remained to be seen.

Once the waiter had brought their dishes Gayle allowed the tone of the conversation to change. 'So, let's get down to business. How long have you been married, Donna?'

'Six years. We have two little boys, as I said, and I only started noticing things after Patrick, the youngest, was born.'

'What sort of things?'

'Nothing you could really put your finger on, I'm afraid. No lipstick on the collar. No love letters. But Brad didn't want to start making love again after my six-weeks' check-up. The doctor said it would be okay, and I thought he'd be pleased.'

'Does that mean you hadn't made love for . . . what, nearly a year?'

She nodded. 'I don't feel like it when I'm pregnant. But it wasn't only the lack of sex. Brad seemed more off-hand with me, like I was just an employee hired to look after his kids. Then he started coming home late from the office. He said he had to do lots of overtime, but when I phoned him at the office one evening there was no reply. He told me he'd popped out for a beer, but he sounded shifty. I know I could be wrong. I hope I am. But . . .'

'But you'd like to know for sure. I understand, Donna. Sometimes the uncertainty, the suspicion, is worse than the truth. Believe me, I've been there.'

Donna pushed away her plate. She had barely touched the food. 'So I thought if I could get someone to check him out I might find out if he was straying. Then I read about you in the local paper . . .'

Thanks, Jim! Gayle thought. All those drinks she had bought that reporter had at last paid off with some free advertising. The article had described her, euphemistically, as 'often going above and beyond the call of duty in her pursuit of cheating husbands'.

'So you rang me. Well, there are various lines I could pursue, some more costly than others. Have you given a thought to the budget?'

Gayle liked to be up front about payment from the start. Was Brad going to have to pay for his own fidelity test, she wondered, or did Donna have funds of her own?

'I have about a thousand pounds to spare out of my own savings,' Donna said. 'I'd rather not spend all of it, but if I have to . . .'

'Look, these are the options. We could start with some surveillance, or I could try to get information out of friends or colleagues. Both of those are open-ended, could go on for weeks and might get us nowhere. It depends what you want to know. I could find out if he's having an ongoing affair with someone more easily than if he's going for casual one-night stands.'

'I just want to know if he's still faithful to me,' Donna said miserably.

'In that case, I could test him out myself. I would meet him in a bar or somewhere and come on to him fairly strongly, see how he reacted then report back. Do you trust me, Donna?'

'Oh, yes! I know you'd only be doing your job.'

'It would be the quickest and cheapest alternative. But even if he responded to me, you still wouldn't know how many other women he'd bedded. Would you mind that?'

'If I could show I knew about him and you, he might confess the rest.'

'Or come clean about whatever's bothering him. You should consider the possibility that it might be something else entirely. Worry over work, perhaps. Or even a health problem. I could check out those areas too, only it would take time, and time is money in my job.' Donna was tearing her serviette into little strips beneath the tablecloth. Gayle reached over and touched her arm. 'Whatever you decide, I promise I'll do my best.'

Donna frowned. 'But what if he turns you down? I still won't know if there's anyone else.'

'I'll try to get as much information out of him as I can. And if he does respond I'll see how far he's prepared to go. I've had a lot of experience in this work and you'd be surprised how much men will reveal to a strange woman when they have a few drinks inside them.'

Donna still seemed uncertain, but when Gayle detailed the charges she made up her mind to go for a one-off encounter. Gayle questioned her about the best place to meet him, they shook hands on the deal, split the restaurant bill and went their separate ways.

As she drove back to her house in Chorlton, Gayle felt the usual mixture of elation and unease that accompanied taking on a new assignment. Women like Donna evoked her sympathy, yet she hated the idea of being the harbinger of bad news. Only her own memories of sleepless nights, furtive rummaging through pockets and eavesdropping on phone calls reminded her of why she had gone into this work in the first place.

A few days later Gayle received a letter from Donna containing details of the pub her husband frequented on Friday nights, a recent photograph and a cheque for a hundred pounds on account. While she didn't want to appear too mercenary Gayle knew from experience that an advance signalled both her determination to be paid for the job and satisfied the client that she was in this for the money, not for kicks. In the past people had made unkind and unfair allegations about her, sometimes insinuating that she must be some kind of nympho, or little more than a prostitute. Her attitude had consequently become more businesslike and down-to-earth over the three years that she'd been doing this work.

The Greedy Goat, on a Friday night, was full of lively Mancunian youth. They tanked up on ale then moved on to the club down the road where they danced till dawn. The regulars tended to congregate in The Snug, a small bar at the back of the pub. When Gayle entered, black leather skirt hitched high to expose her lean thighs and a skinny cropped top showing an inch of tanned midriff, she knew she would be taken for a 'raver' who had somehow got into the wrong bar. It would be up to her to spot the subject and move in on target quickly, before she got too many hostile looks.

Entering the quiet area of bentwood chairs and small, marble-topped tables, Gayle flopped down on a stool with a smile for the barman.

'Whew! It's so hot in there!' she declared, fanning herself with a beer mat. She looked around the room. The – mostly older – men were into serious drinking and didn't give her a second glance. There were a few wives or girlfriends, who looked at her with casual dismissal.

Gayle soon identified Donna's husband. He was sitting on his own and regarding her thoughtfully as he finished his pint. His photo hadn't done him justice. Brad Lewis was really quite a dish. Gayle had a brief impression of light brown hair and clear blue eyes, a broad chest and long legs. She flashed him a quick smile then turned back to her tonic water at the bar, making sure that most of her right thigh was exposed.

It didn't take him long to come sauntering up with his empty glass. Standing next to her at the bar he gave her a sidelong smile. She decided to take the initiative.

'It's much quieter in here, isn't it? I was supposed to meet someone at eight. Oh well.'

'I can't imagine anyone not turning up for a nice girl like you.'

His voice was soft and low, almost conspiratorial. Gayle gave him a full smile, saw his eyes light up with interest. 'It's no big deal. I prefer the company in here anyway.'

A hand with long, lean fingers was held out to her. 'My name's Brad.'

'Good to meet you, Brad. I'm Sharon.' Gayle never used her own name on jobs like this.

'What are you drinking?'

'Same again, please.'

She gambled that the barman would not reveal that she was only drinking tonic. Brad ordered himself another beer and they took their glasses back to the table he had vacated. Gayle crossed her legs, offering him a glimpse of red silk panties as she did so, and saw his pupils dilate. Her own libido was rising now, despite her determination to remain neutral. Careful! she warned herself.

'So, Brad, do you live round here? Is this your local?' she asked, when they were settled.

'Oh no,' he lied. 'I'm from the other side of town. Hazel Grove.'

'Really? I used to live there once. Maresfield Road. Do you know it?'

He frowned. 'Can't say I do. Where do you live now, Sharon?'

He's getting out of line, she thought. Must pull him back on track. 'Actually, I don't live in Manchester at all. I'm visiting relatives. Going back to Sheffield tomorrow.'

She knew that if he was into one-night stands that would make her enormously appealing. Was it her imagination, or was he edging a little closer to her, showing a tad more interest?

'Nice place, Hazel Grove,' she continued. 'Good place to bring up a family. Do you have a wife and kids?'

'No, I'm . . . divorced.' He hesitated, but only for a fraction of a second. Gayle continued to survey him coolly, waiting for the next clue to his state of mind.

'Me too. Guess I'm not cut out for long-term relationships. I prefer to play the field.'

More bait. He downed his beer swiftly and she watched his Adam's apple jolt up and down. God, but he was attractive. Even without the benefit of alcohol Gayle could feel her pulse rate was up, her hands slightly moist and the dark chasm between her thighs even moister. For the first time she felt uneasy about this assignment, unsure if she could maintain the necessary self-control when the time came.

'Very wise. You're still young and beautiful. Time enough to settle down when you're past your prime. Of course, it's easier for men than it is for women.'

You can say that again, Gayle thought. Time to probe a bit more. 'What do you do then, Brad?'

'I'm in computer sales. Software, mostly.'

'Really? Does that mean you travel about the country a lot?'

'Not a lot. Most of my calls are in the Greater Manchester area. But let's not talk about work. You look like you're dressed for dancing. There's a hotel I know, has a disco in the basement. Not that ghastly house music, proper tunes. Fancy it?'

Gayle knew that what he really meant was, 'Fancy *me*?' And she didn't have to put on an act when she smilingly agreed to go with him. They drove there in his silver convertible, their knees touching intermittently all the way, and she felt the old itch in her groin growing stronger. Think of Donna, she told herself. But she had to get proof, real proof, that Brad was prepared to be unfaithful to his wife with a total stranger, and that meant going along with him until she had all the incriminating evidence she needed.

'You know, I thought tonight was going to be just another boring night out down the pub. Just shows how wrong you can be.' He grinned at her as they pulled up outside Dene's Disco Den in the basement of the Hazeldene Hotel. Boney M filled the air. Gayle winced.

The cellar bar was filled to bursting with thirty-some-things, shaking their booty like there was no tomorrow. Brad put his arm around Gayle's waist and swung her into the midst of the throng, proceeding to dance very close to her in a slow, sinuous style that made up in sensuality for what it lacked in rhythm. Their hip bones clashed from time to time as they swayed in close proximity to each other and, beneath the familiar scent of male sweat, Gayle could smell the tang of fresh aftershave that he must have sprayed on surreptitiously before leaving the car. His eyes were staring at her in soft focus, his lips mouthing the words of the song as if he needed to keep them occupied. She could tell he was hot for her. Little pearls of perspiration had broken out on his brow and Gayle could feel her cleavage getting hot and sweaty too, making a damp patch in the cotton top.

'Whew! Could we get a drink, please?' she asked him, as one tune faded into another.

'It is a bit clammy in here.' He glanced towards the small crowded bar where a single barmaid was struggling to keep up with the orders. 'Shall we go up to the hotel lounge?'

Gayle nodded, confident now that he had something other than dancing and drinking in mind. She'd had enough experience of men on heat to recognise the signs. In the quiet, elegant upstairs bar he stretched his arm along the sofa behind her as they sipped their drinks.

'Ever stayed in this hotel?' he asked suddenly. She shook her head. 'Well, I have. Years ago, before I came to live in Manchester. You get pretty good service. Nice rooms, too. Kingsized beds in all the doubles.'

The crunch was coming but, before it did, Gayle had to do something. She excused herself and went out to the ladies' in the entrance hall. When she returned, the minute digital tape recorder in her bag was switched on, prepared to record up to two hours of conversation with its ultra-powerful microphone.

'It does seem a nice place,' she smiled as she slipped back into her seat. 'I thought I might stay here next time I visit my sister, as her house is so crowded with the new baby. The receptionist said there are always rooms free at this time of year.'

'Like tonight, for instance?'

He was very close, his right hand dropping over her shoulder to lightly brush the bare skin of her upper chest. Gayle's senses were on full alert, listening for his heartbeat, smelling the musky odour of his arousal, feeling the touch of his fingertips. She was equally aware of her own reactions as her nipples hardened and her labia swelled around her humid cleft.

'Tonight?'

'Yes.' His voice became soft, cajoling. 'You and me.'

Gayle gave an excited giggle. 'Oh no. We shouldn't.'

'Why not?'

'Well, I hardly know you for one thing.'

'But sex is so much more exciting with strangers, don't you find?'

'You mean you've done this sort of thing before?'

'A few times.'

'In this hotel?'

He grinned at her, showing his dimples, his eyes wide and electric blue. 'Maybe.'

It should have been enough, Brad's proposition on record. But Gayle knew from experience that most women wanted more. They needed to know that their errant husband or boyfriend would back his words with deeds. Sometimes actual sex had to take place so that evidence could be gathered for a divorce case.

Gayle felt his hand stroke the top of her breast and knew that he would go further if she encouraged him, much further. She giggled again. 'Well, I don't know about this.'

His lips whispered, 'You want me, don't you? I can tell.'

She felt his tongue-tip trace the inside of her ear, sending shivers down her back. 'Yes, but I don't know what to tell my sister. She thinks I'm going back to her place tonight.'

'Give her a ring. Tell her you've met an old school friend

and you're staying the night at her place instead.'

'You're good at alibis, aren't you?'

He grinned. 'I've had plenty of practice.'

'Okay. I saw a phone in the hall.'

While she pretended to call her imaginary sister, Brad made the reservation at the desk. Gayle felt a knot of excitement unfurl in the pit of her stomach as she contemplated going upstairs with him, letting him begin making love to her. She had her escape plan, of course. But what if it all went wrong?

'Ready?' He was coming towards her now, smiling with all the cocksure confidence of a man about to score. Gayle found herself wondering about his body, his prick. She mustn't let things get that far, of course. Still, it was exciting to speculate.

They took the lift up to the third floor, room twenty-eight. Everything inside was giant-sized: the bed, the TV, the double wardrobe, the panoramic window over the park. Brad eyed her lasciviously, came towards her the second she closed the door behind her and took her roughly into his arms.

'You're a hell of a girl, Sharon!' he murmured, his lips on her throat. 'Great ass, great legs, great boobs. And I bet you've got a great cunt too!'

Gayle hadn't expected such crude talk, but she wasn't fazed even though it sent her sexual temperature rising. Smiling faintly she put her hand down his waistband and felt his firm taut bum. He wriggled and sighed, his lips travelling down her cleavage until his face was nuzzling her breasts. Inside the leather bag she'd flung onto the bed, the tape-recorder was still rolling.

'Why don't you lie down?' she suggested, pretending to stumble. 'I'll take your shoes off for you.'

'And the rest!' he grinned.

'Okay.'

That suited her plan. A nude man would be less likely to come in hot pursuit of her when she made her getaway. Gayle stripped him to his underpants and saw the solid dimensions of his tool, lying diagonally. 'See the effect you have on me?' he boasted. 'Now it's my turn to get your kit off. I can't wait to see you in the buff.'

He sat up and made a grab for her tits. Gayle forced a smile. 'Just a minute, Brad. I have to use the bathroom.'

'Well make it quick. I'm going to roger you senseless when you come out of there.'

There was enough on the tape now, surely? Gayle took her bag into the adjoining bathroom and closed the door. She took a pee then, under cover of the flush, played back a few inches of tape just to make sure she had a good recording. Satisfied, she replaced the machine in her bag and took a deep breath. It was time to make a run for it. Slowly she opened the door a fraction and peered through.

As she'd expected, Brad was still lying on the bed with his eyes closed and his hands behind his head. His face bore a faint smile and she guessed he was fantasising about what he would do to her. For a split second Gayle wished that this was for real, that she was free to play along and indulge in wild, abandoned sex. But this was business, and she'd almost forgotten what pleasure felt like.

The element of surprise was crucial. Gayle flung back the bathroom door and made a dash for the exit, but to her horror Brad leapt from the bed and pulled her to the floor in a flying tackle.

'Changed your mind?' he growled, biting with soft emphasis into her neck. 'I thought you might, but it's no good trying to escape from a rugby player! Come on, sweetheart, let's see what you've got to offer. You didn't really think I'd let you go now, did you?'

He was pulling the clothes off her, dragging down her skirt, whipping the top over her head. Gayle cursed the fact that she'd turned off the recorder. She might have had him for rape. Yet even as the thought entered her head she knew that would be unfair. The knowledge that she wanted him, had desired him ever since she first set eyes on him, was making her cream herself now, sending voluptuous currents of pure lust swirling around her innards, opening her up to him.

The red silk knickers were on the floor, exposing her fluffy dark blonde bush and the full, pink lips to his avid gaze. Before she could register what was happening his mouth had fastened on her open vulva and he was sucking at her like a piece of melon, siphoning off her juices, probing with his tongue into the warm, wet cavity. Gayle gave up all thoughts of fight or flight and squirmed with lust, forgetting everything but the immediate sensation of blissful acquiescence. She looked up at Brad from where she was spread out on the carpet, his hands about to force an entry beneath the taut casing of her bra, and felt the first stirrings of an orgasm gathering in her belly like a coiled spring.

His groping fingers managed to get inside the cups and fasten on her bulging nipples, pinching them to even greater prominence. Gayle felt the fastenings ping at her back and the bra hung there useless as he plundered it to get at her breasts. She sighed to feel his hands on the smooth mounds of her flesh, squeezing and stroking, pleasuring her as well as himself. His face surfaced from her pussy long enough for him to breathe, 'God, Sharon, my dick will burst if it doesn't get inside you soon!'

Gayle saw him tear off his pants and his penis sprang up like a dowsing rod, pointing at her cunny. It was huge and angry, purplish-red at the tip. He groped for a condom and she shuddered at the thought of it driving into her deeply, forcefully, over and over again until she came. It had been such a long time since any man had done that. How could she have forgotten how good it was, how utterly irresistible?

Brad didn't thrust straight in but teased her for a bit by letting his glans hover at the entrance to her cunny, like a shy visitor. She could both feel and hear him squelching in her juices, making her overflow with lubrication, readying her for penetration. Now she wanted it cruelly, her clitoris pulsing out its signals with increasing frustration as his hands fondled the deep pink tips of her breasts to their maximum firmness.

Gayle would never have believed herself capable of begging for it but, taken to the limit of her endurance, she heard herself plead, 'Now, Brad, for heaven's sake. Come into me *now*!'

To her utmost relief he obeyed, sliding smoothly down the length of her like a vessel being launched down a slipway, and uttering a long, satisfied moan as he did so. She clasped him to her with everything she had: arms, thighs, tight vaginal walls. He filled her like a dream. At the top of her pussy her clitoris throbbed against the thick root of his shaft, waiting for the rub. Slowly he pulled up and out, his hardness caressing her sensitive tissues until he was poised to descend again. This time his thrusting continued, giving her the rhythmic pounding she craved, gathering force and speed.

'Oh, Brad!' she heard a faraway voice exclaim as the spring in her belly quivered and let rip. The release filled her with hot spiralling bliss, shooting stars that exploded deep inside her and left glowing trails behind them. His pace quickened then slowed as the fire spewed out of him, propelling him into the same timeless space.

Afterwards they flopped where they lay on the deep-pile carpet, unable to so much as crawl over to the comfort of the big bed, both of them utterly spent.

Sometime in the night Gayle must have crept into bed because, when she awoke, that was where she was lying, alone. Brad was still sprawled, face down, on the floor. By the light of the bedside lamp Gayle managed to find the hotel key and she hastily dressed then let herself out. The cool dawn air revived her and she soon hailed a cab to take her home.

Back in her Chorlton semi, Gayle stripped and got under the shower until she was thoroughly cleansed. She needed it, she felt unclean. Tonight she had made a big mistake and even if she were never found out there would always be that nagging memory to haunt her, the memory of the night when she had let her animal passions usurp her professional control. Thinking about it now she felt sick. How could she have been so stupid?

Putting on a clean cotton nightie, whose long sleeves and buttoned-up neck provided an appropriately penitential garb, Gayle lay in bed trying to understand why she'd let things go so far. Brad had been attractive and persuasive, but so had several other straying husbands that she'd targeted. Hitting the playback button of her recorder, she sought clues in the steamy exchanges between them but only succeeded in getting herself worked up again. At least there was enough incriminating evidence on the tape to convince Donna. Waves of guilt washed over her as she thought of Brad's wife. Had she made matters worse, instead of better? Sighing with remorse, she turned over and attempted to complete her night's sleep.

* * *

Gayle felt a guilty pang as she drove past the Greedy Goat on her way to Donna's house. It was the middle of the afternoon and Brad was at work so she was quite safe, but the memory of meeting him there left a nasty taste in her mouth. Beside her, on the front seat, was her bag containing the recording. There was plenty of damning conversation on the tape and Gayle still wished that she'd left it at that and not let her seduction of Brad reach its logical conclusion. What on earth had made her go that far? She still didn't know.

Donna lived in Burnage, near one of Manchester's few hills. There was a kiddy's trike and a football in the front garden. She rang the bell with a heavy heart, sorry to be the bringer of bad news. Still, she'd only been doing her job. Donna answered the door looking drawn.

'Come in, I've just put the kettle on,' she said, unsmiling. A toddler stared up at Gayle as she followed down the hall, big blue eyes beneath a yellow fringe. Her depressed mood deepened. She tried to tell herself that it wasn't her concern if Donna's marriage crumbled, that she shouldn't get involved. But two little boys! It was always the kids that got hurt worst.

'Put the telly on, it's time for your programme,' Donna told her son, who toddled off into the next room. 'My eldest is at school,' she explained. 'Tea or coffee?'

Once the drinks were poured, Gayle placed the battery-run recorder on the kitchen table. 'I hope you're ready for this, Donna. It's not good news, I'm afraid.' The woman nodded, obviously trying to prepare herself. 'We met in the pub and then he suggested we should go to a disco. It was in the basement of a hotel.'

'Which hotel?' she asked, her voice grimly even.

'The Hazeldene.' Again Donna nodded, knowingly.

'Anyway, he suggested we should book a room for the night. I tried to back out, but he was very persuasive. I'm sorry.'

'He booked the room? Paid for it, and everything?'

'As far as I know. I went up with him, let him go so far . . .' She tailed off, unwilling to lie. Instead she pressed the play button. 'You can hear for yourself.'

Donna sat through it stony-faced. At the end she said, simply, 'How much do I owe you?'

'I've made out the bill.' She found the envelope in her bag and handed it over. Donna's face showed no expression as she reached for her cheque book.

'I don't suppose you'll be needing my services again, not now you've got the proof you needed,' Gayle said, watching her write out the cheque in a careful hand. 'But in case you do, I'll leave my card.'

'Thank you. I intend to divorce him, you know. I'd already decided that.'

'I wouldn't be too hasty if I were you, Donna. Think of your boys.' She took the cheque, thanked her and rose. 'You might try contacting Relate, seeing a counsellor. The courts prefer you to try reconciliation these days. For the sake of the children.'

'Thank you, Gayle. If I need you again I'll give you a ring.' Her tone was dismissive, suggesting that she wanted to be alone with her feelings.

The same applied to Gayle. Driving home, she wondered yet again why she had allowed herself to get so stupidly caught. She had behaved in a shamelessly unprofessional manner, yet what disturbed her even more was the memory of how she had felt, fucking a guy she'd only just met and who meant nothing to her. It had been bloody marvellous!

Chapter Two

'She says she still loves me, and all she needs is some space for a while.'

Harvey Boyd had heard it all before. He tried to seem sympathetic as the poor bastard went on about how much he loved his fickle fiancée, but he needed all his acting skills. He would rather have advised his client to get out while the going was good, find someone more ready to commit, but then he'd be talking himself out of a job.

'Okay, so she goes out with her girlfriends on Friday nights. I can't see the harm in that,' Harvey said. It was clear he was dealing with some degree of obsession here and that could be dangerous. More than once he had been violently attacked as the bearer of bad news.

'I just need to know if Mandy's playing around.'

Chris Laughton was in his thirties, and ready to settle down. He had a good job, a house of his own and a steady girlfriend to whom he was unofficially engaged. Harvey didn't think checking up on her was a good idea, but he was the hired hand and would do as he was told.

'Okay, I think our best bet is surveillance but it could become expensive. Could you give me some idea of how much you're prepared to spend?'

'I thought a few hundred.'

'Hm. Let's start with one evening and see how far that gets us, shall we? Now tell me what you know about these hen nights. Where does she meet her friends? How does she get there?'

'She doesn't use her car. They meet in the Crown, have a drink and go on from there to a disco or a club. It's what happens after that I'm worried about.'

'Okay. Do you have a photograph?'

Chris fished one out of his pocket. She was a classy tart all right, but with dyed blonde hair. Nice eyes and mouth, good figure. The kind of woman he might have dated himself, once upon a time.

So Friday night found Harvey waiting in his car opposite the large Victorian house where Mandy had her flat. It was eight-thirty; he'd been there an hour and a half and so far nothing had happened. God, he hated surveillance work! Interviewing was what he was best at, sizing up a subject, getting into their heads and under their skin.

Sometimes Harvey wondered if he was cut out for this work at all. He had drifted into it when he was dismissed under a cloud from the police. As an ambitious young detective he'd been tempted to flout the rules for the sake of quick results and been accused of entrapment. Most of the others had done similar things but perhaps he hadn't been as good at covering his tracks. Or else they'd been better at hiding their contempt for their superiors. At any rate, he found himself out of the force at thirty-two and more or less unemployable.

It had been hard at first, having to take on every case, even the non-starters and obvious nutters. Gradually he'd been able to be more choosy. He was building up a good record with child custody cases, which at least made him feel that he was doing something worthwhile. Jobs like this latest one were a piece of cake, but not nearly so satisfying.

A cab drew up outside number thirty-seven. Harvey was instantly on full alert. The door opened and Mandy appeared, wearing a pink mini-dress with a long black cardigan and strappy, high-heeled black shoes. She was fully made up and had dangly gold earrings. If he hadn't known otherwise, Harvey would have assumed she was meeting her boyfriend.

He drove up the street a little way, made a right and then another until he came out into Mandy's road. He waited until the taxi drew away then began to follow. It started up the Stockport road in the direction of the city centre. Harvey got into the stream a couple of vehicles behind. Ideally he would have had a colleague in another car to back him, but this was a low-budget job. Fortunately he knew the taxi firm. Josh, the black guy who ran it, had helped him out before and would tell him Mandy's destination if need be.

This time he was in luck. He tailed the cab all the way to the Hanky-Panky pub, which he suspected had been named as a disrespectful jibe against Mrs Pankhurst, the founder of the first Women's Liberation movement, who had lived nearby. One day he would check it out.

Tonight, though, he had another liberated woman's movements to check out. He parked nearby and waited until Mandy had entered the building. A banner on the front of the pub proclaimed that it was a 'Ladies Only Night' upstairs in the large function room. The downstairs bar was open to all, however, and that was probably where she was meeting her friends. Harvey wondered whether he would need his camera or pocket tape recorder. Probably not, but he decided to take them anyway.

Harvey was in luck: an old mate of his – another ex-cop – was on security duty that night. He stood next to Bob at the door for a while, surveying the scene. Mandy was with two other girls at the bar.

'What gives?' Bob asked him. 'Are you on duty here too?'

'Kind of. Keeping watch on someone's missus.'

'Bit of a comedown after busting villains, isn't it, Harv?'

Harvey shrugged. 'It's a living. How about you?'

'I prefer this to being in the force. You get to chat up more women!'

'Yeah. I seem to recall that's why they busted *you*!'

Bob laughed, glad to be thought of as a womaniser. The banter over, Harvey made his request, keeping his voice low. 'If I needed to take a peep upstairs, could you get me in?'

'Only if you put on a posing pouch, mate! They've got some Chippendales-type act on for the girls. Better take your earplugs, too.'

'Is there any way I can get to see what's going on?'

'Projection room. They show movies up there, local film club. You'd get a view of the whole show.'

'Audience too?'

'You betcha. Grab yourself a beer and I'll take you up there, but we'd better be quick. The stairs will get crowded once they start letting them in.'

'Thanks, pal. Anything I can get you?'

'I'm not supposed to drink but I could murder a Boddy's. Get an extra bottle.'

Clutching the beers Harvey followed Bob up the stairs, glancing in at the empty room as he did so. There were a few chairs and tables dotted around the sides but the main floor area was clear. A couple of hunks stood in the middle of the room surveying the stage and arguing about something with a fat, balding man.

'The slaphead is Reg, the manager,' Bob explained. 'Better keep out of his way.'

The projection room was small and hot, but the shuttered window offered an excellent vantage point. They sat in the dark space swigging beer until Bob said he had to go.

'You'll be okay up here.'

It was more of a statement than a question. Harvey nodded. 'Thanks. I owe you one.'

'Don't worry, I always call in my debts!'

Harvey was bored at first, but once the women started to flock in he began to practise his observation skills. It was easy to tell which of them had been to a show like this before and which were there for the first time. The bold ones egged on their more nervous friends, assuring them that they would have a great time. Most of them had brought drinks up from downstairs and an atmosphere of heady excitement was building even before the performers appeared. There was disco music blaring out, getting them in the mood, and some of the women were dancing in a wild uninhibited way, showing off their wobbling breasts and shaking bums. Harvey felt his dick start to respond to the wave of female energy that was wafting up from below. His balls felt hot and heavy.

At last he spotted Mandy and her friends. A fourth girl joined them and they quickly formed a tight knot of suppressed excitement near the stage. Mandy seemed perfectly at home in the crowd and he guessed she had been to this kind of event before. It seemed harmless enough to him, but he would have to check out what happened later. The show was specifically designed to get the female libido going. What happened to these rampant women at the end of the evening? Not all of them would be going home for sex with their husbands and boyfriends, that was for sure.

There was a drag act first, by way of a warm-up. Harvey felt sorry for the tacky Madonna look-alike miming to 'Like a Virgin', who was greeted with boos and catcalls from the impatient crowd. When two bronzed and muscular guys came prancing onto the small stage there was a great uproar from the women. They screamed and roared, stamped and whistled, shouted encouragement and obscenities. Harvey had never witnessed such a display of sexual aggression in his life and it was frightening. He was grateful for his dark hideaway, vague memories of ancient Greek myths returning to haunt him: men torn to bits for daring to spy on just such exclusively female rites as these.

How can they get so worked up over a pair of fake-tanned greaseballs, Harvey wondered, as the men began to wiggle their tight arses and flex their over-pumped biceps. Their faces were like mahogany masks, grins stretched permanently wide, eyes unnaturally bright. He watched them lower their bulging torsos to the deck and do a series of press-ups. You could hardly call them strippers, they were stripped almost naked already. Stripped and ripped. One had long black hair in a pony-tail, the other had a mass of blond curls. The women were reaching out for them, begging for a grope. Those guys had to be quick on their feet or their tackle would be out on display in no time.

But it seemed the men were prepared to sail close to the wind. The blond guy beckoned a woman up on stage, one of Mandy's friends, and handed her a bottle of massage oil. Blushing, she massaged the grease into his sculpted pectorals while he continued to grin at the crowd and they hooted their approval. Her hands moved to his flat stomach and the uproar increased, with cries of 'Get in there, girl!' and 'Lower, lower!' filtering up to where Harvey was. The dark guy called another girl up on stage, a cheeky-looking redhead who made a grab for his lunch packet. He dodged, knelt down on one knee and invited her to bend over his other knee while he playfully pulled up her mini-skirt and slapped her lace-trimmed bottom, much to the delight of the audience.

Some of the women were taking off their panties and throwing them into the air. The blond guy caught a black nylon pair and wiped his sweaty brow with them, then threw them back into the heaving, screaming throng. Two women fought over them and got half each. Then the other poser decided to go one better. Picking up a pink satin pair he thrust them into his pouch and rubbed his tackle with them, grinning and rolling his eyes as he did so to the ecstatic delight of the crowd. When he threw the musk-laden knickers back they were ripped into several pieces and Harvey noticed that Mandy got one of them. She stuffed it into her cleavage, grinning at her mates.

The atmosphere was heavy with the scent of female arousal and some of it was getting through to the projection room. Watching all those women getting hot in the crotch, Harvey felt his cock harden massively. He could see Mandy shouting, egging on her friend, blonde hair streaked across her sweaty brow. It was getting too much for him: he was feeling the heat in more ways than one. Realising that she couldn't get up to much while the show was on, he left the stuffy little room and went back down to the bar for another beer.

When he returned, the fair-haired guy had been stripped of his leopardskin pouch and was now wearing what looked like a black condom. He was well endowed – presumably that was the main qualification for the job – and the girls were going wild as he swung his tackle round in time to the music. The blond fella had his back to the audience and was flexing his lean buttocks rhythmically. What a pair of plonkers, Harvey thought. No self-respecting man would do that for a living. Or was he just envious?

The show reached its climax with the men standing, legs apart and backs to the audience, ready to strip off the last vestiges of their clothing. Harvey scanned the audience. Everywhere he could see red cheeks, sweaty brows, faces distorted into expressions of raw lust. He would never have imagined that women could behave in such a brazenly uninhibited fashion. It was amazing! Any minute now he expected the guys on stage to be mobbed and treated to the equivalent of a gang-bang.

It didn't happen, however. Although the women were obviously creaming themselves at the sight of those tanned, swaying buttocks and the way those thongs were creeping down the lean thighs, they remained at a respectable distance. There was a sudden hush as the men were stripped totally naked and the music halted. The atmosphere became tense, almost reverent. Harvey recognised that moment of breathless concentration: it was like the pause before the cataclysm, the pre-orgasmic hiatus. Both men raised their arms in the air and slowly turned around to display their impressive erections for a few seconds, then the lights went out and the music blared. The pair slipped off the stage, two fleet shadows, and the show was over. Harvey found himself breathing a sigh of relief on behalf of those two guys. Whatever else you thought about their performance you had to admit they had guts!

The audience began to trickle out of the room, but Mandy and her friends went over to a table that had been vacated and sat down for a chat. They were giggling a lot, and Harvey guessed they were asking the girl what it had felt like to massage oil into that hairy chest. Mandy was leaning forward with her arms on the table, showing off her cleavage, and the sight was doing nothing to deflate Harvey's erection. He had a real hard-on now, thanks to the sight of all those randy women.

At last the four girls rose and crossed the room, making Harvey leap for the door. What would they do now? He glanced at his watch: ten-thirty. Maybe they were heading for the bar. As he reached the bottom of the stairs, however, he saw two of them saying goodbye to Mandy and her friend. She tried to persuade them to stay for another drink, but they wouldn't. Hovering at the foot of the stairs, Harvey waited until the remaining pair had gone into the bar then casually sauntered in after them.

The women outnumbered the men in there, making him feel uncomfortable. There was still a scent of raw desire in the air, sweat and hormones making a heady cocktail. Harvey ordered another beer and looked around for Bob, seeking moral support, but his friend was nowhere to be seen. He found a seat in the far corner and tried to keep out of the way while still keeping watch on Chris's girlfriend. Already he was mentally composing his report. It would make reassuring reading.

Then Mandy came up to the bar to order. She was quite near him, exuding perfume and sexiness. He looked away, but when he glanced back he caught her eye. She smiled at him. He frowned and looked away in the direction of her friend but discovered that she was not there. Had she gone home, leaving Mandy alone?

It certainly looked like it. The girl bought only one drink and remained by the bar, surveying the room. She looked his way again, but this time he managed to avoid her eyes. Maybe it was time for him to leave. He could always watch the pub from his car to see when she left and whether she was alone. Quickly he rose from his chair but a crowd of women suddenly barred his path, forcing him to linger right next to Mandy until they made way for him. She reached out and touched his arm.

'Excuse me!' He tried to pretend he hadn't heard, but she tugged at his sleeve more insistently. 'Excuse me!'

Harvey was forced to acknowledge her presence. 'Yes?' he said, his tone slightly irritated.

Mandy put on a charming smile. 'I suppose you wouldn't have any change, would you? I need some for the cigarette machine.'

She waved a five-pound note at him. He felt in his pocket, pulled out a handful of coins. Mandy squeezed his fingers as she pressed the note into his hand. It was a definite signal. Harvey became ultra-conscious of the bulge in his crotch.

'Thanks very much.' She slipped from her stool, breasts thrust momentarily into his face. Harvey swallowed and tried to get ahead of her as they moved through the crowd, but she squashed herself against him, clinging to him like a limpet. The cigarette machine was in the hall of the pub and he thought he would lose her there, but when they reached it the machine said 'Out of Order'.

'Damn!' she turned her appealing blue eyes towards him. 'I suppose you wouldn't have a fag, would you? I could really do with one.'

'I don't smoke. Sorry.'

He was breaking his first rule of surveillance: don't let the subject get a good look at your face. Further spying from this close would automatically be ruled out now. Harvey cursed his carelessness.

'Pity.' She was still smiling at him, as if there was something else on her mind. Then she said boldly, 'You can take me home, if you like.'

Harvey's refusal was on the tip of his tongue until he realised that this was a perfect opportunity to pump her for information. He was unlikely to get another chance now that she'd had a good look at him, and so far he had nothing very tangible to offer his client. Brusquely he nodded. 'Okay. My car's out the back.'

Mandy slipped into the front seat, smelling of *Loulou* and something more intimate. She grinned up at him, a slip of a thing really, her cleavage damp with sweat. Overcome by the heady scent and warm presence, Harvey almost forgot to ask where she lived.

They moved out, heading for the Stockport road, and Harvey reminded himself that he had little more than ten minutes to find out what he could. He started by commenting on how the houses in her area had almost all been turned into bedsits. 'Have you got a nice flat, then?' he asked. 'Plenty of room?'

'It's okay. I'd like a garden flat really, but mine's on the middle floor. It's near the bathroom, though.'

'You live alone, then?'

She gave him a wry, sidelong look. 'What's it to you?'

'Nothing. Just interested. I'm looking for a place myself, as a matter of fact.'

'Why – wife kicked you out?'

'Cheeky bitch!'

'Sorry, I couldn't resist it. Are you married, though?'

'Nope. Never have been.'

'Me neither.' She stretched her legs out in front of her as far as she could. 'Don't fancy it yet. I'm only twenty-two. Far too young to settle down. I've got a sister who was married at nineteen and divorced by the time she was my age. It puts you off.'

This was promising. Harvey tried to sound casual as he asked, 'No steady boyfriend, then?'

'Not really.' She sounded hesitant, a bit vague.

He decided to press her. 'But you do have a boyfriend, is that it?'

'Mm. We both see other people, though. It's nothing serious.'

It occurred to Harvey that he should have had his recorder running, but it was too late now. Then he saw a petrol station and pulled in, pretending to be low on fuel. While he went into the office to pay he switched on his pocket recorder and returned to the car. It was time to get some hard evidence on tape.

'So you're young, single and fancy free then, are you?' he reiterated, fastening his seatbelt.

'That's about right. Why, are you interested?' She giggled and nudged his elbow as he put the car into gear.

'Maybe. You're a really attractive girl, Mandy. You must have lots of fellas chasing you.'

'I don't do so badly.' As they moved out of the forecourt she added, 'As long as the guy understands that all I want is a physical relationship. I'm not interested in emotional involvement, if you know what I mean.'

'Absolutely! I feel the same myself, right now.'

'You feel the same as me?' she giggled. 'I doubt it!'

'Why's that?'

'Well you haven't spent the evening watching two incredibly gorgeous guys strut their stuff in the nude. God, were they hot! I've not felt so lecherous in ages.'

Harvey was unaccountably miffed. 'Well, we can't all be Chippendales or Gladiators.'

But then he felt the touch of her hand on his shoulder, followed by her husky voice in his ear. 'You look good enough for me, darlin'. I don't go for that pumped-up look. I prefer a man with style, know what I mean?'

Mandy nibbled his earlobe briefly, sending his libido into

overdrive. Harvey nearly crashed the car, but managed to steady the wheel in time. 'Don't do that when I'm driving, crazy woman!'

She gave a trilling laugh that echoed dizzyingly through his brain. What a tease! No wonder that poor bastard wanted her tailed. It was only now that he realised Chris's suspicions about his girl were fully justified.

They entered the road where her flat was and Harvey drew up outside. 'Coming in for a coffee?' she invited, confidently.

Harvey knew if he did he'd be lost. He shook his head. 'No thanks. I'd better get going.'

'Why? Girlfriend waiting up for you?'

Mandy's eyes were challenging him as she slowly unlocked her seatbelt. She thrust her small breasts forward, displaying her wares. Harvey sensed that she wasn't used to having men turn her down. She took his chin between her thumb and forefinger and drew his face near to hers until those blue circles were mesmerising him with their focused intensity.

Harvey opened his mouth but no words came. Instead her lips approached his with relentless purpose. She pressed both soft cushions against his mouth, a slip of a tongue passing between them to meet his own. He groaned, knowing he was as good as lost now anyway.

Swiftly Mandy undid his seatbelt and then the belt of his jeans. She was small enough to slip down into the space in front of the seat. Harvey tried to push her back but she unzipped his fly and her nimble fingers found the bulging hardness within before he could utter a syllable. All he could do after that was groan.

While she extricated his cock from his pants, Harvey reached down and felt her firm little breasts. The neckline of her top gaped, and he was able to put his hands in to feel the warm flesh. The bra was flimsy, offering no resistance. He put in his thumbs and pulled out her plums, two juice-dark nipples that reared up provocatively over the constraining garments. Mandy moaned softly as he twiddled them, and then bent to take the end of his prick into her mouth. Harvey leaned back in his seat, watching the orange glow of the street lamps turn hazier and hazier.

The heat coursed through his belly, building up like a furnace as Mandy pushed her mouth further down his shaft. His glans met the roof of her mouth, caressed the soft palate, making her gag a little. She adjusted the angle so he could push into her throat while her busy fingers freed his balls and began to play with them, juggling them around in their sac. Harvey knew he couldn't hold out much longer. The fire was melting his guts, his testicles were tensing to shed their load, his penis on a hair-trigger. The caress of her tongue on his glans followed by one more thrust did it. He exploded full into her mouth, sending a jet-stream of hot liquid into the yawning cavern. Mandy swallowed it all greedily.

Exhausted, Harvey flopped back in his seat wondering how the hell he would find the energy to drive home. He could feel her wiping him with a tissue, packing his kit back into his pants, zipping him up again. Slowly he opened his eyes to see her pulling her top over her delectable little tits, a self-satisfied grin on her face. She looked up at him and opened the car door behind her back.

'Maybe next time you'll come in for coffee!'

He made a noise somewhere between a groan and a sigh, but before he could say anything she was gone. Bleary-eyed he stared through the windscreen at the orange blobs, trying to get a grip on himself. He didn't fancy spending the night in a Levenshulme back street. In his pocket the recorder continued its silent running. He played back a couple of seconds: moans and groans. Maybe he'd edit that bit out to save Chris's sanity. On the other hand, perhaps he should know exactly what that horny bitch was capable of. He recalled a case, not one of his, where a girl had been murdered by her irate boyfriend after just such a piece of taped evidence. It was a dilemma he would have to face in the morning. Fastening his belt, Harvey switched on the engine and put the car into gear.

Driving back slowly in the early hours he wondered how he had allowed things to go that far. Maybe they'd both been turned on by that tacky show. Even now the thought of all those women on heat made his prick stir in his pants. Plus the fact that he hadn't had sex for a long time. Far too long, obviously. He recalled the way his last girlfriend, Fran, used to gush like a soda fountain when she came and his erection grew. It was dangerous, being this frustrated. You thought you could forget about sex, pretend it didn't matter, but it made you vulnerable without you realising. Then, when opportunity knocked as it had tonight, you just couldn't help yourself. Maybe I'm in the wrong job, he thought, not for the first time, as he turned into the street where he lived.

The following evening Harvey took the tape to Chris Laughton's house. He played it to him poker-faced, letting the conversation speak for itself, watching his client's face crumple progressively then disappear in a welter of despair behind his hands.

'God, I was afraid of this!' he whimpered at the unmistakable sound of a zip being undone.

'The tape ran out after that,' Harvey lied.

'What happened?' He raised fearful eyes, wanting and not wanting to know.

Harvey shrugged. 'I told her to go home to bed, like a good girl.'

'Thanks, mate! But she'd have done it, wouldn't she? Right there in your car. The cow!'

Harvey nodded. 'She was all worked up by that show, Chris. Pity you weren't there in bed waiting for her. You'd have had the time of your life!'

'I don't know what to do!' he moaned. 'What should I do, Harvey? You must have met men in my position before. What would you do?'

'Lay down the law, I reckon. Tell her "commit, or quit". But be prepared to lose her.'

'I think you're right,' Chris said, quietly. 'Anything's better than this uncertainty. If she gets out of my life now at least I have a chance of finding someone who wants the same as me.'

'Now you're talking sense.' Harvey handed him the bill. 'I could go on tailing her for a couple more nights, but I don't see the point. You're better off giving her an ultimatum and having done with it.'

As he drove away from the pleasant suburban semi Harvey heaved a sigh. That guy deserved a break. He moved down street after street of similar homes wondering what secrets they hid, how many potential cases for him to handle, and felt sickened. Something had gone sadly wrong with society. Men and women didn't trust each other any more. Love had become a dirty joke. And he was making money out of people's mistrust.

Then he passed the end of Cedar Drive. Halfway down was the home of Maggie, the divorced mother of young Richard, whose father had tried to take him off to Singapore without his ex-wife's consent. She'd been sure that he intended to keep their son there against his will. Harvey had been hired to trace the boy and, after a dramatic confrontation at Heathrow, Richard and his mother had been reunited.

Harvey smiled. Maybe the job had its compensations, after all.

Chapter Three

For weeks Mark McCade had been pestering Gayle for a date. She'd met him through a mutual friend and although she found him attractive she'd been growing tired of his constant phone calls. Now she was having second thoughts. Maybe a boyfriend was just what she needed to save her from getting into awkward situations at work. The incident with Brad had shaken her and she didn't want it to happen again.

So when Mark next phoned she surprised him by agreeing to go out to dinner the following night. He responded enthusiastically. 'That's great, Gayle! Do you like Italian food? There's a new place opened up on Oldham Street.'

'I love Italian!' she assured him. 'Will you pick me up, or shall I meet you there?'

They arranged to meet at La Casa Rosa at eight-thirty. But late that afternoon Gayle had a phone call from a woman named Janice who sounded agitated. 'Can I see you this evening?' she asked. 'I really need to see someone. If you're not available, I'll have to try someone else.'

Gayle thought quickly. If the interview didn't last too long she could still keep her date with Mark. She decided to risk it. They arranged to meet in a café-bar in town, not too far from the restaurant. She tried to phone Mark but he'd already left the office and there was no reply at his home number. Well, she had to put business before pleasure. That woman had sounded distraught on the phone. It must be something pretty serious.

Much to her annoyance, Janice was late. It was gone eight by the time she showed up, full of apologies. She ordered a black coffee and they sat at a quiet table at the back of the café, near where some musicians were setting up on a tiny stage. Quickly Janice gulped down the coffee and ordered another, then lit a cigarette.

'I've never been to see anyone like you before,' she began. 'And it took me ages to make up my mind to phone.'

'How did you hear about me?' Gayle always asked that question, since she didn't advertise in the Yellow Pages.

'A friend recommended you: Susan Marsh.'

'Oh yes.' Gayle remembered that case. Susan's father had suffered from amnesia after an accident and was eventually found living like a hermit in an abandoned cottage on the moors. 'How do you think I can help you?'

'It's not another missing person, I know exactly where he is.' Gayle noted the tension in her voice. 'I'm talking about my fiancé, Sid Morrow. He works at Cannings, he's their senior export manager.' Despite her obvious anxiety she couldn't keep a note of pride out of her voice.

'What's the problem, then?'

'Well he's asked me to marry him, but I'm not sure. Maybe I'm being stupid, not trusting him, but I can't forget how he and I got together.'

'I don't follow. Can we take this more slowly, please?'

'I'm sorry. I'll start at the beginning. Sid and I met because I went to work at Cannings as a temp, and became his secretary. I was only there three months, but during that time he and I got close and after I left we carried on seeing each other. That was eighteen months ago now.'

Gayle could feel the minutes ticking by but there was nothing she could do except hope that Mark would wait. She tried to hurry her up. 'Can we get to the point please, Janice?'

'Sorry. Well, the point is that Sid made a pass at me in his office. If I hadn't fancied him something rotten I suppose I could have charged him with sexual harassment. Instead, I ended up getting engaged to him. The trouble is, I know there are still temps working at his office, so I can't help wondering if he's making a play for them, too.'

'I see.' Gayle took a sip of her blackcurrant juice. 'So what do you want me to do?'

'Test him out, I suppose.'

'What, offer him some sexual temptation?'

'You do take on that sort of work, don't you? Sue said you did.'

Gayle nodded. 'Sometimes. But I'm not sure it's appropriate here. I mean, what are you trying to find out?'

'Just whether or not I can trust him. I'd rather know before we marry than after.'

Gayle nodded. 'Well, if this is really what you want, I suppose I could pose as a temp for a while. Do you know which employment bureau Cannings uses?'

'Quick Tempers.'

'No problem. I know Linda, the boss. Leave it with me. We might have to wait a couple of weeks for an opening, so I hope you're not in too much of a hurry.'

It was nine before Gayle could leave. She arrived at the restaurant just after ten past, but Mark had already gone. She phoned his number but there was no reply. Feeling bad, she ordered a take-away pizza and drove home.

When she did manage to get through to Mark, two days

later, he was polite with her on the phone, but she knew she'd blown it. Still, business was business. Meanwhile, she got in touch with Linda at Quick Tempers and explained that she needed to go undercover at Cannings as soon as possible. She had a couple of other cases to be working on in between, but one evening, ten days later, Linda gave her a ring at home.

'Cannings need a temp for the rest of this week. It's for that Mr Morrow. Is that okay?'

'Linda, you're a real pal! Remind me to buy you a drink sometime. For this job my name's "Karen Taylor", by the way!'

The following morning Gayle spent some time over her make-up. She put on lashings of mascara, a curly auburn wig and a turquoise mini-dress in clingy jersey. Looking vaguely like a Seventies' swinger she sprayed on some appropriately cheap perfume and drove to the big clothing warehouse off Ancoats Street where Sid Morrow was in charge of exports.

'Oh, you must be the new temp,' the receptionist smiled, eyeing her with faint suspicion. 'Mr Morrow's office is down that corridor. Third door on the left. The ladies' is second door opposite, in case you want to freshen up, do your hair or anything.'

Her tone suggested that Gayle needed it.

When she presented herself to her new 'boss' she was surprised by his suave appearance and manner. She had been expecting someone altogether less refined. Serves me right for thinking in stereotypes, she told herself as she shook hands with him. His voice was deep and cultured. If she hadn't been forewarned she would have been taken in by his charm, but now she noticed the slightly predatory way his eyes swept over her, lingering on her crossed thighs, and the throaty inflexion in his voice.

'It's good of you to help us out at short notice, Miss Taylor,' he said.

'Not at all,' she answered brightly. 'That's why I'm with the agency.'

He showed her the ropes, telling her what he wanted done on the word-processor that morning. Fortunately Gayle knew how to merge files, insert graphics and address envelopes, all skills that had been included in the course she'd done. At the time she'd thought she would never need to use them but now she was glad she knew what she was doing.

Sid seemed pleased with her. 'You've got through that lot in half the time I was expecting,' he grinned. 'Why don't I treat you to lunch? There's a decent Chinese place down the road.'

Knowing she had to play along, Gayle agreed. The place was full of businessmen and women, buzzing with chatter. Sid asked her whether she was married or had a steady boyfriend. It was pretty obvious that he was a fast worker. She could feel his eyes raking over her and felt like goods on display. It was not a pleasant sensation.

'How about you, Mr Morrow?' she asked at last. 'Are you married?'

'No chance!'

'Engaged, then?'

He gave her a wry smile. 'My girlfriend thinks we are.'

'Really? Isn't that something you should sort out between you, then?'

'All in good time. I'm in no hurry to be tied down, Karen. Makes a man more attractive to a woman if she has to chase him a bit, don't you find? By the way, what's with this "Mr Morrow"? Call me Sid, there's a good girl. Everyone does.'

'And I bet that's not all they call you!' Gayle thought, cynically.

When the meal was over and they were walking back to the office, Sid asked if she was busy at the weekend. Gayle said she was. 'Pity,' he sighed, theatrically. 'My girlfriend's going away this weekend and I could do with some company.'

That evening, she phoned Janice and told her what Sid had said.

'The lying rat!' she exploded. 'I'm not going anywhere. In fact, he promised to take me to the cinema on Saturday night.'

'Do you want me to "change my mind" about a date, just to see how far he would go?'

There was a long silence at the other end of the line. Then Janice said, 'No, I can't let you do that. Just see how he behaves for the rest of the week, would you?'

It was no skin off Gayle's nose. In fact, she was doing rather well out of it. Not only was she getting paid by Janice but she was getting a cut from Linda, too, for the temp job!

The following morning Sid buzzed her as soon as she arrived. 'Will you come into my office please, Karen. I want you to take dictation.'

His words had a certain old-fashioned ring about them. Something in his tone put Gayle on alert, so she started the tape running in her miniature recorder then put it into the breast pocket of her tailored blouse, since there was no room to spare in her skintight mini-skirt. She went in with her pencil and pad, glad that she'd taken a shorthand course when she'd had a brief spell as a reporter for the local rag.

Sid Morrow was sitting behind his desk wearing a smug grin. He leaned back in his chair tapping his hands together over his chest. 'That's right, Karen, you sit there.' She sank into the only other chair in his office, a low-seated one that made her skirt ride up as she sat down. It was a warm day and she wore no tights or stockings. As she attempted to cross her legs she was sure that her black panties were on full view.

'Now then, take a letter please. "Dear Miss Taylor" . . .'

Karen looked up, startled. 'Excuse me. Did you say *Taylor*?'

'That's right.' His smile deepened, making her realise that it wasn't just coincidence or a slip of the tongue. He meant to address the letter to her. Or, at least, to her pseudonym. 'Carry on please, Karen.'

Dutifully she bent her head to the task, wondering what was coming next. It was a good thing she had the recorder running. She had a feeling she'd be glad of it by the time this 'dictation' was through!

'Ready? Dear Miss Taylor, Since you have come to work in my office I have been unable to take my eyes off your gorgeous pert breasts, tight little arse and long, long legs . . .'

Gayle felt she must make a token protest. 'Mr Morrow, I really can't continue with this.'

'Do as you're told, Karen, or there will be consequences. Now then, are you ready to resume?' She nodded, eyes down. 'Full stop. I think you know exactly what you are doing to me as you wiggle that cute ass of yours around the office. And I know exactly what I'd like to do to you. First I would rip the clothes off your nubile young body . . .'

'Mr Morrow, are you aware that this letter could be construed as sexual harassment?'

Sid chuckled. 'You ain't heard nothin' yet! Keep writing, Miss Taylor . . . Nubile young body, then I would make you lie face down on my desk with your legs spread and your tits hanging over the edge where I can fondle them. By then I know you would be secretly dying for it, but first I would cover your delectable firm buttocks in mayo from my pastrami salad sandwich, making sure that some of the dressing went right down into your crack to make you nice and greasy.'

Gayle looked up. 'Ugh, that's disgusting!'

His beady brown eyes stared back at her, arrogant and unrepentant. She could see the slavering lust reflected there and wondered how long he would be content merely to dictate to her. What a wanker!

'Continue if you please, Karen. I would put my finger into your arse and wiggle it about until you opened up to me, then I would put in the rest of my fingers and give you a good fisting. You love it up the bum, don't you, Miss Taylor? I can tell. When I was quite sure that you were ready for me I would place my king-size prick between your deliciously rotund cheeks and—'

Gayle jumped to her feet, genuinely disturbed. 'I don't want to hear any more of this!'

He rose and came round the desk towards her, his eyes gleaming hotly. Snatching the notebook from her hand he put both hands on her shoulders and stared deep into her eyes. Gayle thought she knew how a rabbit must feel when mesmerised by a snake.

'Do you want me to tell the agency that you've been a bad girl, that you refused to take dictation?' he said in a low, threatening tone. 'They won't send you on any other jobs, you know. You'll be finished as a temp, and it's hard to get any kind of job these days. You might end up on the streets, just to make ends meet.'

'Don't be ridiculous! I could take you to court for this!'

Gayle tried to back away, but he held her firmly and she began to feel frightened. The man was some kind of sex maniac and she'd walked right into the trap.

'It would only be your word against mine, and I have friends in high places. You do as you're told, my dear, and I'll give the agency a good report.' He tried to give her back the notebook. 'Come on, I've not finished this letter yet.'

'You know as well as I do that this is not a proper letter.'

'No, it's an improper letter!' he guffawed.

'You know what I mean. It's not office business, nor do you intend to send it, so you're wasting my time and yours.'

'It's for me to be the judge of that, my dear. Now then, where was I? Ah yes, with my magnificent cock positioned between your . . . I mean *Miss Taylor's* . . . softly cushioning buttocks.'

Gayle tried to walk out, but he was too quick for her. Dismayed, she saw him lock the door and put the key into his trouser pocket. She could feel her heart beating rapidly, but was it fear or excitement that was causing her adrenalin buzz?

'All right, if that's how you want to play it I'm afraid you must be punished. Kneel on the floor, Karen, and bend over the arm of that chair.'

She stood defiant, arms crossed over her chest where she could feel the faint whirring of the recorder in her pocket. It was a relief to know that everything this bastard was saying to her was being recorded and would later *incriminate* him.

'I said, bend over!' he repeated harshly. Still she stood there, defying him. He swiftly tripped her up and pulled one arm behind her back, forcing her down across the padded leather arm of the chair.

'Ouch! You're hurting me!' she squealed. 'I'll sue you for assault!'

'I told you, my word against yours,' he said softly in her ear. 'There are no witnesses.'

That's what you think. She smiled to herself, touching the small, hard square in her breast pocket as the brown seat cushion came up to meet her. Pinning her down with one hand, her 'boss' groped beneath her short skirt and she felt his palm caress her buttocks over the flesh-toned nylon. Helplessly she wriggled, grinding her bulging mons against the leather padding.

'That's a good girl,' he crooned. 'The sooner you co-operate, the more you'll enjoy it.'

Sid hitched a finger under the waistline of her knickers and pulled them halfway down her thighs, exposing her bottom completely. His hand continued to stroke the soft cheeks with a circular motion until, without warning, he gave her an almighty slap on the left buttock. Gayle gasped at its stinging impact, but before it had ceased smarting another smack was delivered to her right buttock, making her tingle all over.

He released his hand from her shoulder and, thinking she had a chance to escape, Gayle slid away. Then strong arms seized her from behind, but she was hobbled by the panties around her knees and, in the ensuing struggle the recorder fell from her pocket and dropped to the floor. Horrified, Gayle tried to grab it, but he got there first. Holding it high, out of her reach, Sid gave a sardonic laugh.

'What's this? Some kind of dictaphone?' He went behind his desk and pressed the rewind switch, then the play button. His own voice came forth, heavy with insinuation, and Gayle winced. His smile widened as he rewound it to the beginning. 'Ah, so we have a spy in our midst, do we?'

Throwing it onto the desk, Sid darted back to where Gayle was and pushed her down over the chair again. She could feel her heart thumping wildly, afraid of what he might do to her now that her treachery had been exposed.

'We were just playing before. Now it's serious!' he snapped. 'You must be severely disciplined to teach you not to play silly buggers with me again.'

Quickly he stripped off her panties, and before she knew it he was using them to tie her hands behind her back. Gayle gasped as he turned her round and undid the buttons of her blouse, his eyes dark with desire. He pulled the straps as far down her arms as he could, then lifted her breasts out of the cups. She shuddered as her nipples grew to prominence on contact with the air – or was it something else that was stimulating them? Annoyed with herself, Gayle tried to remain impassive as he leched over her exposed body.

'What gorgeous tits!' he grinned, pinching the nipples hard and making her eyes water. 'You know what I'd like to do to you now? Make you give me a tit wank. But I won't. Not yet, anyway, because you might get off on that and we want to make sure you're well and truly humiliated first, don't we?'

Gayle just shrugged, staring at him with contempt. She was furious with herself for allowing him to get hold of her recorder like that. Now she would only have hearsay to report to Janice. The thought of that poor girl living in a romantic dream while this beast tormented any poor temp that came his way made her want to puke. How the hell had he got away with it all this time?

She heard him rummage in a drawer then return with a plastic ruler which he flexed in front of her. 'This should do the trick!' he smiled. 'Bend over, Miss Cleverclogs. You've had this coming ever since you arrived, wearing that prick-teaser of a skirt! Six of the best on each side, that should do it.'

There was nothing for it but to obey. Gayle leaned over the chair again, her bottom trembling with anticipation and her naked breasts thrust forward onto the seat cushion. The first couple of whacks weren't too bad, but it was clear that she wouldn't be let off lightly. Sid soon got into a thumping rhythm that left her sore and aching.

'Oh, you bad little bitch!' she heard him groan, and guessed that he was becoming extremely aroused by his actions. She wondered if he would make her suck him off. The thought evoked a mixture of feelings, some pleasant, some not so pleasant. Gayle warned herself to stop her imagination from wandering and bear in mind that she was here on a job, but it wasn't easy. A curious atmosphere of complicity was being built up between her and Morrow that was powerfully seductive.

When he had delivered the twelve strokes Gayle felt searingly numb from the waist down. He untied her hands, then made her lie face down on the carpeted floor. She wondered what was coming next. Was he about to fulfil the fantasy he'd described in that fake letter? A few seconds later the feeling of some wet gloop being rubbed into her buttocks seemed to indicate exactly that, and Gayle felt real panic strike. 'What are you doing?' she gasped, terrified.

Sid continued to rub her buttocks gently. 'It's all right, girly,' he murmured. 'You can relax now. The punishment's over and it's time for your reward. Lie still, now.'

His fingers did slide down her arse crack a little but he made no attempt to penetrate her. Instead he began to massage her pussy from behind. The oil, she now realised, was not mayonnaise but some scented unguent that soothed her with its herbal smell as well as its warm, smooth consistency. For the first time during their encounter she gave herself up to him, letting his fingers go wherever they wished, revelling in the warm afterglow that was spreading from her bottom all around her lower region and down her thighs.

As the slow strokings continued Gayle felt something gathering force inside her, the familiar build-up towards orgasm. No, she thought, I can't let this bastard make me come. But it was difficult to imagine how she was going to prevent it. Since she had so shamelessly given in to the temptation that was Brad Lewis, her libido had been hovering on the threshold, ready to take full advantage of any similar situation she might find herself in.

Consequently, when Sid placed one hand on her breast and began to squeeze it, simultaneously rubbing against her bulbous clitoris, it proved altogether too much for Gayle's self-control. She felt the first wild spasms rack through her with joyous abandon, making her groan aloud, and soon she was in the throes of a fierce climax that made her gasp as it pulsed its way through her nervous system, reaching every part of her. Once it had begun to fade she collapsed on the carpet, utterly exhausted. She was dimly aware of the sound of a door being unlocked and a heavy tread leave the room, abandoning her completely.

When Gayle eventually sat up she saw that Sid had hung a notice on the door handle saying 'Gone to Lunch'.

Feeling both physically and emotionally battered Gayle rose, found her pants and put them on, then made her way to the ladies' across the corridor. There she bathed her lower quarters in warm water, splashed her face with cold, combed her hair and returned to the office. She found her recorder on the desk in Sid's room. It was still whirring away, having come to the end of the tape, but when she went to play it back she found he'd wiped it clean.

Gayle cursed softly. What a fool she had been! Somehow she had walked straight into the trap that Sid had set her and come out of it without a shred of evidence to convict him.

Feeling in need of some creature comforts, Gayle left the

building and went for lunch at a sandwich bar across the road. She took her time over lunch, debating what her next move should be, but when she returned there was a note on her desk. Sid wanted her to continue with yesterday's work and said he'd be in a meeting all afternoon.

'I'm damned if I'm going to stay here a moment longer,' she decided. Since there was no way she could obtain any further evidence from this undercover job she might as well jack it in. Too bad if it left Cannings in the lurch. Her own self-respect was more important to her, and Linda would understand when she gave her an edited account of what had happened.

But what about Janice? Gayle was dreading making her report, but knew that she had to do it. If she went home right now she could finish it by late afternoon and maybe see the poor girl again that evening. The sooner she got shot of this unsavoury case the better.

Before she began making her report, Gayle phoned Janice. She was taken aback when the woman suddenly gave vent to apologies. 'I'm terribly sorry, Gayle, it was all my fault. I spoilt everything for you, didn't I?'

'What do you mean?'

'Well he found out, didn't he? Looked at the stubs in my bank book, the swine, and saw your name where I'd written out the cheque for your advance. I had no idea he was keeping track of my spending. Anyway, he asked me who you were and, in the end, I'm afraid I told him. He . . . he always manages to get things out of me in the end.'

Gayle could well imagine it. Then she had a horrible thought. 'Just a minute – exactly when did he find out about me?'

'This morning, after we'd spent the night together. I tried to phone you after he'd gone to work, but you'd already left and the switchboard at Cannings wouldn't put me through, Said he'd stopped all calls. I'm really sorry. Did he give you a hard time?'

Gayle gave a disgusted laugh. 'You could say that!'

She was flabbergasted. So that prick had known all along that she was a private investigator! He'd just been playing games with her. Her anger welled up like a poisoned spring. What could she say to Janice now? The idea that he had seduced her out of some kind of revenge against his fiancée was sickening.

'So what happened?' Janice asked.

'He wiped the tape I'd made,' she said, snatching at the one piece of truth she felt comfortable relating. 'So even if he had made suggestions I'd have had no real evidence.'

'Ah well, never mind. It's all over between him and me anyway. The idea that I'd hired someone to spy on him made him furious. I suppose he must have had something to hide, or he wouldn't have reacted like that.'

'So do you want to leave it there, then?'

'Yes, I think so. Just send me the bill, don't worry about making out a report or anything.'

Gayle felt rotten after she'd put the phone down. Her professional pride had been badly hurt, and she racked her brains trying to work out how she might have avoided trouble. Perhaps by not taking the case on in the first place. Certainly she should have raised the alarm when he locked the door and began coming on to her. She hated letting Sid Morrow go unpunished. Now he was free to cheat on some new young innocent, and there wasn't a thing she could do about it. Worse, she felt humiliated by the fact that she'd allowed him to pleasure her. Was she so desperate for it that she could let a sod like that make her come?

Once again she considered getting herself a regular

boyfriend and thought of Mark. He'd been relatively understanding about their broken date. Would he be willing to give her a second chance? She picked up the phone again and dialled his number.

To her relief, Mark seemed pleased to hear from her. Heartened by his warm tone she made a date for the following evening and this time she was able to keep it. Over dinner in a quiet restaurant, he plied her with questions about her work and she answered as frankly as she could whilst maintaining client confidentiality.

'Have you ever bedded a guy just to get information, or set him up?' he wanted to know.

'Mm . . . as good as.'

He grinned, his grey eyes shining mischievously. 'So how do I know this isn't a set-up?'

'You don't. But if you're telling me the truth, you don't have a regular girlfriend at the moment. Not one who would have any right to be jealous, anyway.'

'That's true. But suppose, just suppose, you got really involved with me. Would you use another private investigator to check me out?'

'I might.'

'You're that cynical, huh?'

'Well, this job does give you a jaundiced view of human nature in general, and men in particular.'

'I'll bet!'

She began to realise that Mark was more interested in Gayle Webster the detective than Gayle Webster the woman. Still, once he'd exhausted his curiosity she would find out if their relationship had any more mileage in it.

After the meal they took a leisurely stroll down by the canal where, hidden under a bridge, Mark pressed her to the wall and kissed her passionately. Gayle responded in like fashion and soon his hands were everywhere, creeping beneath her loose top to caress her breasts in their smooth-cupped bra, then undoing the button at her waist so that his roving fingers could slip down to feel the warm mounds of her bottom. She knew she wanted him, but after her experiences with Brad and Sid she was cautious. If this was going to be something worthwhile she wanted to move more slowly.

'Shall we go back to my place?' Mark murmured, urgently.

'Not tonight, if you don't mind. I have to make an early start tomorrow.'

It was true; Gayle was travelling to Liverpool on a new missing person case, but she still felt mean putting him off. He shrugged philosophically, taking her hand to resume their walk. 'I hope I can see you again, though.'

'Oh yes, of course!'

Gayle sounded more enthusiastic than she felt. Much as she liked Mark, she wondered if he could stay the pace. The thought of what her previous boyfriends had had to endure returned, memories of dates broken at the last minute, calls in the middle of the night, anxiety about her work. Even as she made another date with him she was wondering if she'd have to break it.

Chapter Four

Despite the attractions of cafés spilling out onto pavements and women spilling out of skimpy dresses, summer in the city was not Harvey's favourite season. It seemed to bring out the nut-cases in droves. Like the man who was convinced that his dog was inhabited by an alien life form, and who wanted Harvey to keep watch on its kennel in case the mother ship landed in his backyard. The woman who was convinced her husband turned into a transvestite the minute he was out of her sight. A mother who swore her son's father was Elvis, and who wanted a sample of DNA collected from the King's grave so that paternity could be proved. Some unscrupulous investigators would take on loonies like these, humouring them, feeding them lies until they'd milked them of their cash. Not Harvey. You couldn't build a business, or a reputation, on that sort of trade.

There were a few small jobs that Harvey considered more or less routine: checking on moonlighters for the DSS, a couple of credit checks and insurance fraud suspects. He had built up quite a few useful contacts amongst the local lawyers, too, who put work his way on a fairly regular basis. Then, when things slackened off, there were always the longer-term investigations to pursue, mostly missing persons. But by August he was itching for something to get his teeth into. So when a small Irishwoman called Eileen O'Donnell phoned him saying she wanted to find out if her son Sean was gay, it seemed quite an attractive assignment.

'I know he's seeing someone,' she said, when they met in Toolan's. 'But he's very cagey about it and that's what makes me think it's another man. He's never been so shifty before.'

'How old is he?'

'Twenty.'

'Old enough to make up his own mind, I should have thought. It's legal at that age now.'

'Well, yes, you're right of course. But I'd still like to be sure, one way or another. I've already tried another investigator, a nice young woman. She specialises in leading men on, you know, to see if they're faithful to their wives and girlfriends.'

'Her name wouldn't be Gayle Webster by any chance?'

'The very same! You know her?'

'Not personally, but I read a profile on her in the Evening News.'

'Well I thought if she flirted with Sean he might tell her he was gay to put her off, sort of thing. I'm glad to say he didn't take the bait. I wouldn't like to think my son's the kind to pick up strange women in bars. But there was no mention of him liking men more than women or anything, so I was none the wiser. And Gayle said I'd be wasting my money to use her again.'

'That was honest of her, anyway. So how do you think I could help, Mrs O'Donnell?'

'Just keep an eye on him, would you? Find out the company he keeps. I thought if he goes to gay bars or clubs it would be better to have a man tailing him than a woman.'

'Hm. Maybe.' Harvey had made a few forays into Manchester's 'Village', visiting bars like Metz and Cruz 101.

He'd even attended a gay night at the Paradise Factory, all in the course of duty. But on the whole he preferred to steer clear of the gay scene.

'Actually, though, I don't believe he does that . . . what do they call it, "sailing"?'

'I think you mean "cruising", Mrs O'Donnell.'

'That's the word! Anyway, I don't believe he does that. I think he has a steady relationship with someone. He had this letter arrive for him one day, and wouldn't tell me what it was. He acted ever so strangely, so I think it was from his friend.'

'Does he go out regularly, same nights each week?'

'Fridays and Saturdays. He goes to church on Sundays. He's a good son to me, Mr Boyd.'

Harvey could see incipient tears in the woman's eyes and knew that he had to take the job on. Somehow he didn't think she would give her son a hard time if he did turn out to be gay. She just wanted to know for sure, and evidently Sean couldn't bring himself to tell her. Well, he would see what he could do to solve the mystery.

The following Friday night Harvey watched Sean O'Donnell leave the little suburban dwelling he shared with his widowed mother and get into his red Escort. He tracked him down Bury New Road to a large detached mansion in Prestwich, on the other side of the city. This is getting interesting, Harvey thought, as he cut a small, neat spyhole in his newspaper and settled down to view the proceedings in his wing mirror. He didn't see who opened the door to Sean, but in his experience he was more likely to get a glimpse when they said goodbye. Lovers' partings were invariably more drawn out than their meetings, when they couldn't wait to get off the doorstep and into bed.

It looked like the case might be solved that very night, but

Harvey knew better than to count his chickens. There might be a dozen or more reasons why Sean had driven right across town that night. Still, Eileen O'Donnell hadn't asked him to discover whether her son was on drugs, contacting the spirit of his dead father or receiving acupuncture. The brief was to check out his sexual orientation, and Harvey would stick to that. He'd learnt from bitter experience that any extra information he might glean on the way was best kept to himself

Switching on his car radio, kept tuned to JFM, Harvey relaxed into the gentle strains of Stan Getz as he pretended to scan the paper in front of his face. This could be a long wait. If Sean was having an affair it could be two in the morning before he emerged. His mother had said he often came home in the early hours after seeing his mysterious lover. Harvey looked longingly at the two cans of low-alcohol lager and the cheese sandwich he'd brought with him. He couldn't afford to start on them too soon.

Eventually Harvey abandoned his pretence of reading the News and took out a paperback crime novel instead. Although surveillance from a parked car was one of the most boring aspects of his job it was definitely one of the easiest, and he could never avoid feeling guilty that he was charging so much for his time. He found his mind turning to Gayle Webster. Did she get much job satisfaction out of giving strange men the eye? What if Sean O'Donnell had responded to her, would his poor mother have been relieved that he wasn't gay, or upset that he could be so easily seduced? It had obviously never crossed that sweet woman's mind that her son could be bisexual!

Harvey's personal feeling was that investigators like Gayle gave his profession a bad name. Okay, so he'd succumbed to temptation himself recently, but he hadn't intended to let that tart Mandy seduce him, only to observe her behaviour. There was a world of difference between what he did and what Gayle and her fellow 'mate-checkers' got up to. The newspaper article had suggested that they nearly always got their man, but what did that prove? Simply that most men couldn't resist a pretty girl who made a play for them. Big deal! The more he thought about it, the more distasteful their *modus operandi* seemed.

Around ten Harvey drove down the road a little way, still keeping his eye on the house, and ended up parked in a different position. He could see the front door more directly now, and settled down with his beer and sandwich. Afterwards he reached down under the passenger seat for the hot water bottle he always took with him on long observation jobs when he couldn't risk leaving his post. Undoing his fly he took a long, satisfying leak then stoppered the bottle tightly, replacing it under the seat.

The hands of his watch crept slowly on towards midnight and the faint, soporific tones of JFM were in danger of sending him to sleep. Then, when it was almost one, he saw the hall light come on behind the stained glass panel in the front door and was instantly alert. He knew he might only have a few seconds to see who kissed Sean goodbye. Fortunately there was a street lamp right outside the gate, giving extra illumination. Harvey was only half aware that another car had entered the road and was approaching him on the other side.

Then, just as the front door opened and the figure of Sean appeared, the car drew up alongside him and someone rapped on his window, forcing him to look away at the crucial moment. He cursed, and glanced back to where Sean was hovering on the doorstep. There came another insistent rap and a woman called his name. He looked round with a scowl. The other driver had rolled down her window and was leaning towards him. It didn't take him long to realise that he knew her: Marianne Simon, an old flame.

With a scowl, Harvey opened his side window and hissed, in a stage whisper, 'For God's sake, Marianne, I'm on surveillance!'

'Oh, I'm so sorry, Harvey. I had no idea! I'll go, then.'

But as Harvey's anxious gaze returned to the house he found the damage had been done. Sean had reached the gate and the front door had closed again, concealing the identity of the occupant. Swiftly Harvey considered whether anything could be salvaged from the fiasco. Realising that Marianne afforded him a useful alibi he decided to continue their conversation. If he was in luck, Sean's lover might reappear to put out a milk bottle or something.

'No, wait. Keep talking, Marianne, I need to linger. Haven't seen you in ages. How are you?'

'Separated from David and soon to be divorced,' she told him with a grimace. 'I should have married you, Harv.'

It had never been on the cards and they both knew it, but Harvey played along all the same. 'I warned you about Dave. All mouth and no trousers, as my mother would say.'

'Actually his mouth was very useful, when it wasn't talking shite! But seriously, I could use some advice. Maybe we could have a chat sometime? I've got Jake Fisher on my case but I'm not sure he's the best man for the job.'

'When it comes to divorce, you could do worse.'

'Mm, but there's complications. He's been screwing me.'

'Marianne! You never change, do you?'

'Anyway, can I see you for a drink sometime soon?'

Harvey nodded. Sean was pulling away now and the light in the hall had gone out. There was little point in sticking around any longer. 'How about right now?' he suggested. 'I know an all-night bar near the centre. We could talk there.'

'Fine.'

As Harvey led the way to the Sun and Moon his irritation with Marianne was fading. There was something appealingly irrepressible about her that always won him over. Besides, she'd had no way of knowing that he was on a job when she came across his car that evening. These little hiccoughs happened every so often. He'd already decided to charge Eileen half-price for this evening's work and he would try again tomorrow, if Sean visited his lover again.

Chatting cosily with his old girlfriend over a hot chocolate with brandy, Harvey soon mellowed out. Marianne had lost little of her allure, although it was over five years since he'd seen her and a good deal longer since he'd bedded her. Flashes of how she'd been with him kept returning. Like a young tigress mostly, he recalled. Hungry for it at all hours of the day and night, and not given to pulling her punches. If anything she'd become even more attractive, maturity filling out her body to a luscious roundness and the crinkles in her face adding authenticity to her smile. She smiled a lot, too, and touched his hand from time to time, making it clear that he'd retained his attraction for her. Harvey was flattered.

'So how come you got involved with Jake?' he asked her.

'Oh, it was pretty inevitable really. All those late-night chats about my marital problems. Stupid though, really. I mean, he could get himself struck off or whatever lawyers get done to them. He should drop the case now, shouldn't he?'

'Of course he should. I'm surprised. I always thought of him as rather straitlaced.'

'Must be my irresistible charm, then!' She grinned seductively, as if to prove it. Harvey felt his prick stretch itself. 'Pity, I'm sure he would have been able to screw David for my share of the house. I put some of my money into it, but because I gave up work when we married David is trying to say I don't have a claim on the proceeds when the sale goes through.'

'Sounds complicated.'

'Yes. Well I always seem to complicate things, don't I? Anyway, this thing with Jake has gone far enough and I want out. I don't want him to handle either me or my case any more. He wasn't that good in the sack anyway. Not like you, Harv!'

'You flatter me!'

But she looked serious, her dark brown eyes meltingly soft. 'I mean it. Still, you don't want to listen to me all night. I'd rather hear about you. From the look of you, you haven't made a mess of your life. Quite the reverse.'

Harvey grinned. It was true, his business had grown splendidly over the past year or so and he was proud of his achievements. While he talked to Marianne about some of his more interesting cases he warmed to her even more. It was going to be difficult to tear himself away from her at the end of the night. He could feel his erection reaching maximum proportions within his boxer shorts, straining for release. And, judging from the flush in her plump cheeks and the bright sparkle in her eye, Marianne was pretty well turned-on too.

At two-thirty they rose to leave but continued their conversation on the pavement outside. It was obvious that they were reluctant to part. At last Harvey decided to risk a direct approach. After all, he knew Marianne well enough by now. If she was going to rebuff him she would do it kindly, he was sure of that.

'Er . . . look, I must get back. I don't suppose you'd consider coming with me, would you?'

She gave a grateful sigh. 'Thank God for that. I thought you'd never ask!'

Marianne rode in his car, leaving her own parked in the centre. Harvey had offered to run her in again in the morning since he had to be in town by nine-thirty. That gave them around six hours for wild, uninhibited love-making. Whoopee!

Harvey drove back through the almost-deserted streets with Marianne kissing his neck and running her fingers through his hair, making it quite difficult for him to concentrate on driving. Almost as soon as they were through his front door he pinned her to the wall in a long, passionate kiss that had them both gasping for it. Her mouth tasted sweet and hot, and as his hands roamed eagerly around her curves he found she was delightfully pneumatic, having put on a bit of weight since he last knew her intimately.

'Let's go upstairs,' he whispered hoarsely, when the fire in his belly was threatening to spill out of his prick.

He half-dragged her up the dark stairs to his bedroom, still in disarray since that morning but with fairly clean sheets on the bed. Marianne fumbled in her bag and, while he kicked off his shoes, she pulled out something metallic that clinked. She held them up with a smile, and Harvey felt himself recoil from the sight. Handcuffs?

'I've discovered I like it better if I'm locked into these.' She smiled. 'Put them on my wrists, tell me I've been a naughty girl. You know the script.'

He didn't, but he could have a good guess. In the investigation business you found out a good deal about what people got up to behind closed doors and nothing much could faze him. Even so, he was unused to such practices himself. While he hesitated, Marianne writhed impatiently on the bed and he knew he had to placate her.

'Give me your hands!' he said sternly, advancing towards her. 'You've been a very naughty girl and I'm placing you under arrest.'

'Oh dear, officer. What will happen to me?'

'That all depends on how you behave.'

He clicked the cuffs over her wrists and she lay back with a sigh. Harvey studied the way her breasts were heaving beneath the blue silk blouse and the bulge of her mons beneath the tight black satin jeans, and knew he wanted to take her without preliminaries. Somehow he guessed that was how she wanted it, too. He roughly undid her buttons until the white lace bra was fully exposed, her honey-coloured bosom filling out the cups. He pulled at the lace with both hands until the brown beads of her nipples were accessible and tweaked them mercilessly.

Marianne groaned and thrust her round tits into the air while her hips rotated eagerly. Harvey felt for her zipper and pulled it down until he could see the white of her panties with the pink lacy heart in front. Above it a few strands of her dark bush showed, making him want her even more. He groped with his own fly and pulled his erection out of his pants. The heat was gathering in his groin, blood pumping into his penis until there seemed no more room for expansion, the skin stretched tight over shaft and glans.

'Talk dirty to me!' Marianne pleaded softly from the bed.

'Okay, you've had this coming to you, bitch!' he snarled, beginning to enjoy himself. He pulled at the pink heart and at once the whole of her pubic hair was visible, with the slitted pouch in the centre. 'I'm going to push right into your wet little cunt and fuck you over and over, till you beg for mercy!'

Harvey felt in the drawer beside the bed and drew out a

foil-wrapped condom. When he opened the packet he saw that it was a black one, a sample he'd had from some men's magazine. So much the better. As he rolled it down his cock the thing became transformed into a gleaming instrument, slick and alien. It made him feel absurdly macho.

Marianne gave an excited squeal. 'Ooh! You're not going to use that on me, are you?'

'Too right I am, bitch!'

He plunged his forefinger into the tangled hair and felt her moist vulva with the hot, wet depression at the centre. She was ready for him all right. As he withdrew, his fingertip passed over her most sensitive spot and she gasped with pleasure. 'Yes, do that again! Please touch me there again!'

Harvey rubbed all around the area of her clitoris, feeling the thing swell and tingle as it responded to stimulation. When she was fully lubricated he swung his thighs between hers and, after yanking down her satin pants, thrust his penis home. Straight into her willing pussy he plunged, feeling the deep smooth walls envelop him until he could go no further, and a hot rush of energy went fountaining up his spine.

Marianne's manacled hands were raised above her head so that her full breasts were uptilted and pert. Hitching himself higher up her body, Harvey seized one mound in one hand and took the solid nipple of the other between his lips as he shafted her, making her wriggle deliciously. She was accelerating the movements of her pelvis, co-ordinating her motions with his so as to maximise the friction on her sensitive love-button. Her breath was coming in hot little gasps now, punctuated with moans.

Harvey's own climax was imminent. He couldn't hold out for long against those erotic sounds, and down below his prick was a driving piston of pure pleasure, taking him relentlessly towards his destination. He could feel her walls rippling around him, tightening, slackening, giving his cock a thorough massage as it wove in and out of her cushioning flesh.

Then came the first juddering spasms of her orgasm and Harvey felt his balls tighten, ready to shed their load. He groaned out his relief as the bliss-laden juice poured from him into the black tube between his legs, releasing all the tension in him. Marianne was still moaning softly when he withdrew. Quickly he unlocked the handcuffs with the key she'd placed on the bedside cabinet. She hugged him close, kissing his face and neck, then collapsed in his arms.

For a while they lay silently, comfortably. Then Marianne said, 'I knew I could trust you not to go too far. Not like that bastard I married.'

'David? What happened?'

'He hurt me, Harv. Really hurt me. Once he found I liked being tied up he took advantage, wouldn't listen when I begged him to stop.'

'That's despicable! Those games depend on mutual trust or they degenerate into S & M without consent.'

'Exactly. That's what I tried to explain to Jake. I admit it's a bit of a grey area as far as the law is concerned, but he didn't seem to understand. I just like the feeling of being helpless, you know? It doesn't have to go much further than that.'

They drifted into sleep, and in the morning woke too late to have time for chatting. In the car, however, Harvey recommended another couple of lawyers experienced in handling matrimonial disputes. When he dropped Marianne near the centre she seemed grateful. 'Maybe we should meet again, soon,' she suggested with a smile.

'Maybe,' he grinned back. 'I'll ring you.'

It was only after she left that he realised he didn't have her phone number. Oh well, she knew his. Yet he had a gut feeling that she wouldn't contact him again. They had met by accident and used each other for a night, but there would probably be no sequel. Once, he had thought about settling down with Marianne, but her unreliable nature and flirty ways would have made it a disastrous match. If ever he did settle for one woman she would have to be someone he could depend upon, someone who could be an equal partner. Furthermore, she would have to be independent and understanding enough to put up with his antisocial hours and unconventional lifestyle. In short, he thought with a wry grin, Wonderwomen only need apply.

Harvey called in at the Sun and Moon and was greeted by Mal, the barman, who was still on duty from last night. He drank a black coffee at the same table he'd shared with Marianne while he skimmed the morning papers. It felt like he'd never been away. He used this bar as an unofficial office, being unable to afford city centre rents. It was a bit of a cybercafé, with a few computers linked into the Internet upstairs together with reprographic facilities and fax. There were four phone lines, too. Best of all, he was allowed an account there.

As soon as his caffeine injection was done, Harvey made his way upstairs. He checked to see if any of the requests for information he'd sent out using the *Smoon* address had elicited a response and was pleased to note that there were two leads to follow up on missing persons. Then he moved to the phone. He dialled Eileen O'Donnell's number and when she answered told her that his tailing of her son last night had failed to bear fruit.

'Oh, that is a shame,' she answered. The tone of her voice suggested that Sean was within earshot, so he was careful not to ask her any questions that might reveal the nature of his call.

'With your permission, I shall try again tonight. If he goes to the same address in Prestwich, that will at least confirm your suspicions that he's seeing someone regularly. I can check the address on the electoral roll, see who the householder is. And if we're lucky, this time I might get a sighting. Do you want me to go ahead? Just answer yes or no.'

'Yes. Yes please.'

A trip to the Town Hall yielded the information that the house was owned by a Mrs Delia Goldman. Harvey did a bit more research for another case, then decided to follow up the leads he'd been given through the Internet. After a sandwich at Smoon's he decided to go back home. It was Saturday, and he was entitled to take half a day off. Relieved that there were no messages on his answerphone, he decided that the City v. United match could wait. After switching on his video to record the game, he went back to bed.

By six he was ready for another stint of a different game, Harvey Boyd v. Sean O'Donnell. It was beginning to feel like that. Although he knew that Eileen's son hadn't deliberately given him the slip last night, and that Marianne turning up at precisely the wrong moment had been sheer bad luck, it still felt as if he'd been outwitted. Perhaps tonight luck would be on his side.

Sean left his home a little earlier and was already halfway down the road when Harvey arrived. He had to do a turn and nearly missed him. Losing sight of him down the Bury Old Road, he was nevertheless confident that his target was going to the same address. When he turned into Delia Goldman's road and saw the now-familiar red Escort parked outside her house, he gave a sigh of relief

Settling in for another long evening, Harvey switched on his radio. In a few minutes, however, he heard a door slam and was instantly on the alert. Yes, he was in luck! Sean had emerged, followed by a woman in a navy jacket and white skirt – presumably Mrs Goldman. Was there a Mr Goldman? he wondered as he picked up his Polaroid camera from the front seat. They must be going out for the evening. Well, a photo was always useful. But then, as he operated the zoom lens, he had shock. As soon as the woman came into focus he could see that she was sixty-five if she was a day. Old enough to be young Sean's grandmother!

Maybe she *was* his grandmother, he thought, as he snapped away. But then he saw Sean kiss her cheek and noticed the light in her eyes as he whispered into her ear. No, they were definitely lovers, no doubt about that. Harvey had enough experience behind him to recognise lust when he saw it. But no wonder the lad was scared to tell his ma. Unfortunately, it was now down to Harvey to break the news to her instead.

There seemed little point in hanging around outside the house. Harvey watched the lovers walk to the end of the road and turn the corner. He drove after them and, just as he reached the next road, saw them slip into the Green Man pub on the corner. After driving into the car park he followed after them.

They were sitting in a corner seat, locked in intimacy. Harvey ordered a pint of Boddy's and sat reading the paper in the opposite corner, glancing over towards them every so often. In his pocket was a directional mike capable of picking up conversations within a twenty-metre radius. It was linked to a miniature tape-recorder. Harvey's ears were good, but not that good. He would have to take pot luck and see what he'd managed to pick up on the tape later.

The pair left after about half an hour and Harvey followed at a discreet distance. It was obvious that they were going back to her place so he returned to his car and replayed what he had recorded. It was soon obvious that they were discussing whether or not to tell Mrs O'Donnell about their affair.

'She'd never understand,' Sean was saying. 'I mean, she'd like grandchildren and all that. It would be too hard for her.'

'But if you don't tell her I shan't believe you're serious about me.'

'Look, give me time, darling. It's hard even for me to get used to the idea, you know?'

'Me too,' Mrs Goldman giggled. 'But here's to the future, darling boy. Cheers!'

Harvey switched off the tape. There was always something nauseating about eavesdropping, although it often had to be done. In this case, however, he decided not to use the tape. The photographs would probably suffice to show Sean's mother who he was with, and Harvey suspected that once he was confronted with the evidence, her son would come clean. His conversation had seemed to indicate that, at heart, he wanted his mother to know.

It was still only nine-thirty, so Harvey decided to take the photos round to Mrs O'Donnell straight away. She was watching the television but switched it off the instant he entered the sitting room, her face tense and expectant. He suggested she should sit down because she might be in for a bit of a shock.

'Are you telling me he *is* gay, after all?' she began.

Harvey shook his head. 'Not as far as I know, but his relationship is not exactly conventional. I want you to take a look at these photographs. This is the woman your son has been visiting. Her name is Delia Goldman.'

'But she's older than me!'

'Precisely.'

'Well then, he couldn't possibly . . .'

She looked up at Harvey in mute appeal. He shrugged. 'It does look as if they're having an affair, Mrs O'Donnell. I've had some experience in these matters and I can usually tell when a relationship is platonic and when it isn't. I tailed them to a pub and observed them for about twenty minutes, and there's no doubt that Sean is emotionally involved with her.'

'I've heard of some men liking older women, but this is ridiculous! She must be drawing her pension.'

Harvey decided to wax philosophical, to hide his embarrassment. 'Love is a funny business, you know. I've seen couples you would never have believed would be attracted to each other. Yet they often make more of a go of it than supposedly conventional couples. Something to prove, I suppose.'

'But what do I do now?'

Harvey realised that Eileen O'Donnell was bewildered rather than distraught. 'That's up to you, but if I were you I'd do nothing for the time being. He may tell you in his own good time, or the affair may fizzle out. Either way you've nothing to lose.'

'Really? You think I should say nothing at all?'

'You wanted to know if your son was gay, Mrs O'Donnell, and you've found out he isn't. Like I said, if I were you I'd leave it at that. I could run a check on the woman, of course, but would that be wise? If Sean found out you'd been snooping around he might be so angry that he'd cut himself off from you altogether. It's a delicate situation.'

'Well, you've had more experience of these things than I have, that's for sure. I think I'll sleep on it, see how it looks in the morning. Thank you for all you've done, Mr Boyd.'

He left his bill and went off into the night, but he couldn't help wondering whether Eileen O'Donnell was better or worse off for knowing the truth about her son. From his perspective the truth often hurt, but it was generally less painful than deception. He got into his battered Peugeot and drove to the Sun and Moon. At this time on a Saturday night it was likely to be filled with barflies, posers and students, but somehow Harvey felt more at home amongst them than with so-called 'normal' people. Maybe that was because he was a bit of a weirdo himself.

Chapter Five

Much to her relief, Gayle was able to keep her date with Mark. They spent a Sunday afternoon wandering along the banks of the Mersey and ended up at a pub for dinner. He continued to question her about her work, showing great interest in some of the cases she described although she was always careful to maintain client confidentiality. She suspected that he had an over-romantic view of what her job entailed.

In return, Mark told her about the photography course he was doing. Apparently he was interested in becoming a press photographer, and his present job was just a fill-in until he was taken on by a newspaper. After they'd spent a pleasant evening chatting, he took her home. By that time Gayle was fancying him something rotten. Since her divorce she'd put all her energies into her work but, after the episode with Brad, it was as if her sexual fire had been ignited again and would not be dampened down.

Once the token coffee had been drunk, Mark took her in his arms on the sofa and they began to kiss. Gayle felt herself relax, letting the sweet wetness of his tongue invade her mouth, feeling the corresponding wetness between her thighs. His hand found her breast and her nipple tingled as he squeezed it, making her crave the warm brush of skin against skin.

'Why don't I take this off?' she said hoarsely, already lifting the hem of her T-shirt.

She wore no bra beneath. Mark gasped his approval as her perfectly proportioned breasts appeared, topped with pinkish-brown nipples that were already hard and hungry to be seized. Soon it was Gayle's turn to gasp as he nibbled at one, grazing it softly with his teeth, while he fingered the other. She felt her breasts swell and tighten, the tingling sensations travelling in a spiral path down to that other centre of arousal below. Within its secret niche her clitoris bulged and throbbed.

Mark was tearing off her jeans now with unseemly haste, followed by her pants. She wanted him to lick her pussy, but before she knew it he had undone his fly and pulled out a smallish but very ready prick which he proceeded to envelop in rubber. Without further ado he slipped his penis into her and after a few fierce thrusts she felt him come. Disappointed, she lay there on the sofa cushions with her pussy still in heat and juices oozing out of her.

'Sometimes I have trouble getting it up when I've been drinking,' Mark admitted as he backed out of her. 'So I have to strike while the iron's hot, so to speak.'

'That's okay, so long as I get my turn later,' she smiled. 'How about giving me a bit of a licking while I'm all hot and bothered down there?'

A look of distaste passed over his face. 'Sorry, Gayle, I don't do that.'

'But you can touch me, can't you? I need it, Mark. I need it bad.'

'You do it,' he urged her, sinking exhausted onto the floor beside her. 'I like to watch.'

Suspecting that he was just too knackered, Gayle decided that a spot of DIY was the best she was going to get right then. Her clitoris was demanding immediate attention so she pulled her labia apart and touched it delicately, the way she knew was best for her. Soon she was subjecting the hard nub to continuous friction, working herself up towards an orgasm with effortless ease. As the first tremors hit her she moaned at the release from tension, letting the satisfying waves pass right through her.

When she regained awareness of her surroundings, she found that Mark had disappeared. Upstairs she heard the loo flush and knew he'd heeded a call of nature, but she felt miffed. Had the spectacle really been that boring? Something about the guy put her on alert. She was used to sniffing out weirdness, and Mark seemed to have a strange way of behaving when it came to sex. Still, for the time being she would give him the benefit of the doubt and put it down to too much alcohol.

While Gayle was still lying there, enjoying the feeling of utter relaxation in her limbs, Mark came back down. 'I'm sorry, Gayle, but I just threw up.'

'Was it something I said, or something I did?'

'Look, I'm really sorry. It's my own stupid fault for mixing drinks. But I think I ought to be heading home.'

'You're welcome to stay. I'll put you to bed and look after you,' she offered, but he shook his head.

'Thanks, but I don't want to impose. I'll be in touch, okay?'

'Hey, you're in no state to drive home . . .'

But he was already out of the front door and Gayle was stark naked. She shrugged. So much for their first night of rapturous pleasure! Maybe Mark was feeling embarrassed. She would ring him tomorrow and let him know that she didn't hold it against him.

On Sunday morning, however, she had an unexpected

phone call herself. It was from Donna Lewis. Gayle was astonished to hear her voice again. She'd thought that case was closed but Donna explained, 'I need more evidence, for the divorce. I want to make sure Brad doesn't get sole custody of the boys. He says he'll take them from me, and I couldn't bear that.'

'I'll do whatever I can to help,' Gayle assured her.

'I need photos, if possible. My lawyer says it'll make all the difference to my case.'

Gayle pondered a while. She had a feeling that Brad would still be interested in her. All she had to do was turn up at the Greedy Goat again on a Friday night and she was pretty sure he'd welcome her with open arms. But how to set up a photo session?

Then she thought of Mark. If he was so fascinated by the idea of her work, and keen on photography, maybe he'd like to be her accomplice for one night only. The more she thought about it the better the idea seemed. It would be a way of reassuring him, boosting his confidence. 'Look, can I get back to you on this one?' she asked Donna.

As she'd expected, Mark was overjoyed to be asked to help. They met for Sunday lunch and she quickly outlined the plan. If he was hoping for a chance to redeem himself sexually, however, he was to be disappointed. She had to drive to Sheffield that afternoon to meet a client and make arrangements for an early-morning assignment next day.

The Sheffield job went well, clearing her desk for the Brad Lewis photo opportunity. After carefully checking the details with Mark, she made her way to the Greedy Goat on Friday evening as before, and was relieved to see Brad in the back bar just as she'd hoped. He greeted her with a warm smile, his blue eyes filled with the light of desire.

'Sharon! I was hoping I'd see you again. You disappeared

into the night like a beautiful dream, so we didn't get a chance to swap addresses.'

'Yes, sorry about that. I suddenly remembered I had to get home and feed the cat.'

If he suspected another motive he didn't show it. 'Would you like a drink?'

They were soon chatting freely and the erotic temperature began to rise. Gayle had forgotten how strong the sexual chemistry was between them. Being with Brad was like wallowing in a warm bath, with all her defences slowly dissolving. She began to have doubts about whether she should have agreed to meet him a second time. But then she remembered that this time Mark was on hand, primed to interrupt the proceedings before they got out of control. All she had to do was make sure they returned to the same hotel where her accomplice would be waiting in the wings, camera at the ready.

'How about going back to that hotel disco?' she suggested at last.

Brad needed no persuasion. 'Back to the Hazeldene?' His eyes smouldered at her, making her insides swoop with blatant lust. He put his lips close to her ear whispering, 'I've got a better idea. Why don't we skip the disco and go straight for the alternative entertainment?'

Soon they were speeding towards the hotel, where Gayle hoped Mark would already be awaiting them. When they arrived she suggested a quick drink and as soon as they entered the hotel bar she was relieved to see her boyfriend sitting in the corner with a pint and a tourist guidebook. After giving him a discreet wink, she asked Brad to get her a champagne cocktail. While she sipped it he went out to book the room, and Gayle felt her pulse begin to race. What if the hotel were fully booked? She hadn't bothered to arrange a 'Plan B'.

Her luck was in, however. Not only did Brad throw the room keys down on the table in front of her, but he went off to the gents' immediately. While he was gone she signalled the room number to Mark with her fingers: twenty-three. This time, surely, nothing could go wrong. Mark had been instructed to wait ten minutes after they went upstairs and then to burst in with his camera snapping. She knew Brad was a quick worker and they should be in a compromising position by then. Mark's sudden entrance would both interrupt the proceedings effectively and get Donna the necessary evidence. Of course, it would blow Gayle's cover for good, but hopefully that wouldn't matter once the film was in the can.

As they left the bar Gayle threw Mark a backward glance just to make sure he'd noticed their exit. He was closing his book lazily and finishing the last of his pint, giving her a nod as he did so. Good old Mark! Perhaps he would turn out to be useful on other jobs, too. She often needed some back-up and it would be good to work with someone she knew well.

Soon, however, all her attention was being commanded by Brad as he drew her into the empty lift. Once the door was closed he pulled her into a passionate clinch that left her hardly able to stagger out onto the landing. Her body was on fire all over, and from the way that Brad was panting she guessed he was pretty hot for her too. They entered the bedroom and before Gayle could take stock of her surroundings she was being dragged to the king-sized bed and stripped of her clothes. Hungrily Brad's mouth closed over hers.

While he thrust his tongue into her mouth, making her ache with wanting him, Gayle undid the buttons at Brad's throat until she could put her hands inside his shirt and feel the hot, hairy flesh of his chest. He paused and took it off, then unbuckled his belt and eased himself out of his jeans until he lay there in his underpants, his prick making a visible hump in the cotton. Gayle reached down and pulled out his erection, feeling the solid weight of it against her palm. She closed her fingers around it, squeezing gently, and the impatient organ thrust against her wrist in a reflex action. 'Don't!' Brad groaned. 'I don't want to come too soon!'

So Gayle contented herself with stroking his muscled chest and enjoying the increasingly wet kisses that he was giving her. She could still feel the tip of his rampant penis moving against her stomach and the tip of her own clitoris pulsating through her labia in ecstatic response. Hurry up, Mark, she said to herself, afraid that it might all be over by the time he arrived with his camera. If he came soon, however, he would get some excellent shots.

Gayle was half-expecting Brad to thrust straight into her, as Mark had done last time, but instead he put his head between her thighs and slowly opened her labia with his fingers revealing the deep pink folds within. She heard the soft sucking noise that her love-lips made as they parted and felt a gush as new secretions increased her lubrication. Brad groaned and put his mouth to her pussy, ready to lick and suck at her fresh juices. Despite herself Gayle dropped her guard and began to relax, lying back against the pillow in voluptuous anticipation of the sensual pleasures to come. She even began to hope that Mark wouldn't make his dramatic entrance before she'd had at least *one* orgasm!

One thing was for sure, Brad Lewis gave excellent head. His tongue was long and flexible, getting to the parts that other tongues couldn't reach. Right inside her quim it probed, working round the extra-sensitive entrance to titillating effect, then withdrawing so that the tip could play on her protruding love-button. Back and forth it flicked with rapid precision, first to one side then the other, filling her with a deeply gratifying warmth. Gayle could feel the knot of energy tightening inside her, moving her towards the inevitable conclusion, and she took hold of her breasts, caressing their smooth sides and fingering the taut nipples to hasten her arousal. She shuddered as an exquisite quiver occurred deep inside her, a tantalising foretaste of things to come.

It wasn't long before she was arching back in abandoned bliss, feeling the flood of wild sweetness course through her veins. Although her clitoris was throbbing violently, Brad didn't seem to notice. He just went on licking as if he was in a world of his own, drunk on her wine. Gayle could hardly believe her luck. His tongue left the over-sensitive area at the top of her vulva and plunged into her again, making her grunt with the sudden revival of her rapture. She pinched her nipples and the spasms intensified, taking her into another mind-blowing climax. As her arousal peaked she found herself praying, 'Not yet, Mark, please – not just yet!'

But hardly had she come down from her second orgasm when she heard the door being thrust open, and knew that her fun was over. There was a series of flashes. Brad's surprised face looked up from between her thighs and then grew dark with anger. 'What the fuck—' He leapt off the bed but Mark was too quick for him and backed away, out of the door, still clicking. Gayle grabbed her clothes and dashed into the bathroom, locking the door behind her. She had her story prepared: Mark was nothing to do with her, he had been hired by Donna to get evidence of adultery. Even so she found herself trembling as she hastily scrambled back into her clothes.

When she came out Brad was sitting on the bed in his

underpants, head in hands. 'My wife!' he moaned. 'My bloody wife! I should have known.'

'I thought you were divorced.'

'Not yet. In the process. Now she'll really have some ammo to throw at the judge, won't she? The bitch!'

Gayle shrugged. She couldn't go so far as to express sympathy for him. It was time to go, but she had to do it tactfully if she wanted to avoid suspicion. 'I think I'd better leave, Brad. You look as if you want to be alone.'

He reached out for her, his eyes dark and faraway. 'It's not your fault, Sharon. I don't want you to feel bad about this.'

Gayle buried her guilt, reminding herself that she was still working. Even so, she found it hard to be totally detached. Giving him a hug, she swung her bag over her shoulder and left him to his thoughts.

As arranged, Gayle met up with Mark in a nearby café-bar where he was already sitting moodily over a coffee. 'Well, you looked like you were enjoying yourself all right,' he accused her, as soon as she arrived.

'For God's sake, Mark, it was only a job!' she told him. However, she found it hard to convince herself, let alone him. She ordered a cappuccino and tried to change the subject. 'Job's done, now where shall we go? I've heard there's a good disco on in town.'

'Don't you want to know if the photos have come out?' he asked, in a sneering tone.

'I'm sure you're a very competent photographer, Mark.'

'But you're secretly *dying* to see him licking you, aren't you? Go on, admit it!'

Gayle sensed a hidden agenda but she didn't know what he was on about. Was Mark jealous, was that it? If so, he had no cause. Brad Lewis had been an assignment, that was all, and now it was over. Still, it might be as well to put the lid on this once and for all.

'You want me to develop the film right away, is that it?'

He nodded. Gayle sighed. There was only one lab she knew of that worked through the weekend and that was Dave Burrows', but he charged the earth.

'I could do it,' Mark said. 'At the college. I've got a key to the dark room.'

'Okay, if that's how you want to spend your Friday night . . .'

Apparently, it was. Much to her surprise, Gayle found herself driving across Manchester and being let in through a side door to the dark-room of the photo lab. In the claustrophobic gloom she watched Mark take the film out of the camera and start the developing process. His face, illumined by a red bulb, took on the eerie likeness of a B-movie alien and for a few moments she felt afraid. How well did she know this guy, after all? Nobody knew they were here, after hours in the deserted building. Had she put herself in jeopardy?

Soon he was absorbed in the printing process and Gayle, forgetting her fear, was growing bored. There were other pictures on the film, research shots taken on longer-term assignments, and only the last few would be relevant to the Lewis case. But already Mark was scrutinising the film closely, as if he had some personal involvement in it. He seemed more interested than her in the results. Gayle found his behaviour more and more weird, and her unease waxed and waned as she sat there observing him.

At last the developed prints were hung up to dry and they opened the dark-room door. The lab, dominated by the huge rostrum camera, was full of shadows. Gayle wandered around, peering at the displays on the walls, while Mark lurked in the doorway. She sensed that he was not happy, but she wasn't sure why.

At last he called her back into the dark-room. He'd switched on the light and ranged the six significant photos on the bench for her inspection. There was Gayle lying on the palatial bed with her hands on her naked breasts, her head thrown back and a look of abandoned rapture contorting her features. Between her legs was Brad, head down in the first two shots and busily at work, but then his startled face was looking directly at the camera, as he realised what was going on. His large erection was very obvious in three of the prints.

'Well done!' Gayle commented, briskly. 'I'm sure my client will be very pleased with these.'

'And I hope you're pleased with yourself!' Mark snarled, alerting her once again to the fact that all was not well.

'What do you mean?'

'Did he bring you off then, when he sucked you? Good, was it?'

Suddenly Gayle remembered that Mark had an aversion to cunnilingus. Was it possible that he was jealous of Brad's uninhibited and enthusiastic tonguing of her pussy? It was certainly looking that way.

'I was doing a job, Mark,' she said, evenly. 'Sometimes it's necessary to lead a man on so I can get the evidence I need. In this case, it's worked a treat. You performed your part to perfection, and that rat's wife has all the evidence she needs to make sure she gets custody of their two sons. That's what I do it for, Mark. Not just for thrills.'

'Really!' His tone was sarcastic, and he turned away, gathering up the prints and handing them to her with a scowl. Then his grey eyes caught hers in their searchlight beam. 'So you were faking it, were you?'

'Look that man means nothing to me, okay? The job's done and I'll most likely never see him again. It's you I'm concerned about, Mark. Now why don't we get out of here, find somewhere to have a quiet drink and start to enjoy what's left of the evening?'

Reluctantly he tidied up, then locked the door. They left the building and went to where Gayle had parked her car. But once they were inside it Mark said, 'I think I'd rather you drove me home, if you don't mind.'

'Sure.'

She followed his directions and they were soon at his flat. Mark invited Gayle in for a beer, but she wasn't at all sure whether he wanted her there or not. He was still acting strangely. Nevertheless she followed him upstairs, and when she was seated in a battered armchair he went through to the tiny kitchen and took a couple of beers out of the fridge.

For a while they sat drinking in silence and Gayle felt distinctly uncomfortable. Then Mark suddenly said, 'That wasn't the first time you'd been with that guy, was it?'

'No.' She told him about the previous occasion. 'But I've only ever seen him at the request of his missus. I can't work out why it seems to bother you so much.'

'How many other men have you laid in the course of duty?'

'Mark, I don't generally "lay" them, as you put it. The idea is simply to lead them on until they incriminate themselves, then I report back to their wives or girlfriends.'

'It's a good way to try men out though, isn't it? Find out who's got the biggest dick. I mean, if you came across someone who really turned you on, wouldn't you be tempted to go on seeing him?'

'No I wouldn't!' Gayle felt anger rise in her as she realised that what she was dealing with here was definitely jealousy, and of an almost pathological kind. 'Look, Mark, listen to me. You know the kind of work I do, and if you can't take it then I suggest we call it a day. I'm not going to change my job just to suit you. If you can't believe that I'm in this for the money rather than the kicks, then that's your problem, but don't lay your trip on me. Okay?'

He rose from his chair and stood over her, menacingly. Gayle's adrenalin began to flow and she automatically started to plot her moves. With thudding heart she calculated how quickly she could get to the door.

'When we made love, the other night, was it as good as it was with him? His dick's bigger than mine, isn't it?'

The nature of Mark's obsession began to reveal itself, but Gayle was in no mood to psychoanalyse him. She tried to keep calm. 'Size doesn't mean anything, Mark, as I'm sure you know. It's how you use it that counts.'

'So what do you give me for last time then, a two? I know you didn't get off, so don't try and pretend you did. But *he* made you come, didn't he? That bastard who's cheating on his wife! *He* satisfied you!'

'Don't be ridiculous, Mark. Look, I think I'd better go . . .'

Gayle made for the door, scared stiff that he would try to stop her, turn violent even, but he stood by and let her pass. She heard him mumbling incoherently as she struggled to open the lock, and at last the door stood open. 'I'm sorry, Mark,' was all she could say as she hurried down the dingy staircase and out through the front door into the night. As she made for her car she expected him to come crashing out of the house at any moment, or at least to start shouting after her, but nothing happened. With a sigh of relief she put the car into gear and drove off back to Chorlton.

That guy has problems, she told herself as she sped through the city streets. Much as she felt sorry for him, she knew that there was no way she could take on such a disturbed individual. Her life was complicated and tricky enough as it was, and her work took almost all her energy. If she was to have a boyfriend it had to be someone she could relax with, someone she felt perfectly at ease with, or she would rather be alone.

Donna was taken aback by the photos at first. Gayle thought perhaps she hadn't realised how far things had to go between Brad and her to get explicit shots. But she agreed that they would provide valuable evidence.

'We want to prove that he's the kind of man who would pick any woman up in a bar. Not the sort of rôle model I'd want for my boys. But I'd like to ask you another favour – would you be prepared to testify in court, Gayle?'

It wouldn't be the first time she'd done it, but there could be a problem. Since she hadn't actually taken the shots herself, an aggressive lawyer might require the photographer to take the stand as well. 'Who is your lawyer?' she asked.

'Jacob Fisher.'

Gayle nodded. She knew Jake of old. 'I'll have a word.'

'Thanks very much, Gayle. This means an awful lot to me, and to my boys. Although they're too young to know much about it, thank God!'

Gayle phoned Jake a week later, when he'd had time to see the photos. He understood her reluctance to appear in court. A lengthy custody hearing would make inroads into her valuable time with no financial recompense. Still, he seemed to think that a signed affidavit should suffice.

Mark made no further effort to get in touch with her, and Gayle presumed that their short-lived affair was at an end. She couldn't help feeling that it had been a mistake from the start. The way he'd pestered her should have put her on alert, together with the unhealthy fascination he'd seemed to have for her work. She regretted that she'd ever become involved with him.

Once again she was led to the conclusion that her work was incompatible with a serious love affair. It would take a very special kind of man to tolerate broken dates and unsocial hours, let alone the sexual encounters that were an integral part of her job. Sometimes she contemplated getting out, finding a more normal occupation and a more conventional lifestyle, but always she ended up telling herself she would give it just another year. Gayle was fast coming to the conclusion that, if the truth be told, she really loved her work.

Chapter Six

Harvey sat in the lounge bar of the Criterion feeling ill at ease. This wasn't the sort of place that he normally met clients, but the woman on the phone had insisted on it. She'd said something about the place being 'discreet'. It was certainly that. In an atmosphere of sepulchral gloom, aged waiters with silver platters bearing drinks drifted around like butlers from some bygone age. He sat self-consciously, feeling out of place in his sand-coloured jacket, reading a copy of the *Evening News*, as arranged.

'Mr Boyd?' Harvey started to hear his name. Looking round he saw a well-groomed woman in her forties: immaculate hair tinted an ambiguous shade of platinum-grey; make-up that emphasised the blue of her eyes and tinted her lips coral pink; figure kept nicely in trim and now subtly displayed in a smart navy and white dress. She exuded a faint scent of *Femme*.

'Mrs Goodman?'

'Call me Lorraine, do. Shall we sit over here, where it's nice and quiet?'

He followed her to the corner by the window, away from the trio of businessmen, and ordered a glass of white wine and a beer for himself. From the way in which Lorraine Goodman plonked her navy bag down on the table he knew at once that she meant business and would come straight to the point.

'My husband's name is Paul,' she began, looking him squarely in the eye. 'Does that mean anything to you?'

'Paul Goodman?' Harvey frowned. It certainly had a familiar ring. Ah yes, now he had it! That name had been seen all over town a month or two back, splurged across the smiling face of an American-style evangelist. 'Your husband is part of the "Joy of Jesus" campaign, right?'

'No, Mr Boyd. My husband *is* the "Joy of Jesus" campaign! It was his brainchild, and he is the prime mover. But for him, thousands of people would never know the joy of Jesus Christ.'

Harvey began to feel decidedly uneasy. He had nothing against people being religious, as long as they kept their feelings and convictions to themselves. But starry-eyed evangelical types gave him the heeby-jeebies. 'I see. Well, how do you think I can help you?'

'It's a very delicate matter, but I want you to investigate my husband. I have reason to believe he is not all he appears to be.'

'In what way?'

She leant forward, allowing him to glimpse half an inch of cleavage between her generous breasts. 'In the worst possible way for one who pretends to be a devoted family man. I am talking about licentiousness, lasciviousness. The shameful abuse of power that leads him to take advantage of young, vulnerable women. Not to put too fine a point on it, I am talking about adultery, plain and simple, Mr Boyd.'

'I see.'

'Not with the same woman, you understand. He would not be so foolish as to have a lasting affair. No, I think we are dealing with opportunity and temptation here. You must understand that my husband is a very charismatic man. He draws people to him, especially susceptible young girls. He holds private audiences, absolving them personally of their sins. It is during these private sessions that I believe he goes too far and sometimes actually abuses the young women.'

'Have there been any complaints?'

Lorraine Goodman gave a sharp laugh of mockery. 'Complaints? I should say not! These girls are filled with rapture when he touches them. To be alone with the great, the divine Paul Goodman is more than they could have dreamed of.' Her face grew dark, bitter. 'They would gladly lay their virginity down on the altar of my sainted husband's egotistical vanity and unbridled lechery.'

Harvey was struggling to remain calm in the face of so much barely-controlled anger and jealousy. He had seldom met a woman so eaten up with emotion. It was clear that she wanted revenge in the form of public humiliation for her husband. If this one broke in the national press, Paul Goodman's evangelical career would be ruined. 'What would you like me to do?'

'Catch him out! Get photographs, the best you can. I want proof. After that, you can leave the rest to me.'

'Where is he now?'

She thrust a leaflet at him with a list of tour dates, just like a rock band. He saw that the road show was in Glasgow that night, then Liverpool, Manchester, Sheffield, Birmingham.

'I've been staying here with my sister for a few days, but I'm going back to London with our children tomorrow,' she said. 'He prefers it if I don't tour with him – I'll leave you to guess why. I have the names of the hotels he'll be staying in. He generally holds these private audiences in his hotel room, with men on guard outside.'

'Sounds tricky . . .'

'Well I thought you might be able to get taken on as a bodyguard. I can tell you the man to get in touch with. They generally hire them locally, just for one night. I know he hasn't got one for Manchester yet because I heard them talking about it.'

'You seem to have done your homework, Lorraine. Can we talk finance? Even if I'm paid for a night's work as a bodyguard, there are still my expenses.'

'No problem. I'll make sure your fee will come out of campaign funds. I think that's only fair, don't you?'

She flashed him a rather cheeky smile, taking him by surprise. If she weren't so embittered, Harvey thought, Lorraine Goodman would be an attractive woman. He imagined she was a good wife and mother, too, in a very conventional way. What on earth would make a man like Paul risk everything just for the sake of a quick thrill with a star-struck young devotee?

A rampant libido, presumably.

As he drove home Harvey realised that he was glad of the chance to expose that hypocrite. He had taken a dislike to the man, or at least to his squeaky-clean image, and to confirm his wife's suspicions that he really was a lecher would give him a good deal of satisfaction. The crucial question was whether he could persuade his head honcho, a man called Stephen Treblant, to hire him as a bodyguard.

Harvey rang the number Lorraine had given him as soon as he got in. Apparently Mr Goodman and his mates were out feasting, but Mr Treblant would ring him back when they returned. Much to Harvey's surprise he actually did, two hours later.

'What can I do for you, Mr Boyd?' came the voice of a smooth operator at the other end of the line.

Harvey explained that he'd heard a bodyguard was needed for the Manchester gig. He was gently reproved. 'Convocation, please. Yes, we are short of a man for the night. What experience do you have, and what are your rates per hour?'

He quoted a fee that he knew was very reasonable. After detailing a few of the places he'd worked at, and people he'd worked for, Harvey sensed that he had got the job.

'Please come to the Victoria Crown Hotel at four-thirty on Wednesday. We shall issue you with identification and give you your orders. It is essential that you turn up on time.'

'Don't worry, I'll be there.'

Although it went against the grain, Harvey had his hair cut for the occasion. He wanted to fit in, and knew that image was everything. His dark suit had been cleaned, his black shoes polished and he was well-scrubbed behind the ears. When he finally presented himself to Stephen his reward was a brief nod of approval.

'Here is your identity badge, Mr Boyd. It will get you anywhere you need to go, including backstage. I'm also issuing you with this radio, so you can keep in touch with me throughout. Your duty will be to keep Mr Goodman in sight at all times and warn me if you have the slightest suspicion about anyone in his vicinity. When he returns to this hotel you will ride in the following car with me. You will then stand guard outside his room until you are relieved, and your duties will not end until you are dismissed by me personally. Is that clear?'

'Very clear, thank you, Mr Treblant.'

What was certainly clear was that they weren't prepared to rely simply on the good Lord to look after His own. The whole operation was being run with military precision. Why? Was it simply to protect Paul Goodman from harm, or did he have something to hide? That was one of the things Harvey intended to find out.

There were three other bodyguards on duty that evening, and they were to work a rota system whereby they would be allowed a ten-minute break at set intervals. They were to keep strictly to schedule. If they missed their break for any reason, too bad. There was to be no slacking on duty. Although nothing had been said, Harvey had the impression that at least one of the others was armed. They were certainly formidable-looking guys, making him feel quite a weakling by comparison.

They were driven to the hall in a sleek black limo and Harvey was taken backstage to meet the man himself. Paul Goodman was surprisingly short, but he had startlingly blue eyes, a tanned complexion, a head of thick, dark hair – and something extra. Was it to do with his bearing, Harvey wondered, or did a subtle aura of power surround him? Whatever it was, Harvey was impressed despite himself.

'Welcome to our team,' Paul said, shaking him by the hand with a firm and slightly lingering grip. Then he fixed him with the piercing blue eyes and asked quietly, 'Are you a believer, Harvey?'

The question was unnervingly disconcerting. Harvey stammered, 'Well . . . er . . . not altogether. I mean, I don't go to church but . . .'

'But you believe in God, right?' Why was his tone ironic? Harvey felt as if he were caught in the middle of some game whose rules he didn't know. He shrugged, laughing nervously.

'I'm not interested in whether a man believes or not,' Paul continued. 'I only want people to *know*! If you don't know the Lord intimately, then you cannot walk in His ways. Perhaps you will come to know the Lord by the end of the evening, Harvey. I sincerely hope so.' If this man's a hypocrite, Harvey concluded, then he's a pretty successful one.

Backstage it was hot and cramped, but Harvey had to share a small room with two of the bodyguards until seven, when the doors opened to let the people in. They drank Coke, since Paul forbade alcohol entirely, and the other pair played chess while Harvey read. He could hear speakers being tested, people shouting orders, furniture being moved around. The all-male atmosphere was different from those he'd encountered before. There was nothing of the pub, club or locker-room about it. Harvey thought maybe it was more like being in a monastery. He wouldn't know.

At seven they were summoned to Paul's room for prayers. Harvey felt ill-at-ease hearing the impromptu invocation made on his behalf, but he muttered 'Amen' with the rest of them, then waited for his orders.

'Adam and John, front of house please,' Stephen said crisply. 'Harvey and James, I want you in the wings, one each side. I'm going down into the auditorium now to test out your radios.'

Once the hall started filling up Harvey felt an air of excitement building which he knew would reach its peak when Paul made his appearance. There was a gospel-type choir with their own live band, and they began to croon softly as the rows of seats filled. At the back of the stage a huge banner proclaimed 'Joy of Jesus', and there was a bank of flowers all along the front of the stage with huge sheaves in the wings. Harvey had to peer through the giant gladioli to get a clear view.

At last, when the hall was full to bursting, Paul Goodman came to stand in the opposite wing. He wore a dark suit, white shirt and bright red tie with a large gold cross embroidered on it. Harvey watched him psyche himself up to make his entrance while one of his minions sang his praises accompanied by the choir. When the crowd was keyed up to the highest pitch of anticipation, Paul walked forward into the spotlight and the whole place erupted.

The man was a preacher, not a healer, and yet there were people in wheelchairs and on crutches sitting in the front. Inspired by their hero's charismatic presence, several of these stood up and waved their arms around. Young and old lined up to be blessed, some selected individuals testified to the change that the Lord had wrought in their lives, and over it all Paul Goodman reigned supreme.

There wasn't much he didn't know about crowd manipulation. His speeches were carefully orchestrated to reach their climax at the point of maximum emotional appeal, subtly reinforced with music. His hand gestures, his posture, the tone and volume of his voice were all carefully choreographed. To Harvey it was all very familiar. Where had he seen such techniques practised with such mastery before? Ah yes, those films of the Nuremberg Rallies!

Harvey felt himself being carried away despite his scepticism by the sheer power and infectious euphoria of it all. When the show was over, Harvey noticed that Stephen had taken aside several attractive young women and was talking to them earnestly. Curious, he tried to saunter over to eavesdrop but one of the other bodyguards stopped him.

'Mr Treblant is busy right now,' he was told, firmly. 'Take a ten-minute break then report to the dressing-rooms.'

Harvey went backstage. There was a guard posted outside Paul Goodman's door. A small queue of people were waiting, but when he tried to talk to one of them the guard frowned and waved him on. He went to where cold drinks were being dispensed and had an orange juice.

For a while he wandered around the hall aimlessly, listening to the excited chatter of the converted. Eventually he was paged by Stephen. 'Convene at the entrance in five minutes. We're returning to the hotel.'

Harvey felt his heart-rate rise once more. The four bodyguards were driven in one car, Goodman with several aides was in another, and Stephen followed in a minibus with darkened windows. Harvey had a suspicion that it was full of adoring young women. The convoy set out for the Victoria Crown, and as soon as they arrived the bodyguards were sent ahead to check the celebrity suite. Harvey was sent to make a thorough search of the bathroom. It would have been the perfect opportunity to plant a bug, if he'd thought of it.

At last he heard a buzz of voices in the lounge and went out to see Paul standing with two other aides. Stephen came up to him. 'You are to stand right outside the door with James. No one must be allowed into here unless they have my personal authorisation. Is that clear?'

Harvey nodded. He was pleased that he would be in a position to see exactly who came and went. As he passed Goodman on his way out the man gave him a brief nod of acknowledgement. Harvey was amazed that he felt gratified.

The corridor seemed full of people, but James was standing there coolly with an air of disinterest. Harvey gave him a smile but received only a stony stare in return. Stephen came out and went into a room further down the corridor, ignoring the two guards. He returned in a few seconds with a pretty brunette of around twenty. Her eyes were filled with the same starry light as most of the other people at the convocation. Harvey heard him say, 'I'll see if Mr Goodman is ready for you now.'

For a few seconds the girl hovered between the two guards and Harvey could sense the pent-up exhilaration within her. She was filled with a strong erotic charge, ready to explode into orgasm or the spiritual equivalent. It would be very easy to take advantage of such a vulnerable young woman.

She was let into the suite by Stephen, who went off down the corridor again. Harvey's ears strained for tell-tale sounds, but he could hear nothing. Eventually Stephen returned with a second devotee, this time a blonde. She looked even younger than the first and gave Harvey a dazzling smile which he returned.

'Oh, this is so wonderful! I never thought I stood a chance of getting near him.'

'Mr Goodman likes to give as many personal audiences as he possibly can when he is on tour,' Stephen commented, po-faced.

'What do I have to do?' the girl asked, full of nervous excitement. 'I mean, do I kneel before him or anything?'

He's not the Pope, Harvey thought. Stephen said, 'Allow him to lead the proceedings, my dear. Act as the Spirit moves you, and you can't go wrong. Trust in the Lord to guide you.'

'Oh, yes!' she breathed, her blue eyes misting.

When the brunette appeared, she was weeping. Stephen ushered in the second girl then accompanied the first back to the room down the corridor. Harvey caught James' eye. 'I knew there'd be tears before bedtime!' he grinned.

James gave him a steely look. 'It is a very emotional experience for these young people.'

'You can say that again! Anyone would think he was a pop star, or something.'

James did not deign to reply. Stephen returned with yet another young lady, a beautiful Asian girl with hair to her waist. The 'audience' with her lasted about twenty minutes and had Stephen looking impatiently at his watch. All in all, twelve young women were ushered into Goodman's presence that night and almost all of them emerged in tears. Harvey decided that it was definitely suspicious. The trouble was, there was no way he could get in there to check on what was happening. Not even Stephen could know the full story, unless there were hidden cameras. He began to wonder if he could introduce them on another occasion.

There was no chance to talk to the women afterwards as, one by one, they were taken downstairs by two aides and either met up with their friends and relatives or were sent home in a taxi. Most of them seemed to be in another world, and Harvey doubted whether he could have got any sense out of them anyway.

At midnight, when the last of the girls had gone and everyone looked tired, Harvey was handed his wage packet and dismissed. He left the hotel feeling stupid. The work for which Stephen Treblant had employed him had been carried out to everyone's satisfaction, but the job he'd been hired to do by Lorraine Goodman had been hopelessly botched. All he could report was that her husband did indeed see a succession of pretty young women in private. He had no proof that anything improper had taken place.

Even so, he was duty-bound to report back to his client. Next morning he rang her in London, as arranged, and tried to convince her that he'd done his best but had failed to get any actual evidence.

'That's what I was afraid of,' she sighed. 'I know how carefully he protects himself It's a pity you're not a young woman yourself, Mr Boyd. We might have had more success then!'

Her flippant comment struck an immediate chord in Harvey. 'Look, I'd like to give it another go. It's Birmingham in three days' time, isn't it?'

'Yes. We've a strong youth following there, so the rally will be like a rock concert.'

'Okay. Well, I think I might be able to nail him next time, as long as I can get some help. Can I get back to you on this?'

'Of course. And good luck.'

As soon as he put the phone down Harvey looked through his address book. There were several women he'd used as accomplices in the past but none seemed likely to help him now. Hazel, the ex-cop, had married and had a kid recently so she was out of circulation. Lynne had gone to live in France with her millionaire boyfriend. Kath had said she didn't want to work for him again. Who on earth was left?

Then he thought of Gayle Webster. Much as he despised her method of working, Harvey had to admit that she sounded perfect for this particular assignment. He looked for her ad in the Yellow Pages. There wasn't one. Eventually he found her number in the residential section. Presumably she preferred to maintain a low profile. He got her answerphone and left a message, hoping she'd get back to him soon. That evening, just as he was settling down to his cod and chips, she rang. Her tone was crisply professional. 'Harvey Boyd? You wanted to speak to me. Gayle Webster.'

He explained that he was a fellow investigator and was looking for a woman to help him on a case. She didn't exactly jump at the chance. 'I've quite a busy case-load myself at the moment. What kind of job would it be?'

'Something that I believe you specialise in. I've been asked to took into the morals of quite a well-known public figure, someone who sets himself up as an example to others, so to speak, and I'm sure you'd be perfect for the job. It entails travelling to Birmingham on Friday. Could we meet somewhere to discuss it?'

'Friday?' She paused, probably to consult her diary. 'Yes. I could be free then. Shall we meet tonight, at Kennedy's? I've another client to see nearby at eight. Say, seven-thirty?'

Harvey got there early, sat where he could see the door and tried to spot Gayle before she saw him. He identified her at once when she arrived. With her shiny blonde hair in a neat pleat, the voluptuous curves of her figure enhanced by a flowery summer dress and her legs shown off by strappy white sandals, she could have stepped straight out of a Chandler novel. He gave a discreet wave and she smiled at him, coming straight over to his table.

'Harvey?' She held out a hand to him. He felt a warm tingle as he enclosed it briefly in his.

'What would you like to drink?'

'Oh, a lemonade please!' She sank into a chair, fanning herself with the menu. Harvey went to the bar. When he returned she gave him another of those small, wry smiles that made her eyes light up and sent his pulse skittering off course. He could quite see why men fell for her. She must be very good at her job.

Harvey gave her one of the handbills for the 'Joy of Jesus' road show. 'Know anything about this guy?'

She knew better than to repeat Goodman's name aloud. 'Heard of him. Are we talking scandal here?'

Harvey nodded. 'Possibly.' The bar was filling up, becoming an unsuitable place for a confidential conversation. 'When you've finished your drink, shall we take a walk by the canal?'

Gayle understood without question, quaffed her lemonade and followed him to the door. They made their way down to the canalside path, where they could talk undisturbed except by the occasional cyclist or dog-walker.

'His wife put me on to him,' Harvey explained. 'She

thinks he's taking advantage of the young girls who come to
see him . . . I suppose I must say "perform". I've been to one
of his rallies and it really is some performance.'

Harvey told her that he'd been taken on as a bodyguard
but got nowhere. She cottoned on without him having to
spell it out. 'So you want me to pretend to be a convert and
get one of those private audiences?' He nodded. 'You'd want
tapes and photos if possible, I presume.'

'Ideally, I'd like to bug the hotel room. They might take
me on as a bodyguard again, in which case I may get asked
to sweep the place. It's chancy, though, I'd rather have
several different options up my sleeve so I can be sure of
nabbing him. You'd be one of those options.'

Gayle nodded. Her dress blew up with a sudden gust and
she casually brushed her skirt down, but not before Harvey
had glimpsed a long, lean, tanned thigh. He could feel
himself getting the hots for her and cautioned himself to
remember why they were there. It wasn't easy. As a randy
teenager Harvey had often used the tow-path as a courting
ground, and memories of kisses and gropes beneath the
bridges now returned to taunt him.

'Can we talk finance?' she asked at last, and he knew she
was interested.

By eight they had agreed to work together. Harvey went
home and phoned Lorraine, who seemed delighted. She was
also not worried about the cost. 'Whatever it takes,' she told
him. 'He'll pay for it himself in the end. I suspect he's been
misappropriating campaign funds too, but for the time being
we'll stick to the sex issue. When the bubble bursts,
everything will be out in the open and he won't stand a
chance.'

That night Harvey found himself in the middle of a
dream, replaying some of his fantasies about Paul Goodman.

He'd cast himself in the rôle of Stephen Treblant, or someone similar. They were in a hotel room, and he was about to bring in the next young virgin for sacrifice.

'You must test her purity first, in the usual way,' he was told.

While Paul went into the next room, Harvey ushered in the young woman. She was in her late teens, and wore a pretty floral dress with her blonde hair loose about her shoulders, Beneath the summery cotton her breasts were high and proud, her waist and hips slim. Harvey could feel a rush of blood to his cock and his balls grew heavy.

'If you wish to be in the presence of Mr Paul, you must be appropriately attired,' he told her, taking her by the hand.

Laid out on the bed was a simple white shift. She slipped off her sandals then turned passively to allow him to undo the buttons down her back. Inch by inch her smooth, tanned skin was exposed with the white bra across it. As he unclipped the undergarment he felt a further rush to his groin.

The girl stepped daintily out of her dress and half-slip, placing them on the bed, then lifted the bra from her breasts and pulled down her white cotton knickers, When she was entirely naked she turned to Harvey with a dewy-eyed smile. 'Do I put the gown on now?'

He stood there tongue-tied, gazing at the pert uplift of her firm young bosom with the pink nipples hardening as he watched. Down to her flat stomach his eyes travelled, then to the curly blonde bush through which the faint outline of her pussy was just visible.

'Not yet,' he told her, dry-mouthed. 'I have to examine you first. Mr Goodman insists that all the young ladies he sees personally must be completely untouched. Are you a virgin, Miss?'

'Oh yes! I'm saving myself for Jesus!'

Or the next best thing, Harvey thought. He asked her to lie down on the bed and gently pulled her thighs apart until he could see her pink lips protruding between them. His erection was rearing painfully now, crying out for a release that he wasn't sure he'd get. Still, he was under orders to make sure this nubile creature was fit to see his master. Slowly he reached out and let his forefinger probe between the slack labia.

She was deliciously wet within. The girl issued a long sigh as his finger went further in to find the tight barrier of flesh. Satisfied that she was intact, Harvey reluctantly removed his hand. 'Okay, you can put it on now. Mr Goodman will be with you in a moment.'

He went next door and gave the thumbs-up. Paul followed him back into the bedroom where the girl was standing by the bed demurely clad in the shapeless robe, her nipples standing out as hard points beneath the thin cotton. The evangelist embraced her, and Harvey turned to go.

'No, don't leave,' he was told. 'I wish to test the faith of this sweet maiden.'

'How may I serve you?' she asked, humbly.

'By quenching this poor man's fire. He burns with lust, pure one, and only the kiss of an angel such as your sweet self can redeem him.'

Harvey found himself removing his trousers, as if this were a routine they had rehearsed many times. He pulled his pants down over his erection and his prick twitched against his bare stomach. The girl was made to kneel down before him.

'Now take his organ between your lips,' came the order that Harvey had been longing for.

He thrust his way into her warm, wet mouth. She gagged

at first, but then relaxed to accommodate him. Her tongue felt blissfully soft and slippery on the underside of his shaft.

Soon Paul came to kneel behind her, towering over her small frame. He put his hands on her shoulders while she got the hang of licking and sucking in a smooth rhythm. Then Harvey saw him slip his hands over her shoulders and down the front of her robe. He could see the big fingers working her nipples, making her moan softly as her gorgeous lips slid up and down his distended cock. Every so often the hands would squeeze her breasts beneath their white covering, making her groan even louder.

'That's right,' Paul crooned, kissing her on the back of the neck. 'You are doing the Lord's work so well, sucking the devil out of him.'

Harvey could feel the force gathering between his legs and he prepared to abandon himself to the onslaught. Looking down he could see the plump, pink lips working away on his shaft and, every so often, the red tongue that licked his glans with increasing relish, and knew he could hold out no longer. In a sudden torrent the seed spurted out of him and down the open, willing throat. He gasped as all the hot sensation was ripped out of him, every nerve-ending vibrating with bliss as the climax spread throughout his body.

Then, as the orgasm reached its peak, he stared down at the woman's upturned face. She looked back at him with enraptured blue eyes, like some painted saint gilded with heavenly light. For the first time he recognised her: it was Gayle Webster.

Harvey woke to find he actually had come and the bedding was all sticky. It was the first wet dream he'd had for years. That woman must have really turned him on. He smiled as he wiped a tissue over his soggy genitals. If she could do that to him, what wouldn't she do to a randy lecher like Paul Goodman?

Chapter Seven

The prospect of an assignment involving a well-known figure was exciting Gayle as she took a cab to Piccadilly Station, where she was to meet Harvey. The jobs she'd done up to now had been mostly small-time, wives wanting to check out their cheating husbands, or girlfriends needing to test their man's fidelity before they tied the knot. This was different. She remembered seeing posters all over town for Paul Goodman. He had been interviewed on local radio and she'd read about him in the national press.

Then there was Harvey Boyd. In the tough world of private investigation he had a reputation for being hard-bitten and, when the need arose, for sailing too close to the wind. Well, they all did that occasionally; it went with the territory. Now that she'd met him, though, Gayle suspected there was more to him than the stereotyped gumshoe who followed the trail like a bloodhound. She had sensed another Harvey lurking below the surface, a more thoughtful and sensitive man than he was usually given credit for. Well, time would tell.

Gayle also admitted to herself that she was attracted to him. He intrigued her, and that had always been her weakness where men were concerned. A man who evoked her curiosity was halfway to bedding her. So the sooner she solved whatever enigma was at Harvey Boyd's heart the better, or she was in danger of getting involved.

He was waiting for her near the Intercity departures board. 'Platform five,' he told her, without ceremony. 'We have one minute!'

Once on the train Gayle relaxed, accepting Harvey's offer of a beer and sandwich from the buffet car. They would arrive in Birmingham around three, time to get to the Midlands Crown Hotel and check in before Harvey met up with the other guys. It was fortunate that he'd managed to get taken on as a bodyguard again, because he would be around backstage, and later in the hotel, while she played her part.

Harvey returned with the refreshments and said, between bites of his sandwich, 'I think we should check in to our rooms separately. I don't want anyone to connect us.'

Gayle giggled. 'You're making it sound like an extra-marital affair.'

He frowned, his grey eyes darkening a fraction. 'I suppose that's more your style.'

'Do I detect a note of disapproval?'

He gave a wry smile. 'I suppose I can't fool you, can I? Okay, I'll come clean. Yes, I think that what you do is dubious, to say the least. I read that article about you in the *News*—'

'Surely you don't believe everything you read in the papers!'

'But you do put men through a fidelity test, don't you? And you reckon that's fair?'

'Why not? If a man is truly in love with a woman he will be faithful to her. It's a way of assessing whether the relationship has gone sour, or hasn't a hope of succeeding.'

Harvey swilled down a mouthful of beer, his head thrown

back to display his long, lean neck. Gayle felt a twinge of something like lust hit her in the pit of the stomach, but she did her best to ignore it. His grey eyes levelled with hers. 'Don't you think most men would succumb if a sexy woman like you gave them the green light?'

He finds me sexy, Gayle thought, and was disconcerted when her heart lightened a little.

She felt obliged to defend herself. 'Most men who want to be faithful to their women will back out of a compromising situation as soon as they can. I give them plenty of opportunity. They don't *have* to buy me a drink, get into conversation, drive me to a hotel or come into my bedroom. I generally know which way it's going to go within the first five minutes. The good guys make excuses and leave. The slightly naughty ones stop short of the bedroom door . . .'

'But most of them go straight in there, right?'

Gayle laughed. 'Generally I'm not called in unless their women have pretty good grounds for suspicion.'

'Well that's certainly true of chummy-boy. Not only does his wife smell a rat but, after spending an evening around him, I do too. There's nothing that would give me greater satisfaction, professionally speaking, than to see that Jesus-freak exposed as a hypocrite.'

Gayle knew just how he felt. Sometimes she couldn't wait to incriminate some bastard who played the field while his wife suffered agonies at home with the kids. It cheered her to think that, despite his air of detachment and his reputation as a hard man, Harvey Boyd had a heart ticking away beneath that solid chest after all.

'We should meet at some point, Harvey, to check out the equipment, run over contingency plans and so forth.'

'Of course. I have to see Stephen and the others at four-thirty in the conference centre but we can rendezvous before then, in the hotel. I'll find us a dark corner somewhere, then buzz you in your room.'

'Fine.' Gayle settled back into her seat as the majestic scenery of the Peak District came into view. Although she began looking through the window, the mountains soon became a mere backdrop for Harvey's reflection. She studied his features more closely than she would dare to if she were facing him directly. The intelligent grey eyes were shielded by dark, straight brows and fringed with short, spiky lashes. His nose was long and straight and his mouth surprisingly full and sensual making her wonder, momentarily, how it would feel pressed against hers. His dark brown hair was cut boyishly short, curling appealingly around his ears, and he had a good strong chin and jawline. His was not an immediately striking face, but it was one that grew on you the more you observed its range of expressions.

Gayle's eyes slid from the window and she saw that Harvey was staring at the glass right next to her. When their eyes met it was with the sudden recognition that they had been studying each other's reflection. Gayle felt a betraying flush rise in her cheeks.

'Not a good sign, that,' Harvey smiled. She threw him a questioning glance. 'Blushing. A handicap for someone in our field, I'd have thought.'

'Sorry, I just—'

'I know, you were just doing your job. Me too. Give us the chance to observe someone undetected and we'll take it. We can't help it, force of habit.'

They both laughed, breaking any remaining ice between them. Gayle felt inclined to disregard his previous criticisms, and he had apparently decided to take a softer line. She sensed it would be easier to work with him from now on.

Although they took the same taxi to the Birmingham

hotel, Harvey allowed Gayle to go to her room first. She threw off her high-heeled shoes and too-warm jacket, then decided to take a shower. It was deliciously cool after the hot and sticky journey. While she was massaging scented body lotion into her still-damp skin, the phone by the bed rang.

'Hullo, Gayle?' It was Harvey. 'Look, I think we can meet in the lounge on the top floor. We should be safe there. Say, around six? I have to be downstairs at six-thirty.'

'Fine.'

'Er . . . you will wear something alluring, won't you?'

Gayle giggled. 'Teaching your grandmother to suck eggs? Look, I know my job, Harvey. Just leave it to me.'

'Of course. Sorry. I'm just not used to working with another professional.'

'That's okay. Look, I'm standing here butt-naked from the shower . . .'

She heard him groan. 'Gayle, do you have to?'

'I just meant I can't talk. See you at six, top-floor lounge.'

As she put the receiver down a broad grin spread across Gayle's face. She caught sight of herself in the wardrobe mirror and pirouetted, her shapely breasts bobbing as she turned to display her firm pink buttocks. So Harvey Boyd fancied her, did he? Well, when he saw her in her clingy black mini-dress he might just find her irresistible. Pity it was some other guy she had to seduce and not him!

By six she was raring to go. The dress had a low V-neck and she wore it bra-less, showing her natural cleavage. All she had on underneath was a pair of skimpy black lace panties. Her lipstick was pink and frosted, her eye make-up smoky and subtle. Strappy white sandals, gold earrings and a matching bag completed her outfit, but she sprayed on lashings of sultry *Je Reviens* perfume to complete her armoury.

Her reward was to see Harvey's eyes nearly pop out on stalks when she walked into the secluded lounge on floor six. 'Wow, you certainly look the part!' he said, admiringly.

'Do you think they'll let me in, looking like this? It's a religious meeting really, isn't it?'

'It's also some kind of rock concert, remember. I'm sure there will be plenty of young people similarly dressed.'

'That's all right then.'

'Now, have you got the gear in your bag?'

She opened her white handbag. 'This is the camera. It can take in a whole bed when it's strategically placed, and it shoots at intervals of ten seconds, thirty seconds or one minute. It's completely silent. The lens focuses through the middle of this decoration on the bag.'

'Nice one, Miss Moneypenny! What about the recorder?'

'I think that'll work fine in the bag too. It will record up to half an hour of conversation within a fifty-metre radius and it should be pretty clear.'

'Excellent! You certainly know your job, Gayle.'

'My equipment's never let me down yet,' Seeing his amused look, she blushed. 'Oh God, you know what I mean!'

Harvey's eyes sparkled back at her. 'I'm sure you have wonderful equipment, perfectly maintained. Now, here's my schedule for the evening.'

Gayle realised he'd be backstage while she was mingling with the crowd in the hall. Once the show was over, however, she'd get her chance to ask for an audience. Harvey had found out that Stephen always stood at the front of the house afterwards to pick and choose from the queue of young women who were keen to see Paul Goodman personally. It was up to her to impress him, but Harvey was confident that she would.

Gayle felt less confident. She'd be competing with girls younger than herself and, from what Harvey had told her, Goodman preferred them between eighteen and twenty-one. Still, she would do her best.

After the convoy had left for the hall, Gayle remained in her room watching TV. There was a mention of the 'Joy of Jesus' concert on the local news. Apparently the 'Charismatic Evangelical Preacher' would be hosting a 'Rock of Ages' gig at which all ages were welcome. The smiling face of Paul Goodman appeared, urging everyone, young and old, to 'reclaim the devil's music for the Lord!' She stared at it, wondering what the man behind the mask was like. Well, with luck she would find out that very night.

By the time Gayle got there the hall was packed and she only just managed to squeeze in at the back. It was already very hot, despite the air-conditioning, and she could feel sweat trickling down between her breasts, tickling her sensitive skin. Most of the people around her were young, already swaying to the gentle beat that filled the air. There was an electric atmosphere that was unlike any other rock gig she'd ever been to, a feeling of common purpose that she couldn't help but find impressive even though she didn't share it.

On stage, a six-piece band were idling through some hymn tunes waiting for the appearance of the man himself. Gayle thought of Harvey backstage, and felt lonely. She would have been a lot more confident with him by her side, but she knew that although they were working together they must remain apart, at least for the time being.

The tension was growing all around, and every face was turned towards the stage. Suddenly the music stopped and a man hurried up to the mike. 'And now, the moment you've all been waiting for. Here he is, everyone ... PAUL GOODMAN!'

Amidst crashing guitar chords and through a blinding wall of light, a man in a spangly silver-and-black suit appeared. He held up his arms for silence and the music faded to a respectful hum. The surprisingly short figure bent his head and most of the audience did too, but Gayle kept on looking towards the stage. 'O Lord, bless everyone here tonight . . .'

As the prayer proceeded the music grew louder, reaching a crescendo when the crowd roared, 'Amen!' A rock singer bounded onto the stage and began to yell about the 'Joy of Jesus' while the evangelist stood to one side, clapping to the beat. Soon the hall was full of the sound of rhythmic handclaps and Gayle found herself caught up in the music. Before long she was swaying and clapping with the rest of them.

After an hour or so of non-stop music there was an interval where Paul preached a sermon, then passed amongst the invalids in the front row. The proceedings became fast-paced again in the second half, leading up to an exciting climax, and then closed with a prayer. Gayle was surprised to find that she had actually enjoyed the show, but when the audience began to shuffle out she was reminded that she was there on a job and began to work her way to the front. It wasn't easy, moving against the tide, but eventually she found herself amongst the starstruck young women who were thronging just in front of the stage.

She picked out Stephen Treblant straight away. He had a clipboard and identification badge and was trying to shepherd the girls into an orderly line at the side of the hall. Gayle joined them and soon he worked his way down to her. She flashed him a bright smile and saw an answering flicker of interest.

'Name?'

'Sharon.'

'Rose of Sharon,' he smiled, briefly. 'Are you familiar with the Song of Solomon?' Gayle shook her head. ' "I am the rose of Sharon, and the lily of the valleys".' His eyes dropped briefly to her breasts. 'You would like a private audience with Mr Goodman?'

'Oh, yes please!'

'Very well, Sharon. Join the queue over by the stage, will you?'

Gayle felt a surge of triumph. She'd made it! But the hardest part was yet to come.

She looked around for Harvey, but he was nowhere to be seen. Standing amongst the chosen few Gayle could feel how keyed up they were, the mood of excited anticipation almost overwhelming. When a dozen or so of the prettiest women had been selected they were ushered outside and told to get into a minibus.

'I'll remember this for the rest of my life!' one of them exclaimed, climbing into her seat.

'Isn't Paul just wonderful!' another swooned. 'And to think I'll get a few moments alone with him. I never dreamed I'd get this lucky!'

They drove back to the hotel, where Stephen took them to the first floor. There Gayle spotted Harvey and managed to exchange a quick wink. Stephen's party was taken into a room and invited to help themselves to food and drink from a buffet table.

'I couldn't eat a thing, I'm too excited!' one girl exclaimed, and the others murmured in agreement. However they were all so hot and thirsty that they took the drinks eagerly.

Stephen made them sit on a row of chairs in the order in which they would be received. Gayle was around the middle. She drank her orange juice and waited in an atmosphere of nervous silence. Then the girl who would be going first asked, in little more than a whisper, 'Do we need to do anything special? I mean, how should we behave when we get in there?'

Stephen gave a dazzling smile that encompassed them all. 'You just act yourselves, ladies. Mr Goodman doesn't want you to be any different from your lovely, natural selves. He has angelic vision, he can see how pure your souls are. He will give you his blessing, see what your soul needs and perfectly fulfil that need. Trust him, ladies, that's all you need to do.'

What a load of bollocks, Gayle thought, at the same time admitting to herself that there was something impressive about the man. Yet he was only the monkey. It was Goodman who did the organ-grinding.

After a few minutes the first girl was led through the door. She was trembling all over, her eyes glassy bright. The rest of them waited, nervously sipping their drinks. After ten minutes or so the second girl left. Each time one of them went the rest moved up, like musical chairs. Two down, three to go. No one was talking but the air was thick with unspoken thoughts.

At last it was Gayle's turn, and as she rose to her feet in response to Stephen's nod she felt her own legs shaking almost uncontrollably. Out in the corridor, Stephen made her open her handbag. She held her breath, but the camera looked like a leather purse and the tape recorder was disguised as a cigarette case, and he was fooled by them both.

They waited until a door opened and the previous girl came out, dazed and wet-eyed, as if she were sleep-walking during a sad dream. 'In you go, Sharon,' Stephen murmured.

Gayle pushed the door wider and went into the luxurious suite that seemed to be filled with lilies and roses. Paul was awaiting her in a white silk kimono, round his neck a large gold cross with a ruby at its heart. He stared at her with dazzling, pale blue eyes and she felt her heart start to race, her mouth dry out and her knees weaken even more. She managed to put her bag down on a low table, positioning the spy hole towards the large bed to her left, and unobtrusively twisted the catch that activated both camera and recorder.

Smiling, he reached out his hand. She took it like a drowning man clutching at a straw. His grip was firm and warm. 'Sharon, isn't it?' She nodded. 'Beautiful name. Song of Solomon. I see a rose unfolding for me, an exquisite pink rose that deepens to red in the heat.'

Gayle saw the room swim a little before her eyes. His voice went on, low and insistent, and she was mesmerised by the erotic intensity of his gaze. 'Open your heart to me, Sharon. Let me see that secret jewel deep inside, that no man has set eyes upon. Let me feast my eyes upon your pure loveliness.'

Gayle was swaying now, feeling faint. Her eyes were blinded and she staggered towards the bed wanting only to lie down. She could hear Goodman's voice in her ear, soft and insistent, his arm around her shoulders, guiding her. 'That's right, my dear, just lie down a little. You are filled with the Holy Spirit and your body is overwhelmed. Just lie quietly a while and take nice deep breaths.'

'I feel so hot!' she gasped.

'Then take off your dress. I shall help you.'

He pulled down the zipper at her back, and Gayle was too weak to argue or resist but let the skimpy dress fall to the floor. Thankfully she sank down onto the springy mattress. Goodman sat on the edge of the bed beside her, holding her hand. He continued to speak to her in his quiet, insinuating tone. 'Just relax, Sharon, and let the Lord fill your soul with light. That's right, nice deep breaths. Good girl. Soon you will know the true joy of the blessed ones, the rapture of the chosen ones. "Open to me, my sister, my love, my dove, my undefiled" . . .'

She felt his hand between her thighs, stroking her gently. This is enough, a voice in her head insisted, you should put an end to it right here. You've got enough on film. But she was powerless to resist. It occurred to her that she might have been hypnotised. Her desire to remain there passively, letting him do whatever he liked to her, was stronger than her desire to get up off the bed. She told herself that she could leave any time she liked, but as long as that crooning voice and caressing hand continued to work their magic, she lacked the will.

Even when he slowly pulled down her pants and found the wet accessible cleft of her sex, she did nothing to prevent him. She felt drugged, only half-awake. Her thighs fell apart, opening up to him just as he was inviting her to do. When his fingers dipped into the warm pool of her juices she gave a long, shuddering sigh, and soon his lips were mouthing at her nipples, one after the other, making her squirm with exquisite bliss.

' "I am come into my garden, my sister, my spouse,"' he chanted. ' "I have gathered my myrrh with my spice . . ." Now come for me, come for me, beautiful Rose of Sharon!'

Gayle felt the gathering storm in her belly, knew she was on the verge of a tumultuous orgasm. Her head still said she should resist, but her body was on autodrive now.

The probing finger went right inside her pussy as Goodman's voice urged her to 'Feel the joy! Feel the wondrous transforming joy of love and let it fill you up, let it flood through every part of you and let you have a taste of heaven, the heaven that the good Lord has prepared for his own. Give yourself up to it, Sharon, let the love flow through you . . .'

His finger was rotating inside her, stirring her up, and the fleshy pad of his thumb was pressed hard against her clitoris. Gayle felt her vagina contract as the first gut-wrenching spasms shook through her, confounding her already overburdened senses. She moaned aloud, abandoning herself utterly to the cataclysm that was turning her insides to molten honey. It was sweet and rich, the most satisfying orgasm she'd had in years, and her head was spinning wildly with the sudden impact, making her moan aloud. Dimly she heard the voice of Goodman still encouraging her, 'Oh yes, yes! Make a joyful noise unto the Lord!'

For a while, overcome by the force of her climax, Gayle lost consciousness. When she came to she was dressed again, and something cool was on her brow. Goodman sat beside her, a glass of water in his hand.

'Come, sip this.' He removed the wet pad from her forehead and helped her to sit up, then placed the glass to her lips. 'You'll be fine, Sharon. Sometimes our souls cannot bear too much heavenly fire and light. You passed out, that's all.'

She still felt confused, unsure whether she'd been seduced or not. When she tried to remember what had happened it seemed vague, dreamlike, hallucinatory. Could she have been drugged?

'Can you stand up now, Sharon?' Shakily she got up off the bed. He helped her towards the door. 'That's better. It's been a great pleasure meeting you, my dear. May the joy of the Lord always be with you.'

It took her a few seconds to realise that she had been

dismissed. Picking up her bag from the table she walked in a semi-trance towards the door which seemed to open automatically as she approached. Outside, Stephen took her arm. 'The recovery room is just opposite,' he told her, ushering the next girl in.

There were three girls lying down in the darkened room while a woman in a white coat hovered over them, refilling water glasses and soothing fevered brows.

'Come in, dear, and lie down,' she smiled. 'You'll soon be right as rain again.'

'What happened to me? I feel really weird.'

'It's all right, dear. Most people get to feel a little strange after they've had an audience with Mr Goodman. It's the power of the Spirit in him. If you're not used to it, you can be quite overcome. Just rest a while and you'll soon feel normal again.'

After a few minutes the disorientating after-effects began to wear off. Gayle wanted to talk to the other girls, to share experiences, but there was little chance as long as that nurse-type woman was in the room. She began to realise that the whole operation was an elaborate cover-up for Paul Goodman to indulge his perverse, lecherous urges. But was her experience typical or not? Did he screw some of the women? Did he get them to suck his dick? She was determined to find out whatever she could.

Two of the others began to stir and when they got up Gayle followed suit. 'Are you quite sure you're ready to leave?' the woman asked solicitously. 'None of you has to drive, I hope?'

'No, we'll get a taxi home,' one of the other girls smiled.

The three of them went down the stairs to the hotel foyer, where another of Goodman's aides approached them. 'Happy, ladies?' he asked, with a smile.

'Oh yes!' the other two chorused, their eyes shining.

'Good! Can I call you a cab?'

'Mind if I share yours?' Gayle asked. They shook their heads.

Once the three of them were sitting in the back of the taxi the conversation began to flow. Gayle had set her recorder running.

'Wasn't he absolutely divine?' Sarah, the buxom brunette, sighed rapturously.

Trish, the auburn haired girl, agreed. 'Heaven on earth! I wish I were Mrs Goodman!'

'We never get to see her, do we?'

Trish shrugged. 'Who cares? It's Paul everyone wants to see. And we got to be with him, for a few precious minutes. Aren't we the lucky ones!'

'Can you remember what happened?' Gayle asked. 'I mean, it's all a bit blurred in my mind.'

'Of course I remember. I'll never forget!' Trish said, rather impatiently.

'Did he give you his blessing?'

'Oh yes! He made me one of the Lord's anointed. It was wonderful!'

'You mean he actually anointed you? With oil?'

Trish shivered a little at the memory. 'Oh yes,' she murmured. 'All over, from head to foot.'

Gayle turned to Sarah. 'What about you?'

'He said he would pierce my soul with the fiery arrow of truth, just like Saint Teresa,' she said, dreamily. 'And I felt him doing it, sending this healing energy right through me.'

Behind the pseudo-religious metaphors, the implication was clear. It sounded as if Goodman was in the habit of indulging himself with young women whichever way he liked, under the guise of religious claptrap. That he succeeded in doing so without any hindrance suggested the use of either drugs or hypnosis, or both. Gayle recalled that they'd all drunk the beverages on offer in the waiting room. She decided to take a sample of her own urine at the first opportunity and send it to the lab to be analysed.

Once the two girls were dropped off, Gayle asked the driver to take her back to the hotel. Harvey had wanted them to meet in the top-floor lounge around midnight, but she just didn't feel up to it. Once she got to her room she phoned reception and left a message for him, saying she would see him next day. She took the urine sample, put the bottle into the cool interior of the mini-bar, then went to soak in a warm bath. She felt disgusted by the thought of Paul Goodman's slimy hands on her body and wanted to wash herself clean.

The fact that she distinctly remembered getting off on the experience dismayed her further. However much she told herself that she had not been in control of herself, that he had taken advantage of her while she was under the influence of something or other, she still felt vile. In all her experience as a seductress Gayle had never wondered how it felt to be seduced against your will, to have someone play upon your body as if it were a mechanical toy, pressing all the right buttons. Was this what it was like to be raped? Surely most rape victims had the satisfaction of knowing that they'd at least tried to resist.

It gave her some satisfaction to play back the tape, hearing the bastard incriminate himself with his seductive tone and ambiguous words. When she heard her own orgasmic cries, however, she felt ashamed and switched it off. The film would have to wait until tomorrow to be developed, but she had no doubt that it would prove just as damning.

The following morning, after a deep and apparently dreamless sleep, Gayle was awakened by the phone. It was

Harvey. 'Gayle? I was worried about you. I thought maybe your cover had been blown, or something.'

'No, nothing like that. I was just shattered, that's all.'

'Look, it's better if we don't meet in the hotel. There's a café just down the road, called Papa Joe's. I'll see you there for breakfast in half an hour, okay?'

Dressed soberly, in the clothes she'd worn for travelling, Gayle was into her second cappuccino by the time Harvey arrived. He ordered coffee, croissants and orange juice for two. Gayle was enormously relieved to see him. Last night, in her hotel room, she'd felt vulnerable and alone after her ordeal, yet she hadn't been up to seeing anybody. Today she hoped she could begin to look on the episode as simply another job.

'We can't go into detail here,' Harvey cautioned her, quietly. 'But how did it go?'

'I think I've got what we need to expose him. I need to develop the film. Oh, and I need to have a sample of pee analysed.'

His brows shot up. 'His?'

'No, mine!' she giggled. 'I suspect I might have been doped. I still feel a bit spaced-out.'

'Whew! Can you remember much about it?'

'Enough.' She answered, grimly. 'I can't wait to get home. Just being in this city gives me the creeps.'

'Okay, we'll go to the station as soon as we've got some food inside us.'

Gayle travelled back in a sober mood. Now that there was a distinct possibility that Paul Goodman would be publicly discredited, it seemed a momentous undertaking. The faith of so many of his followers would be shattered. So many young minds disillusioned. Having been there amongst them, if only for a few hours, Gayle now realised the seriousness of the operation. But did Harvey?

He seemed to read her thoughts. 'There's a lot riding on this, Gayle,' he commented, as they reached the outskirts of Manchester. 'The man is more than just a personality, he's a whole business. There's a lot of money involved, people's livelihoods. Then there's the faith people have in him. We have a responsibility to get it right.'

'Yes, I know. Well we should know what kind of evidence we have by tonight. Then, I suppose it's down to his wife.'

Harvey frowned. 'That's what's worrying me. Suppose she decides to keep it all to herself, letting him off the hook. All our hard work will have been in vain.'

Chapter Eight

Lorraine Goodman lived in Wimbledon with her three children. Harvey travelled down from Manchester for the day, so he could speak to her in person. She looked very different when she opened the door to him. Red-faced and harassed, she invited him into a comfortable sitting-room while she dealt with a domestic crisis in the kitchen. By the time she reappeared with a tray of coffee and biscuits, some of her poise had returned.

'I hope you have some news for me,' she said as she put the tray down. 'Good or bad. All I want is something solid.'

'Oh, I've got that all right.' Harvey produced the tape and packet of photographs from his bag. There was also the lab report on Gayle's sample. He had her account on tape, as well as the recording made at the scene. 'It seems you were quite right to be suspicious, Lorraine.'

She looked at him with weary eyes. 'I was afraid you'd say that. I've been praying for a miracle, but my heart told me I wasn't going to get one.'

Piece by piece, Harvey revealed what had happened to his accomplice in Paul Goodman's hotel room. He told her about the other girls, the way her husband was getting through a dozen or so women a night although, as far as he could ascertain, he probably wasn't having intercourse with

125

them. 'Technically we're talking sexual assault, not rape,' he told her.

Suddenly Lorraine crumpled. She put her hands over her face and uttered a high-pitched wail. Harvey, concerned for her children in the next room, put his arm around her. 'Be strong, Lorraine,' he murmured.

She clung to him, lifting her tear-stained face to his. Harvey saw the naked need there and guessed that she'd been denied her conjugal rights for some time. That made her a dangerous woman. 'I don't know what to do!' she moaned. 'If I expose him, it will ruin everything. What about the children?'

Harvey loosened his embrace. 'I'm afraid that's a decision only you can make. But I do urge you to think of the young women he seduces with the aid of drugs and hypnosis. What he does is highly illegal, as well as immoral.'

'I know, I know. What would you advise me to do, then, Harvey?'

'Go to the police. They're the best people to handle it.'

'But what will Paul think when he finds out I hired a private investigator to spy on him?'

'I should think that's the least of your worries.'

She lowered her eyes, dabbing at them with a lace-edged handkerchief. 'You're right, I shouldn't mind what he thinks of me. I believe he already despises me, although I swear to God I don't know why. I've been a good wife to him, a good mother. What more did he want?'

'You shouldn't blame yourself, Lorraine.'

She turned her tear-washed blue eyes on him. 'We haven't had sex since our last child was born, six years ago. I've tried to get him interested in me again, Harvey. God knows, I've tried. Am I so very unattractive?'

'On the contrary,' he smiled, but he had the uncomfortable

feeling he knew what was coming. 'If you should divorce Paul I'm sure you could meet another man, start a new life.'

'Divorce!' Harvey kicked himself for his tactlessness as he saw her face dissolve into tears again. 'Oh God!'

Reluctantly he took her into his arms, found her handkerchief. She pressed her ample bosom to his chest and he could feel the raw sexual heat in her, seeping through his skin. Passionately she clung to him and then, after fixing him with a searing look, pulled his head down and pressed her lips to his.

As her soft, wet tongue probed his mouth Harvey felt his libido kick into action, but knew he had to resist. It wasn't the first time a grateful, or desperate, woman had come on to him at the end of an assignment. With Lorraine Goodman, he should have predicted it. Gently, but firmly, he pushed her from him.

'Now come on, Lorraine, pull yourself together,' he told her. 'This is an emotional time for you, I know. But you should try not to do anything you'd later regret.'

'I'm sorry, I'm sorry,' she sniffled, into her handkerchief. 'You must think I'm terrible.'

'No, just upset. Now why don't you go upstairs and wash your face while I take the tray into the kitchen and make us some more coffee.'

Nodding, Lorraine rose and made for the door. 'Barbara, my eldest, will make the coffee. She's a good girl.'

By the time Lorraine came down again Harvey was chatting to the children. They were nice kids, blissfully unaware of the storm that was about to break around them. He promised to be there for Lorraine whenever she needed him, then left the house feeling faintly sick.

Arriving back in Manchester in the early evening, Harvey went home to change into more casual clothes then drove to the Sun and Moon. He took a look at his e-mail messages, then sat downstairs with a beer waiting for something to happen. It wasn't long before he felt a tap on his shoulder and turned to see Gayle smiling at him. 'Hi! I thought I might find you here. I wanted to know how it went with Mrs Goodman.'

'Let me buy you a drink.'

They managed to find a quiet corner, away from both the other customers and the band, where they could talk freely. Harvey explained that Lorraine Goodman had been upset, but he still didn't know what she intended to do.

He saw Gayle's jaw tighten, her eyes turn cold. 'I want that rat nailed, Harvey!'

'So do I, believe me. But would you be prepared to testify in court, if necessary?'

'Yes.'

'Well, good for you.'

He was impressed. Most of the investigators he knew, including himself, tried to avoid getting tangled up in the legal process at all costs. Gayle, it seemed, was made of sterner stuff and he couldn't help admiring her for it.

Her eyes blazed as she said, 'It makes me mad to think of him still getting away with it. Even as we speak he could be at it. Where is he tonight?'

'Oxford, I think. Or maybe Gloucester.'

Gayle stared moodily into her glass. 'I've never felt so used, Harvey. I guess I had my share of duff dates when I was young, but no one took advantage of me like that. I always felt I had some degree of control over my sexual responses.'

'I'm sorry you had to go through that, Gayle. Maybe I shouldn't have asked you to do it.'

'But I wanted to do it! Someone had to, and at least I was

128

used to dealing with strange men in an intimate situation. I just wasn't prepared for being softened up with that drug then hypnotised. But do you know what hurts the most, Harvey?' He shook his head and she looked away, faintly ashamed. 'The worst part is that my body enjoyed it. I had an orgasm, I couldn't help myself. That's what makes me feel really bad.'

A wicked voice in Harvey's head said he wouldn't mind giving her an orgasm himself.

He touched her hand across the table. 'It's just a . . . a mechanism, Gayle. It's happened to me, to most men I suspect. Anything can trigger you off, even when you're asleep.'

'But I wasn't asleep, was I? I let that slimeball finger me. And now I feel horribly unclean, knowing he was doing it – or something similar – to all those other women.'

For the first time it occurred to Harvey that maybe she needed professional help. 'Do you need to see someone, Gayle? A counsellor, perhaps?'

She smiled, squeezing his hand. 'No, I just need to talk to someone who understands. And I feel you do. You're the only person I know who got close to that prick. I don't think talking to a stranger would help.'

'It's such a familiar story, isn't it? I mean, the charismatic preacher seducing women.'

'Abuse of power, I suppose. Like between rock stars and their groupies. Except it usually happens with consent.' She looked thoughtful. 'But why use underhand methods? It rather suggests that Goodman isn't confident enough to trust his own power of attraction. Or maybe he just hasn't the time, wants quick results. Well, he certainly gets them!'

Her tone was bitter, and Harvey felt miserable. He'd put this woman through some kind of trauma and wanted to make amends. The stereotyped view he'd had of her, as little more than a whore, was beginning to break down. He found himself feeling protective towards her, much to his surprise. 'Let's hope he gets his come-uppance then!' he commented, and she giggled. Harvey added, 'No pun intended!'

Gayle finished her drink and got to her feet. 'I'd better get going. You'll let me know if there are any developments, won't you?'

'Of course. Are you okay to get home now?'

'I'll get a cab.'

'Don't do that, I can run you home. It's no trouble.'

'Are you sure?'

'Come on. I'm parked just down the road.'

He could feel her relax as they drove through the city. Mostly they chatted about how Manchester had changed in the years they'd both been living there. By the time they pulled up outside Gayle's house she seemed happier and Harvey felt his mood soften, his body lighten. Inside his underpants there was a slight stirring, a reminder that she still turned him on. He looked out at the neat little Thirties' semi and smiled his approval. 'Nice place.'

'I inherited it after my divorce. Want to come inside?'

The invitation, although casually delivered, made him wary. Was this a good idea? He suspected that Gayle needed the company, but he also sensed her vulnerability. Well, he'd just have to be a good boy, offer a shoulder to cry on but back off if things got too hot.

Inside, the house was in very good order, stylishly decorated with a conservatory full of exotic-looking plants leading off the sitting-room. Beyond he glimpsed a small but well-tended garden. Yet there was something empty about it all. The place had obviously been set up as a joint home, and a valiant attempt had been made to keep up the standard, but it lacked warmth. Harvey followed Gayle into the conservatory where he sat down on the chintz-covered swing seat surrounded by trailing fuschias and lush vegetation.

'Nice, very nice,' he commented. 'You've put a lot of work into this house, Gayle. You must feel you've put down roots.'

She sighed. 'I'm not so sure about that. When my marriage broke up, three years ago, I redecorated the place from top to bottom. It was a kind of therapy for me.'

'What went wrong? With your marriage, I mean.'

Gayle gave a wry smile. 'The sex seemed pretty good at the beginning, but that soon went sour for both of us. I can't blame him, really. When we were first married I worked regular hours in the *Evening News* office. Then I decided I wanted to be a reporter and had to work some evenings and weekends. That's when Bill started to stray.'

'How come you got into investigation work, then?'

'That didn't happen until I set someone on Bill's tail. Stan Marion, Do you know him?'

'Old Stan? Sure! He's been around for years.'

'Well he helped me prove that Bill was playing around, so I could get a decent divorce settlement. That's what made me realise that PI work could really help people, especially where infidelity was concerned. I'd heard about the 'decoy dames' in America and decided that was something I could do too. At first I worked with two other girls, but then we fell out and I set up on my own. It was good having a challenging job to do. Helped me get my life together again after my divorce.'

'You're a strong woman, Gayle. I admire that.'

'Not every woman is like me. Some just crumple when the love of their life turns out to be a bastard. It doesn't help me gain a balanced view of men, though.'

Harvey grinned. 'You're just a cynical man-hater, right?' She shrugged, grinning back. 'Well you don't look the part, I can tell you that for nothing.'

She smiled, a little self-consciously, and it was all Harvey could do to prevent himself from putting his arms around her, pulling her close. Suddenly she said brightly, 'Would you like a drink? There's beer in the fridge and whisky in the cupboard. That's all, I'm afraid.'

'Beer would be fine.'

While Harvey drank his ale straight from the bottle, Gayle asked about his life.

'I was a DI, in the force. Things were getting a bit hot, so I resigned while I still could.'

'I see. Do you miss it – the camaraderie, and all that?'

Harvey gave a short laugh. 'What, the back-stabbing and arse-licking? No, I don't! I'd rather work for and by myself.'

'Me too.' Gayle's deep blue eyes looked suddenly thoughtful. 'But it does get lonely at times, don't you find?'

'That's why it's been great working with you, Gayle.'

'Really?' Her expression softened. 'I've enjoyed it too. Except for what happened with that bastard Goodman,' she added hastily.

Harvey gave her a quizzical look. Her eyes were lucid, and he felt that he could read them plainly. Yet there was always an elusive aspect to the woman that he couldn't grasp. She was starting to fascinate him, and that was dangerous. He drank down his beer, preparing to leave, but as he half-rose from the swing-seat she came over and took the bottle out of his hand.

'Another beer?'

'No, I really should be going.'

She said nothing, only looked disappointed. Then she went over and threw a switch by the door, and the garden, that had been in darkness, was suddenly illuminated. She laughed at his surprise. 'I like to watch the moths at night, drawn by the outside light. Sometimes I see badgers in the garden too, and foxes. I love all wild things.'

He saw her profile as she stood there by the patio doors, bathed in light and surrounded by green leaves, pink and purple flowers. Her face was classical in shape, refined. Her hair shimmered and gleamed like gold. Her lips, slightly parted, were full and inviting. Her body was both slim and stately, the jutting curve of her breasts adding an earthy sensuality to her otherwise slender figure. There was something extraordinary about her, something exotic and compelling, that was drawing him like one of the moths to her alluring light.

'Harvey, do you see—'

Gayle had turned to point something out to him, but the look on his face stopped her in mid-flow. He knew she'd seen the raw lust in his eyes, but instead of shrinking from it she was responding in kind, her gaze offering a warm, enticing invitation. He reached out and touched her arm, closed in on her and waited a few seconds but she remained still, waiting. Harvey bent his head and his lips found hers easily, filling him with a sense of elation as he felt her mouth open under the gentle pressure of his kiss.

Now he could feel her clinging to him, pressing close to his warmth, inviting him to embrace her more intimately. He touched the silk swathe of her hair, felt the curve of her shoulder, and his prick leapt with joy. God, how he'd been wanting this! Their tongues met lusciously, making him moan with the sweetness that filled his mouth with erotic bliss.

But as their kiss deepened and their mutual need became more urgent, Harvey was beset by doubt. This shouldn't be happening. Only minutes ago she'd been pouring out her soul to him, telling him how bad she'd felt when Goodman had seduced her against her will. Besides, they were professionals. If he continued with this madness, their working relationship would be ruined, and he might need her to conclude the Goodman case. With great reluctance, Harvey disentangled his tongue from hers, loosened his arms and drew away. She stared at him, dazed and wide-eyed, utterly beautiful.

'I'm sorry, Gayle,' he began, awkwardly. 'I just don't think this is a good idea.'

'Why not?'

Beneath the even tone he sensed a degree of hurt. God, this wasn't going to be easy! 'We may need to work together again. Besides, you've been badly hurt by another man recently, and I don't want to—'

'You'd be helping to heal the wound,' she said, softly, taking his hand and leading him back over to the swing seat. They both sat down. Gayle's eyes, reflecting the porch light, shone like clear turquoise water flecked with gold. She kept hold of his hand as the seat began to swing slowly back and forth. 'Harvey, since my divorce I've not slept with anyone entirely for my own pleasure. I've seduced many men, usually stopping short of actual intercourse, and when I was with Goodman my body enjoyed what was happening even though my mind was protesting at some level. That was weird. I did try dating someone recently, but that was a ghastly mistake. What I want now is for someone I find really attractive to seduce me, to make me feel normal again. That's what I wanted from you just now, but I'll understand if it's not what you want. Maybe there's someone else, someone you haven't told me about . . .'

He shook his head. 'There's no one else.' Harvey leaned

forward and drew her into his arms again. She felt light and warm, exquisitely feminine. He breathed in the scent from her hair. 'There's nothing I'd like better than to make love to you, Gayle,' he murmured, throatily. 'But I think we work together really well, and I don't want sex to spoil that.'

'It won't,' she promised. 'But it's up to you. I don't want you to do anything you'd regret.'

Harvey gave a short bark of a laugh. The regret, if it happened, was more likely to be over turning down a chance like this. Rarely did he get such an opportunity to bed a woman he truly lusted after and who wasn't a client or otherwise unavailable. Maybe he needed to know what normal sex felt like too. His lips bent to her hair, her forehead. She closed her eyes and he kissed the trembling lids with infinite delicacy. What a luxury it would be to make love to this gorgeous woman slowly, carefully, to watch her bloom and glow under his tender ministrations. His heart surged and he felt awash with desire. There were other feelings too, subtle variations on what he'd felt with other women, but beneath it all ran an undercurrent of pure terror. Never before had he felt this open, this vulnerable. Was he getting old?

Gayle slipped off her shoes and drew her legs up onto the seat, lying with her head in his lap. She gave a feline stretch, her breasts thrusting upwards beneath her T-shirt. Harvey gave up the unequal struggle to resist and the sense of fear receded. He began to dot whisper-like kisses over her cheeks and forehead, making her sigh contentedly. Beneath the thin white cotton his fingers traced the outline of her bra. His hands passed under her top and encountered the warm, smooth flesh of her stomach beneath. He undid the button of her jeans and pulled the zipper down a few inches until he could see the white band of her pants. Which way to go?

His fingers itched to travel all over her.

With a lazy smile Gayle sat up and put her hands behind her back, lifting up her T-shirt so that she could unfasten her bra. Then she sank back down again into a comfortable pose. Harvey took the hint, replacing his hands on her breasts over her top. Now the flimsy bra slid about beneath, and he was able to manoeuvre it away from her nipples so that they protruded boldly. He worked them between his thumbs and forefingers, making them thrust harder against their cotton shield until they stood out like white acorns. He squeezed and scratched at them mercilessly, enjoying the deep moans of arousal that his actions were eliciting. He wanted to see her naked breasts in all their glory, but not yet. Nothing would be rushed tonight. They had all the time in the world.

After a while, looking down at the sleek, tanned plane of her belly, Harvey wanted to explore new territory. He trailed soft kisses down her neck as he abandoned her nipples temporarily and slid his hands over the bare skin of her abdomen. Her stomach hollowed as his palms smoothed across it, and as his fingertips reached the top of her pants Gayle groaned louder, wriggling her hips to allow him freer access.

The hardness of her mound was softened by the fleece that covered it, like grass over an earthy tumulus. Harvey moved his fingers down until he felt the damp indentation at the top of her cleft with the squidgy button of her clitoris within. He made a circling motion over it with his bunched fingertips and Gayle murmured, 'Mm!' As he continued he could feel the material sticking to her wet pussy.

Within the tight enclosure of his own jeans Harvey felt his cock swelling uncomfortably, but he didn't want to get it out yet. This was Gayle's treat, and just for the moment he was enjoying pleasuring her with no thought for his own gratification. How long was it since he had done it like this, just for the woman? He was ashamed to realise that it had been years. Now he felt he was making up for the hurt she'd suffered at the hands of that bastard Goodman and the emotional high that gave him was almost as good as a physical one.

Not that he wasn't enjoying it on a sensual level too. He loved the voluptuousness of her body, rounded or flat in all the right places. Harvey felt ready to feast his eyes on her now, as well as his hands and lips. First he eased the tough denim over her slim hips. She lifted her bottom to help him, then kicked her legs out. For the moment he left her panties on, turning instead to her top half. She helped to roll up her T-shirt until the tangled cups and straps of her bra could be seen, swathed untidily around the golden globes it was supposed to be supporting. Not that they needed much support. As Harvey lifted the scraps of silk and lace up and over her breasts he marvelled at the way they appeared taut and uplifted despite their size.

Soon she was lying there topless, displaying her beauties for him. Harvey couldn't resist gathering them into both hands, feeling their firm tone as he squeezed them, watching their russet-red tips grow even harder and more inviting as he stimulated the surrounding flesh. He was filled with a sense of unlimited bounty that was his to enjoy, an overwhelming urge to lick and caress anywhere and everywhere before plunging into the soft centre of her with his hard tool. He bent his mouth to her breast and sucked on one huge nipple, making her squirm and groan with renewed pleasure.

It was becoming increasingly difficult to hold back, but she made no move towards him, only lay there in passive appreciation of his efforts. That was the deal, he reminded himself. Yet he could sense that beneath her apparent passivity the woman was an active volcano. His fingers slid beneath the elastic of her pants and found the hairy lips of her sex, sodden with love-juice. While he continued to suck hard at her breast Harvey worked his finger down between her labia, the flesh parting easily as he moved towards her vaginal entrance. When he found her openness and slipped a finger inside she became suddenly active, grinding her mons to increase her own arousal, working her pelvis with an insistent rhythm as if she were limbering up, preparing herself for having him inside her.

Now it was Harvey's turn to groan as his dick strained unbearably and clamoured to be let loose. With his free hand he quickly unzipped himself and pulled his shaft out of the constricting underwear. It thudded against his belly and Gayle turned her head to see it. She reached out and touched its velvety skin with her long, cool fingers, making him gasp. 'Nice,' she murmured. 'Very nice!'

His penis swelled with pride. Sensing that the time had come, Harvey got up off the seat for a few seconds, just long enough to strip off his clothes and slip on a condom. While he did so Gayle rearranged herself, sitting upright with her arms spread along the cushioned back of the swing and her feet on the seat, knees bent and thighs apart, exposing her red-lipped pussy to full view. He knew she wanted him to enter her now, to plunge straight in through that open doorway to paradise, but as he knelt on the seat it began to wobble precariously.

'Put one foot on the floor, as in the old movies,' she giggled. 'Then you can control the swing.'

'You've done this before, haven't you?' he mock-chided her.

She shook her head. 'Only in my dreams.'

Cautiously Harvey placed one knee beside her on the

flowered cushion and left his other leg on the ground. His prick was rearing insistently now, impatient with the logistics of the situation as he tried to maintain his balance while homing in on target. He leaned forward, holding on to the back of the seat for support, and his eager glans nosed towards her wide-open crotch. Gayle lay back, thrusting out her pert breasts and sighing with anticipation. At last Harvey felt his glans surrounded by melting softness and knew he was almost home. He pushed forward and his cock slid in beautifully, cleanly, right up to the hilt.

It felt so good in there, her delicious soft walls enclosing him in the most intimate of all embraces while he steadied himself for the push. It didn't take him long to get the hang of it. When the seat swung back he retreated, awaiting the forward lunge that would let him fill her up again and bring his shaft back into full contact with her pulsating clitoris. The slow back and forth of the swing was perfectly suited to the purpose and Harvey relished the extra momentum that allowed him to be more relaxed. He revelled in the lazy sensuality of the dual movement: in, while the soft walls yielded to encompass his shaft and the tip of his glans kissed the mouth of her womb, then out, while her walls gripped him harder as if reluctant to let him go and his shaft was finally caressed by the soft petals of her labia.

Each movement was blissful in its own way, the one serving to reinforce the other until his appetite for sensation grew and he began to increase the pace. Gayle held on tightly to the back of the seat as the ride became rougher, more exciting. Her breasts bobbed delightfully, and although Harvey was unable to let go of his hold on the seat and touch them, he loved to watch their heavy contours sway and heave, topped by the glistening red nipples. As he watched, a deep flush covered her throat and upper chest, accompanied by tremulous ripplings within. Gayle threw back her head and let out a guttural cry.

It was too much for Harvey. He made several short inroads into her heaving cunny, then let the hot ecstasy stream out of him, taking his heart and mind with it. The swing juddered as if in sympathy, making him collapse onto her in a sweaty heap of pure abandon. Only when the fierce spasms were reduced to faint shivers did he lift himself off and let her breathe freely. They lay sprawled side by side on the damp cushions, utterly spent, in a mood of total lassitude until, some minutes later, Harvey found the strength to sit up.

'Can I get you anything?' he whispered, 'A drink, perhaps?'

She opened her eyes and they blinked up at him, blue fire. A slow smile spread across her full lips. 'I think you've done quite enough for me already. Let me get you a beer.'

In the end they both got up and immediately hugged. 'Thank you, Harvey,' she murmured. 'That was exactly what I needed. I feel wonderful!'

'Well, I feel all hot and sticky. Can I take a shower, please?'

After they'd shared a beer they went up to Gayle's well-appointed bathroom and showered together. Harvey's hands ran all over her again, slick with shower gel, and afterwards he lay her down on the fluffy pink mat and licked her clean pussy until she was writhing around in bliss once more. He loved making her come, loved the way she wriggled and flushed and shuddered and moaned. If he had his way he would have carried on all night, making her have orgasm after orgasm until she begged him to stop.

But he knew he couldn't. Tomorrow morning he had a new job on, one that involved him being in Glossop by nine o'clock sharp. Reluctantly he finished towelling himself and pulled on his clothes.

'Do you have to go?' she asked him, with a face like a disappointed child's.

'Sorry,' he shrugged. 'I've a job on in Glossop, first thing tomorrow. You know how it is.'

And he knew that here, just for once, was a woman who understood perfectly.

Chapter Nine

'I've blown it!' Gayle ruefully informed her reflection in the bathroom mirror. 'And he's not the type to give a girl a second chance.'

She was thinking about Harvey Boyd. In fact, she'd been thinking of little else for the past three days, as business was slack. That hot session in her swing-seat was still indelibly printed on every nerve cell in her body, making Gayle long to repeat the experience, but now bitter regret was souring the memory. If only she had waited until they were better acquainted.

Something told her that Harvey was worth more than a one-night stand, that they could have made a go of it given half a chance. But her lust had got the better of her, and she'd ended up proving that she was exactly the sort of randy slut he'd thought she was.

It didn't help much to remind herself that she had been emotionally upset at the time, still wounded by her experience at the hands of that bastard Goodman (a misnomer if ever there was one!). For a while Harvey had made her feel cherished, loved even, and she'd been grateful to him for that. But now, three days later, Gayle wished she had allowed their relationship to develop more slowly. There was something special about the man, something intriguing and exciting, but she had wasted that opportunity and would probably have to wait a long time before anyone equally promising came along.

Gayle sighed, tweaking the last stray hair from her brow and turning away from the mirror. She had some paperwork she could be catching up with, but somehow she lacked the energy. Since that dramatic episode in Birmingham, the prospect of going back to routine cases of straying husbands and cheating fiancés was no longer appealing. It would give her great satisfaction to see that fake preacher in court, but for the time being the ball was in Lorraine Goodman's court. They could only wait and see what she decided to do with the evidence.

Just as Gayle put the kettle on, the phone rang. To her delight, it was Harvey. 'How are you?' he enquired.

Hearing the warmth in his tone her spirits soared, extinguishing her previous doubts. 'Fine. I was just thinking about you.'

'I'm flattered. Listen, Gayle, I need some help again. Something urgent's cropped up and as we've worked together recently I thought of you. Of course, if you've got a heavy caseload at the moment—'

'No!' she broke in, a shade too quickly. 'Nothing I can't put on hold, anyway. What does it involve?'

'A trip to Italy. Child abduction case. Mother's going frantic with worry so we have to get out there as soon as possible.'

Gayle felt her pulse racing with excitement. This was more like it! 'When would that be?'

'Tomorrow.'

'*What*?'

'I'm sorry it's such short notice, but it can't be helped. I take it you've a valid passport?'

'Yes, of course. But . . .' Gayle's head was spinning. The thought of going off on a trip abroad with Harvey was exciting her for all the wrong reasons, and now something in her was urging caution. 'About what happened the other night . . .'

'I'm sorry, Gayle. I took advantage of you when you were feeling vulnerable, but it won't happen again. If you agree to work with me this time I promise it will be on a strictly professional basis.'

It should have been what Gayle wanted to hear, but somehow his words made her feel sad. She pushed her personal feelings aside and questioned him about the job. It seemed that six-year-old Edward had been snatched from his mother's house by his Italian father, Roberto, during an access visit. The parents had only recently been divorced. The flight of father and son from the country had been so swift that the police had been unable to trace them, and the Italian police were not being very co-operative.

'Kate is sure the boy's ex-nanny went with them,' Harvey continued. 'Roberto had been having an affair with her, which is why their marriage broke up. She thinks they would have made for Tuscany, where Roberto's family are. He's most probably hired a villa. The man's stinking rich, apparently.'

'So why do you want me to go with you?'

'Partly as cover, partly so the boy won't be too frightened when I snatch him back. Your job will be to reassure him that we're returning him to his mother.'

'I've never done this sort of work before.'

'I have. You can leave all the details to me. Sometimes it can be a dirty business, but it would be a great help having someone with me who at least knows the basics.'

'Can I have a while to think about it?'

'I'm afraid I need your answer right away, Gayle. I have to book the airline tickets, check us into a hotel. We'd be travelling as a couple and sharing a room, but I'll make sure there are twin beds. What do you say?'

Gayle hesitated. The thought of sleeping in the same room as Harvey, even with separate beds, was making her weak at the knees. Would she just be storing up trouble for herself? Being so close to him, day in, day out, would she be able to exercise the necessary self-control? If not, she might prove more of a hindrance to him than a help.

'I'm not sure I'm the right person for the job, Harvey.'

She heard him give an exasperated sigh. 'Do you think I'd have bothered to phone you if I didn't think you could handle it? I've seen you in action, remember, and you dealt with a difficult situation admirably. I admire your professionalism, Gayle, and furthermore I think we work together really well. Besides, quite frankly there's no one else I can call on at this short notice. Please don't let me down, love. I need your help.'

It must have been that sneaky word 'love' that did it, Gayle reflected as, seconds later, she put down the phone after agreeing to go. Harvey's voice had been warm as the Italian sun, his tone as persuasive as a gigolo's. He knew just how to manipulate her into doing what he wanted, she reflected wryly. Something told her that she might be making a big mistake, but she had committed herself now and wouldn't let him down. Hurrying into her bedroom she began the tricky task of assembling a minimal wardrobe.

They had to look like holiday-makers, Harvey had told her, so she selected a couple of bikinis, some shorts, brief tops and sundresses. This isn't a holiday, she reminded herself, but somehow the message didn't seem to reach her heart, which suddenly felt as light and carefree as a soaring bird's.

The following morning Gayle took a taxi to Manchester Airport, where they were catching a flight to Pisa. When she saw Harvey waiting for her near the check-in desk, her heart flipped. He was wearing a denim suit and open-necked cream shirt that set off his light tan and made him look really sexy. As she walked towards him carrying her holdall, his face broke into a grin. He came up and kissed her affectionately on the cheek, then took her luggage.

'Hullo darling,' he said. 'Looking forward to our holiday?'

Gayle giggled, deciding to play along. 'Of course! Have you booked the hotel, sweetie?'

'Yes. We'll be spending our first night at the Pensione de' Cacciatore, in a small village near Lucca. I think that will be a good centre for us to begin our explorations.'

'Mm! All those lovely Chianti vineyards and hilltop villages. I can't wait!'

Gayle realised that the journey was going to be a bit of a strain. They would have no privacy on the flight, and they'd have to keep up the pretence even on the taxi ride from the airport. Only when they reached the privacy of their hotel bedroom could they talk freely about the job in hand.

During the flight Gayle kept having to remind herself that she was not on vacation and Harvey was not her boyfriend. For a while she drifted off into make-believe, imagining that they were on their honeymoon and that night would be repeating the wonderful love-making that they had already shared. But she soon stopped when she realised that she was only torturing herself with impossible dreams.

It was a relief to be stepping from the plane into the mellow sunshine of an Italian late afternoon. Feeling the full force of the glare on the crown of her head, Gayle reminded herself to buy a sunhat. They were soon sitting in an air-conditioned taxi, being whisked down the autostrada towards Lucca, then turning into a lane that led between terraced slopes of vines.

The quiet country inn seemed perfect for their purposes, but when the landlady showed them upstairs, instead of the expected twin beds, one large *letto matrimoniale* dominated the room. 'I asked the tourist board for twin beds,' Harvey said, clearly embarrassed. The woman looked blank. '*Two* beds, not one,' he explained.

She shrugged. 'Only this room free. You no like?'

'It's a lovely room,' Gayle assured her, looking through the shuttered window onto the balcony which gave a view of distant hills. 'But we wanted twin beds, not a double.'

'No double?'

The woman was starting to look distressed. Harvey said, 'I'm sorry, Gayle. I was quite specific with the woman at the tourist agency. There must have been a mix-up.'

'It's getting a bit late to chop and change. Why don't we accept it for tonight? I'm sure we'll manage. And we intended to move on tomorrow anyway.'

'Well, if you're sure you don't mind. Hey, you don't think I'm pulling a fast one, do you?'

'Harvey! Look, if your conscience is pricking you that much, you can sleep on the balcony.'

'Thanks!'

They managed to reassure the woman, who left beaming, then began to unpack just what they needed for one night. The smell of Italian cuisine drifted up from below and Gayle began to feel hungry. First, though, they had some business to attend to.

'I have to call at the Post Office in Lucca tomorrow,' Harvey said, hanging up his jacket. 'I've a contact here, an old mate called Luigi, who might have left me a message. He's been checking out the family of this Roberto character. Most of them live in the same village, but there's a few big estates around too. His uncle owns a vineyard in San Paolo, about ten kilometres from here. I've a hunch we might find him there, or thereabouts. But we'll see what Luigi has to say first.'

They went for a stroll in the tiny village before dinner, and Gayle was happy to take Harvey's arm. The dark-haired, black-eyed villagers nodded to them as they passed, and the children stopped their play to stare in wonder at the blonde-haired woman. Evidently they didn't see too many tourists in that out-of-the-way spot.

'It's wonderful here!' Gayle exclaimed, seeing the sun going down behind a hill strewn with cypresses and umbrella pines. 'How on earth did you find this place?'

'I hadn't much choice, it was such a late booking. Most tourists stick to the big towns or hire a villa. But I'm glad you like it. Are you sure you don't mind about the bed?'

She threw him a mischievous glance but he looked back at her impassively. 'Harvey, we're here to do a job, aren't we? If we have to spend the night on a railway station or even stuck in a hole in the ground, you won't find me complaining. Whatever it takes, okay?'

He gave her arm a squeeze. 'Spoken like a true professional. But we'll be useless tomorrow if we don't get food inside us and a good night's kip. Shall we go back?'

They dined superbly on bean and fennel soup, osso buco and peaches, washed down with a local Chianti. There were only four other guests: a middle-aged German couple and two Australian women. Gayle had the distinct impression that if they'd been allotted twin beds the two women would have preferred a double. The looks they were exchanging over dinner were decidedly erotic. However, she wasn't going to be the one to suggest a room swap!

After making stilted conversation with the Germans over a glass of *grappa* in the tiny bar, Gayle and Harvey made their way up to their room. It was the moment Gayle had been dreading. She didn't know how they were going to resolve the bed issue, but if she had to share it with him she couldn't answer for the consequences. The skimpy nightie she'd brought with her would offer nowhere near enough protection against Harvey's tempting virility.

'I suppose I'd better camp down on the balcony then,' he said doubtfully, flinging open the doors. There was a table and two chairs out there. He began bringing them into the room.

'You're not going to be very comfortable. Maybe we could take the mattress off the bed.'

But on investigation the bed proved to be not a divan but the old-fashioned type, with bare springs beneath. They managed to find a blanket in the wardrobe, however.

'Don't worry about me, I'll be all right,' Harvey said stoically, folding the blanket lengthways and spreading it on the balcony floor. 'I won't need any covering tonight, it's far too hot.'

'Are you sure? I'll use the bathroom now, then.'

While she showered, lathering the jasmine-scented gel over her body, Gayle felt a deep disappointment seize her. She admitted to herself that she'd been secretly hoping they would share the bed, hoping that their resistance would be broken down in the heat of the night and they would end up making passionate love like before. She was ashamed of her weakness.

When she emerged from the bathroom, clad in her silky nightdress, Harvey was already lying down on his improvised pallet. He was naked except for a pair of navy underpants and gave her a cheery wave through the door.

'I've set my travel alarm for six,' he announced. Gayle shuddered. 'I know it sounds early, but believe me we'll get a whole day's work done here before noon and very little afterwards. Get as much sleep as you can. We have to be fully alert tomorrow.'

'Okay. Goodnight, then.'

'Goodnight, Gayle. And . . . thanks for coming with me.'

It was terribly hot in the big bed, even with the top sheet thrown back. Gayle lay awake looking through the balcony doors at the moonlit sky, imagining Harvey's semi-nude body stretched out in all its masculine glory, like a Renaissance sculpture or painting. The heat that was building up in her wasn't all due to the climate. She could feel the crevice between her thighs growing humid and the itchy spot at the top of the cleft growing more demanding. Her breasts burned with longing to be touched and the nightdress felt like an encumbrance. Impatiently she pulled it up until her torso was exposed with her nipples already turgid on the crests of her full breasts.

Gently she began to caress herself, to ease the aching loneliness. It was easy to imagine Harvey entering in the darkness, shrouded with shadow, creeping into bed beside her and taking over from her own restless fingers. She almost managed to convince herself that it was his hands cupping her breasts, his thumbs that found their way to the peaks and softly rubbed them to fill her with exquisite thrills and awaken her more fully down below.

One hand dropped to her stomach, where she traced a light path with her nails around her navel, relishing the teasing sensuality. She imagined Harvey's lips on her nipples, suckling the way he had before, taking her swiftly into a state of heightened bliss. When she remembered how they'd made love on her swing, his strong repeated thrusts into the soft core of her, she felt her womb convulse with longing and moved her hand quickly down over her bush to find the hard nub of flesh below.

Her strokes became more urgent. Needing the release of orgasm before she could rest, Gayle brought herself swiftly to the point where just a little more friction would tip her over the edge, then slowed, enjoying the sensation of being fully sexually awakened. With her other hand she tweaked her nipples alternately, pulling at them until they felt huge and ripe, hard as nuts. She thought of Harvey on the balcony, his erect penis barely contained by the pouch of his underpants, and wondered how his organ would look standing up straight and tall in the silver light like some exotic lily. She could go out there now and slowly lower herself onto his erection while he slept, riding him like an incubus, stealing his seed. Her vagina contracted at the thought of it.

Gayle took both breasts in her hands and squeezed her thighs tightly together, feeling the warm rush of energy fill her loins. She could bring herself off at any time but she wanted to savour it, knowing that the longer she waited the better it would be. After several nights of wanting Harvey, of longing to repeat their love-making, this was probably the nearest she was going to get to having him and she wanted to savour every minute of it.

When her clitoris was throbbing hotly and she could feel the juices running between her labia, Gayle opened her thighs and felt her vulva delicately with her fingertip. Every surface was soft and runny, like ripe cheese, and when she delved into her opening her finger made little squelchy noises. She stroked the viscous surfaces lovingly, trying to remember how it felt to have Harvey mouth her down there, to spear into her with his tongue and lick her clitoris until she came with explosive force.

Gayle's strokes grew firmer as she increased the friction, wanting it now and unable to wait for it much longer. She bunched her fingers and played at the entrance to her cunny, trying to convince herself that it was Harvey's thick glans that was lodged there, like a great ship waiting to enter harbour. Her breathing was ragged now, filling the air with panting sounds that she made no attempt to stifle, and she could feel her temperature reaching fever heat. Nothing mattered except her impending orgasm.

If Harvey should come into the room now and see her masturbating, so be it. She didn't care. She would let him know how much she wanted him, how desperate she was to be filled by his satisfying prick, and if he was half the man she thought he was, he would give it to her the way he had before. She could picture him kneeling right there on the bed with his lovely big penis rearing up, ready to enter her, while her heart was beating out an urgent love-call.

Suddenly Gayle thrust her fingers deep inside, filling herself completely and triggering the fierce contractions that sent her spiralling into ecstasy. As the climax reached its most intense, she heard herself call out Harvey's name but she was beyond caring. It was only when she was coming down, gently floating back to reality, that she thought she heard a sound out on the balcony.

There it was again, a soft groaning noise. Gayle flopped back on her pillow, exhausted, but then came the unmistakable sound of gasping and moaning that told her, beyond any doubt, that Harvey was engaged in the same occupation. A smile flitted over her face. Had he heard her own self-pleasurings and been unable to resist joining her?

She was tempted to tiptoe over to the balcony door and take a peep, but decided that would be unfair. Besides, a flurry of short gasps told her that it was all over. Perhaps they might both get some sleep now!

It took Gayle a while longer, but eventually she drifted off and slept fitfully until the shrill call of Harvey's alarm awakened her. Soon he appeared in the doorway, framed against the dawn sky as he stretched and yawned. 'Are you awake, Gayle?' he called.

'That thing would waken the dead!' she grumbled.

'Well, hurry up and use the bathroom. We have to be out of here soon.'

As he entered the room she realised that her nightdress was still rucked up above her waist and she hurriedly pulled it down. Why I did that I can't imagine, she told herself. He had already seen her naked, but somehow it was different now. They were there to work, she reminded herself as she leapt off the soft mattress and padded into the bathroom.

Mustering an air of businesslike efficiency, Gayle dressed quickly while Harvey was washing and packed her few things back in her holdall so that she was ready when he emerged. After paying their bill and assuring their landlady that they had enjoyed their brief stay, they took a taxi back to Lucca where Harvey picked up a letter at the Poste Restante desk. As he read it, his face broke into a grin.

'Thanks Luigi!' he said, kissing the notepaper. He gave it to Gayle to read. The Italian had discovered that Roberto's brother had been preparing one of the family villas for guests, and neighbours had told him that a couple and a young boy had moved in. The villa was attached to a vineyard, owned by Roberto's uncle, Enzo Alberti, which was about to be harvested.

'Let's see if Uncle Enzo could do with a hand in the

vineyards, shall we?' Harvey smiled, taking the letter back.

Harvey decided to hire a car. It would be useful for following the targets if they switched venue and it would also serve them as a mobile wardrobe in case they had to change clothes in a hurry. However, when they reached the tiny hilltop village where the villa and vineyard were situated, Harvey said they must park and take with them only what they needed for the time being. 'We have to look like impoverished migrant workers, remember. No holiday clothes. Let's see your jeans and T-shirt.'

Gayle unpacked them and, to her horror, Harvey immediately began to vandalise her clothes. He pulled a couple of buttons off her cotton top, ripped the knee of her jeans and rubbed dirt into them. Then he handed them to her with a grin.

'Harvey, what the hell . . . ?'

'Get behind those bushes and change!'

When she emerged, looking like a tramp, Harvey had got into his own torn jeans and was wearing a faded shirt with the sleeves rolled up. He ruffled her hair and smeared a bit more dirt on her cheek. 'That's better. Now let's parade up the road singing "We're a couple of swells"!'

The villa was very impressive, with lions guarding the gates beyond which a drive wound through shady gardens. Harvey buzzed the intercom and asked for 'Signor Alberti', but when he said they wanted work they were told to go round to a side gate. There they were met by a suspicious-looking foreman who asked to see their passports and work permits.

'We have no permits,' Harvey said. 'We didn't think we needed them. Can't you just let us help in the vineyard for a few days? We're on holiday here, and we ran out of money.'

The man asked if they'd done grape-harvesting before, and Harvey said he had done a few jobs in Bordeaux. The man grunted. 'We do things different here. But we need some more hands. Okay. Come, I take you where you can put your things.'

They followed him down the side wall of the villa and eventually came to a large barn on the edge of the vineyard. Inside were mattresses laid down, and people's belongings strewn about. 'You two go at the end. Water outside. I see you in five minutes.'

Eventually they were shown to the vineyard, where about a dozen people were hard at work. It was coming up for noon, when the harvesting would stop. The foreman showed them which grapes to choose, how to cut the bunches without bruising them and which to leave on the vine. It was a small vineyard, using traditional methods, and great tubs of purple grapes were being loaded onto an ox-cart in the lane.

'You start tomorrow, at dawn,' they were told brusquely.

'Plenty of time to go snooping around!' Gayle whispered, as the man stomped off.

After a picnic lunch in the shade, when they chatted to the other workers, Gayle and Harvey wandered off while most of the others began their siesta. They walked all around the perimeter wall of the villa, finding only two gates where they could see inside. Gayle produced some binoculars from her shoulder-bag and they tried to see into some windows but the only evidence that Edward might be there was a small boy's bike, propped against a wall, and a football half-hidden in the grass.

They went back to the barn and dozed for a while with the rest of the gang, then went up to the village. On the advice of the others, they purchased straw hats from one of the three shops then went to the only bar for a beer. Harvey got talking to the locals and was told that Signor Alberti always had a full house at harvest time.

'His friends and relatives?' Gayle prompted. 'Big family party?'

The barman laughed. 'Oh yes! Always big *festa* if harvest goes well. If not so good . . .' he made an 'iffy' gesture with his hand, 'still big *festa*!' He gave a raucous laugh.

'And everyone joins in, do they? Family and workers together?'

'Yes, of course!'

It augured well. Surely Roberto wouldn't wish to remain in hiding on such an important occasion, and he would want his son to share in the celebration too.

Next morning a loud clanging bell woke Gayle and Harvey at first light. They sluiced themselves under the tap in the courtyard, along with the others, hurriedly drank mugs of coffee and ate hunks of bread and sausage, then made for the vineyard. By the time the sun was up they were already tired. It was arduous work, requiring them to bend over much of the time, and Gayle was very glad of her wide-brimmed hat.

By noon they were feeling shattered and could scarcely drag themselves back to the barn. Despite the gloves she wore, Gayle's fingers were stained purple and red with grape-juice and blood, where she'd nicked herself with the secateurs.

'I had no idea it would be so tough!' she exclaimed, flopping down on some sacks to drink her mineral water. They ate ravenously – bread and cheese, olives and tomatoes, washed down with wine – then it was easy to fall asleep on their mattresses despite the heat.

At around three Gayle woke to find Harvey out in the

yard, splashing cold water over his neck. 'I thought we'd do a bit more snooping,' he murmured as she approached. 'Wake yourself up with a splash then we'll go.'

This time they were more lucky. Just as they reached the main gates and peered through they could see a car parked outside the door of the villa and a basket being loaded into the boot. Suddenly Roberto appeared, instantly recognisable from his photo, followed by Gina leading Edward by the hand.

'Yes!' Harvey exclaimed, grabbing Gayle's hand. 'Come on, we've got to get to our car so we can follow them. Run now, fast as you can!'

It wasn't easy in that heat, but they reached the car just a few seconds before the elegant blue Maserati drove slowly down the village street. Trying not to look too rushed, Harvey unlocked the door and let Gayle into the front seat beside him. They followed the Italian car through the winding roads for around twenty minutes, then came to the bank of a river where a small beach had been created. It was obvious that this was Roberto's destination.

Fortunately there were several other families already ensconced on the shore with deckchairs and umbrellas, so Gayle and Harvey didn't feel too conspicuous. Gayle changed into her bikini in the car while Harvey put on his shorts, and they set up camp with towels, books and bottled water. While Gayle lay on her stomach, Harvey surveyed Roberto and Gina through his sunglasses and gave her a whispered running commentary.

'They're taking Edward into the water now, playing around. He seems happy enough. I think I'll try to get some photos.'

After a while the basket was opened and Roberto tried to tempt his son with some food, but the boy wouldn't eat. He sat to one side, looking miserable, and eventually lay down with his head on a folded towel as if he were exhausted. Gayle saw Gina and Roberto lift him up and carry him into the car, where they laid him on the back seat and shut the door. Then the pair began kissing and cuddling on the beach.

Gina was a buxom girl, and her red shiny bikini showed off her large breasts and slim waist. It was clear that the pair were becoming sexually aroused. Gayle could see the bulge in Roberto's black trunks as he kissed his girlfriend with Latin passion. Suddenly the pair rose and tiptoed to the car, peering in through the back window before going off into some reeds.

Harvey turned to Gayle with a grin. 'Rumpy-pumpy time, I think. Shall we see if we can spy on them, maybe get some shots of what they're up to?'

Gayle nodded. Cautiously they skirted the reeds, through which the red and black of the couple's swimwear was just visible. 'Ever been bird-spotting?' Harvey whispered as they edged closer. 'I think it's time to lie low.'

It was hot and smelly in the reed-bed. Soon Gayle's bikini was filthy and she began wondering about mosquitoes, but she knew that the job must come before her personal comfort. Besides, there was something reassuring about being there with Harvey. It was so nice to be able to rely on someone else for a change, instead of having to make all the decisions and do the dirty work herself. She squirmed out a nest for herself amongst the rotting vegetation and soon had a clear view through the reeds of what the couple were doing.

Roberto was kissing Gina with renewed passion, his fingers deep into her cleavage, while she was wrapping her thighs around his and squeezing hard, her libido evidently at full throttle. Soon he was tearing off her bikini top, exposing breasts that were the size and shape of rugby balls. Evidently she was in the habit of sunbathing topless, for they were an even, rich brown, with large nipples of a darker hue that contracted sharply when her lover pinched them. As Gayle watched she was aware of the nearness of Harvey, his body giving off a sharp scent of male sweat, and she sensed that he, too, was growing randy.

Just as Roberto stripped off his shiny black trunks to display his impressive tackle, Harvey took a photo of the pair and was soon snapping away at intervals. Gina took the end of Roberto's cock between her red lips and began to suck and lick with eager abandon. At the same time he began to squeeze her breasts together, murmuring something in Italian. She took the hint, placing his organ in her cleavage and flicking her tongue across the glans while he moved up and down, his fingers manipulating the giant nipples. Gina began to moan and writhe with abandon. She reached down and pulled off her red bikini pants to expose a very hairy mons beneath which slick pink lips were just visible. Then she began to finger herself as her lover increased the pace of his thrusts.

Gayle was finding the spectacle almost unbearable. She longed to imitate their sex play, to tear off Harvey's skimpy shorts and have him do to her what Roberto was doing to Gina. Only the presence of the camera deterred her, reminding her that they were on a job – not *the* job!

In a few seconds Roberto was shooting straight into Gina's open mouth and she was rubbing herself frantically, trying to match his climax. Just as his groans and spurts faded she succeeded, coming in a series of shudders that set her fat breasts wobbling. The couple sank into each others' arms, covered in mud and sweat, but it wasn't long before they were at it again. This time Gina straddled her lover and lowered herself onto his renewed erection while he reached up and stroked her pendulous breasts. They took it slowly, an expression of bliss on both their faces as they synchronised their lazy movements and extracted every bit of sensual enjoyment from their leisurely screw.

Suddenly Gayle thought she heard a noise, a faint cry of anguish. She turned her head. Yes, it was coming from the direction of the parked Maserati. She nudged Harvey, who nodded to show he'd heard it too, but the couple appeared completely oblivious. While they continued with their intercourse, the cries of the boy became louder and the words 'Papa!' and 'Gina!' could be plainly heard, verging on the hysterical.

'Can't they hear him?' Gayle whispered indignantly. 'The poor kid's getting frantic.'

'They don't care.'

'But this is outrageous. It must be terribly hot in that car, and the boy has no idea where they are. How could they be so selfish and cruel?' Harvey shrugged, taking another shot. Gayle looked back through the reeds towards the beach, wondering what to do. 'Can't we go and get him, right now? Those two won't notice anything. It's the perfect opportunity, surely?'

'No.' Harvey's reply was terse.

Gayle bit her lip. He was in charge, but she couldn't see why they shouldn't carry out the rescue as soon as possible. Surely it would be what his mother wanted? Still, she wouldn't make a fuss. No doubt Harvey had his reasons for preferring to wait.

Loud moans from the reeds ahead signalled that Gina was enjoying another orgasm, and Roberto's soon followed. The screams of the boy were louder than ever now, and although the couple started to put their beachwear back on, they were evidently in no hurry and interspersed their dressing with more kisses and caresses.

'How could they!' Gayle murmured angrily.

They waited until the Italians had got to their feet and started to walk, arms around each others' waists, back to where the car was parked. Gayle stowed the camera in her bag then Harvey cautiously led the way around the reed patch on his hands and knees, so it would look as if they were returning to the beach from a different direction. By the time they approached their car the couple had got into an argument with some other Italians, evidently over the way they had left the sobbing boy alone. Gayle felt so sorry for him. He was standing moodily against the car with a faraway look in his eye, and she guessed that he was thinking of his mother and missing her badly.

'Come on, let's take a dip in the river to get this mud off us,' Harvey said, holding out his hand. His eyes told her that he'd been upset by the episode, too. Hopefully that would make him all the more determined to get the boy back to his mother as quickly as possible.

As they drove back to the villa, Gayle asked why he hadn't seized the child there and then.

'Think about it, Gayle. There were just too many other people about. The boy would have protested, they'd have noted our number and had the police on our tail straight away. When we do take him it has to be a planned operation, and the first thing you must do is have a quiet word with the lad, tell him that we came here from England to take him home. I think the best thing would be to wait until the end of harvest celebrations, next week.'

Gayle sighed. What Harvey had said made sense, but she

couldn't bear to think of that little boy suffering for a day
longer than was strictly necessary.

Chapter Ten

Harvey couldn't remember how it felt to be free from pain. Every morning he awoke to agonising aches in his shoulders, back and calves, while the skin on his arms and legs was burnt raw by the sun. The thin, lumpy mattress didn't help either. He'd had no idea that grape-picking could be so arduous.

But those weren't the only physical problems he had to face. His sexual frustration had been growing worse each day, fuelled by the presence of Gayle. No matter how hard he tried to banish the memories of the way her delectable body felt, inside and out, the self-tormenting continued. He couldn't even have a surreptitious wank beneath the bedclothes, because there weren't any. Night after night he had lain in the barn with his cock bursting out of his pants, forced to observe Gayle's breasts and thighs heaving beneath her thin nightdress without being able to do a thing about it.

If he could have found someone less attractive to be his accomplice he would have done so, but he'd had no choice. Not that he was complaining about her fitness for the job. So far she had done exactly as she was told, quietly and efficiently, but the true test of her professionalism was yet to come. Today was the last day of harvest, and tonight they would be celebrating. With everyone half-drunk and making plenty of noise and bustle, Harvey knew he couldn't hope for a better chance to snatch the boy from under his father's nose.

Last night, walking to the far end of the vineyard, they had laid their plans. Kate had already been alerted by phone and would be arriving in Lucca that morning, checking into a motel near the autostrada. Harvey had warned her that things might not go exactly to plan, but he knew it was vital to have her in the country, ready to reassure young Edward that he was being taken home and not subjected to some new ordeal. He would phone her again that afternoon.

The last morning of grape-picking went smoothly, as most of the harvest was in and it was just a case of going back along the rows and spotting any they'd missed. By noon Harvey felt his physical tension slackening, but his anxiety was increasing. What if they failed, succeeding only in alerting Roberto so that he removed the boy to an even more remote spot?

He felt obliged to warn Kate on the phone that if they didn't pull it off this time, they might not get the opportunity again.

'I know,' she replied, her voice tense. 'But I'm sure you'll do your best, and I'm very grateful to you for trying. How—how was he, when you last saw him?'

'He looked fine,' Harvey assured her.

'What was he wearing – can you describe his clothes to me?'

'Denim shorts and a short-sleeved white shirt. White socks and brown shoes.'

'All new things,' she said bitterly. 'I suppose he has new toys, too. Soon there will be nothing left, no memories of home. Harvey, you've *got* to get him back!'

'I'll do my best. Now you get some rest and stay by the

phone. I'll call you the minute there's any news.'

Harvey put down the receiver with a heavy heart. The pressure was on and he had to deliver. Normally he didn't get emotionally involved in cases, but this was different. He'd seen the child wandering in the garden of the villa a few times, looking lonely and abandoned. And after seeing the way that couple had ignored young Edward's cries, leaving him locked in an overheated car while they carried on fucking, he was determined to get the boy back to his mother by any means possible.

The harvest celebrations began around six, when the barbecue was lit and huge pitchers of wine were carried out of the house onto the long tables set in the grounds. Like the rest of the workers, Harvey and Gayle had taken a shower and put on smarter clothes for the occasion. Their car was parked near the back gate of the villa, ready for a quick getaway, but although Gina could be seen directing operations at the buffet table, as yet there was no sign of Roberto, let alone his son.

'God, I hope the kid shows up!' Harvey murmured to Gayle. 'What if he's been taken off to some other relative's place for the night?'

Gayle smiled. 'Leave it to me. If he doesn't appear, I'll try to find out where he is. I feel as if I've done very little so far, Harvey. Tonight I intend to pull my weight.'

'Don't worry, you've been a great help already. Moral support shouldn't be underestimated in this job. And you've helped me blend in with the crowd, instead of sticking out like a sore thumb!'

Gayle giggled, and his heart lurched a little. Did she know what she was doing to him when she batted those innocent blue eyes at him? The square-necked gingham dress she was wearing made her look like something out of a Fifties musical, all wholesome and folksy and good enough to eat!

Suddenly Roberto appeared, handsome in a pristine white shirt and tight-fitting black trousers, and Harvey was relieved to see that he was holding Edward by the hand. The boy looked well-scrubbed, wearing an outfit that mimicked his father's and with his hair slicked back, but as he surveyed the crowd there was a look of faint terror in his eyes. Gina spotted them and came up all smiles, making a show of taking the boy's hand and leading him down the steps to see the barbecue. Harvey thought of Kate, waiting anxiously by the phone in the Lucca motel, and felt sickened.

The party got going when the local band struck up and, once the sun had gone down and lanterns were lit along swaying overhead wires, Harvey almost succumbed to the festive atmosphere. But he allowed himself only a little wine and his eyes were everywhere, keeping tabs on Roberto and his son. At last he saw Edward sitting on a folding chair by himself and knew it was time to make their move. Roberto and Gina were dancing in the midst of the throng, and there was a clear opportunity for Gayle to talk to the boy.

She had sensed it too, and was starting to approach Edward. Harvey gave her a wink and pointed in the direction of the back gate. He would hide behind a bush, watching and waiting, until Gayle was able to persuade the child to go with her. This was the trickiest part of the whole operation. If the alarm were raised now there would be plenty of willing feet to give chase and hands to hold them down. They wouldn't stand a chance.

Through the dense cover of the bush, Harvey could just make out Gayle's full-skirted form as she reached the chair where Edward was sitting. He saw her bend to talk to him, then she fetched him a glass of lemonade. The boy's face was animated, as if he was glad that someone had noticed him. It was pathetic, really.

Exactly what she said to him Harvey never knew, but whatever it was it worked. He held his breath as Edward rose from his seat and placed the glass carefully on the white tablecloth nearby, then held on to Gayle's hand. She led him towards the shrubbery, glancing over her shoulder as she went, but everyone was enjoying themselves too much to take notice of what Roberto's son was doing with that strange woman.

Soon they were approaching the bush where Harvey was hiding. The music was growing raucous as the players consumed more alcohol, providing useful background noise. Slowly Harvey raised himself from his crouching position and stepped out onto the path.

'Who are you?' the boy asked, startled.

'It's all right, Edward. He's a friend of your mummy's too.'

But this time Gayle's words didn't work. 'I want to go back!' he cried. 'Take me to Papa!' Harvey knew they couldn't turn back now. They must continue according to plan, for the boy's own good. He took hold of his other small hand and tried to drag him along the path.

'Come along, Edward. Your mummy's waiting for you. She's longing to see you.'

But the boy was terrified and beginning to shout for his father. Gayle was obviously unhappy about the way things were going and she let go of Edward's hand.

'We must get him out of here!' Harvey snapped. 'Quick!'

'No, we can't do it like this!' she protested, but the music had temporarily stopped and people were milling around. Soon the boy's absence would be discovered. Harvey picked the child up and threw him over his shoulder in a fireman's lift. Fumbling in his pocket he thrust the car keys into Gayle's hand. 'Go on ahead, start the engine! They'll be after us soon.'

Gayle hesitated, but then began running towards the gate which she left open. By the time Harvey had bundled his living burden into the back seat the engine was running. He threw himself into the driving seat and, with one last backward glance, set off at top speed. They rounded a bend and were soon on the main road, heading for the motorway.

It was a bumpy ride, and Edward was crying noisily in the back seat while Gayle was giving him earache in the front. At last Harvey snapped.

'Look, we got the kid, okay? I'm sorry it couldn't have gone more smoothly, but we aren't out of the wood yet so I'd appreciate it if you didn't give me a hard time. They'll know he's been taken by now and that Maserati is probably already on our tail. I don't fancy our chances of outrunning that speed machine once we're on the autostrada, so we'd better make as much headway as we can.'

Gayle looked chastened. 'Of course, you're right. I'm sorry.'

'Where are you taking me?' came a frightened voice from the back.

'To your mummy. She's waiting for you near here.' Gayle leant back over her seat and tried to give Edward a reassuring pat but he squealed, 'Go away, I hate you!'

'Oh dear!' she sighed, adding in a whisper, 'So much for the sweets I bought. I don't think he'd respond very well to bribes right now, do you?'

'The only thing he'll respond to is the sight of his mother, so we'd better get him there fast. Before we get on the motorway I'll have to ring her and arrange a meeting place. She'll have to book us airline tickets too. Once the police are alerted they'll be watching the airport.'

It was annoying having to stop the car and make that phone call, but there was no alternative. Harvey tried to stem the woman's excited thanks, making sure she got the basic instructions into her head, then he returned to the car. Edward was lying down on the back seat in a sullen stupor. A pang went through Harvey's heart. The boy must feel like a pawn in a game where he had no idea of the rules.

Once on the autostrada, Harvey put his foot down until they reached the turnoff for Lucca. He had arranged to meet Kate in a bar that he'd noticed on his last visit. It was in a quiet back street. When he drew up she was already hovering on the pavement outside, her face a touching blend of hope and anxiety.

'Mum!' The boy threw himself ecstatically into his mother's arms. It was a moment Harvey cherished. He drew Gayle close and they watched the reunion together, but there was no time to over-indulge in sentiment.

'Have you booked the tickets?' he asked Kate.

She nodded. 'I managed to get four on the ten-thirty flight. But they're all single seats. That's all they had left.'

'Doesn't matter. Where's your luggage? Come on, we must get moving.'

He threw her small bag into the boot and she got into the back with Edward. As they drove towards the airport mother and son asked each other dozens of questions, laughing and crying by turns. But Harvey's mind was on the last hurdle ahead. He knew that they wouldn't be completely safe until they were in the air. In an emergency, even a plane could be stopped at the last second before take-off.

Once on the motorway again and cruising at speed, Harvey relaxed a little. They should make the flight in good time. None of them had any more than hand luggage, which would make things far easier. But just as they were approaching the turn-off for the airport he caught sight of a blue car in his wing mirror and his blood froze. The Maserati was gaining on them, zooming up the fast lane like a bat out of hell. Harvey decided to say nothing. He didn't want to alarm the others. Calmly he veered off into the slip road and the other car slowed to follow.

The route to Pisa Airport was clearly marked, but Harvey decided to take a different road.

'Hey, this isn't the right turning,' Gayle protested, but he shushed her with a frown

'What's up?' she whispered.

'They're on our tail. I'm trying to shake them off. Try not to alarm the others, please.'

Gayle looked white as she stared into his mirror. The Maserati was only two cars behind them now, and the grim face of Roberto was clearly visible at the wheel. Harvey slammed his foot to the floor and the car picked up speed, putting some distance between them. It was a risky manoeuvre, however, giving Roberto a chance to overtake and come right up behind them. Fortunately there was a bend in the road preventing it, but Harvey knew that within a few seconds the other car would be right there, and if Roberto honked his horn both Kate and Edward would know about it too.

There was a turning to the left and, acting on impulse, Harvey took it. The road led to a small town but a few hundred yards on there was an even rougher track leading across country. He looked in his rear-view mirror. As yet there was no sign of his pursuers. Quickly he turned off and went bumping down the potholed surface towards a small hamlet.

'Where is this?' Kate asked, anxiously. 'Not the main road to the airport, surely?'

'It's a short cut,' he lied. 'Sorry about the rough ride in the back.'

'We don't care, do we, Eddie? As long as we get back home soon. Tibbles has missed you terribly, darling. Mrs Page is looking after her till we get back.'

Harvey held his breath, grimly steering the car along the increasingly bumpy road towards the isolated cluster of dwellings. Yet there was no sign of the Maserati in the mirror. His gambit seemed to have paid off. For the time being, at any rate.

When they reached the village there was another road leading back towards Pisa, much to Harvey's relief. He glanced at his watch: less than an hour to take-off. It was going to be touch and go. The boy needed to be let out for a pee, and Gayle bought some much-needed mineral water in a garage shop, then they resumed their journey. In half an hour they were delivering the keys of the hired car to the Hertz desk at the airport and taking their hand luggage to the check-in desk.

Before they got to the queue, however, Harvey suddenly froze. He could see Roberto and Gina walking through the lounge scanning the crowd as they went.

'Quick, this way!' He pushed Gayle and Kate towards the ladies' cloakroom. 'Get in there and lie low. They've come straight here.'

'What?' Kate looked round, panic-stricken, but Gayle ushered her off with Edward in tow, and the three of them disappeared into the ladies' while Harvey nipped into the gents' next door. What the hell were they to do? Obviously the Italian pair would be watching the check-in desks like hawks, waiting to pounce on them the minute they turned up.

Then he remembered what he'd done in similar

circumstances before. It was a long shot, but it was the best he could think of. Opening his bag, he took out the fake glasses and moustache that he always kept with him and put them on, adjusting them in the mirror. He exchanged his denim jacket for a black turtle-necked jumper and then left the gents', hoping he was now unrecognisable. Yet *he* was not the problem. Roberto would surely recognise his ex-wife and son straight away, and then the game would be up.

Harvey began a rapid cruise around the airport shops, picking up accessories. It was his only hope now. He purchased a large headscarf, two pairs of sunglasses and a big straw hat. A touch of genius was a toy Batman cape and mask. The idea of turning the four of them into something approaching the Marx brothers seemed ludicrous, but it might just work. If they didn't get onto that plane there would be no hope for them. Roberto would kick up a stink, the airport police would get involved and that would be the end of that.

Tentatively, Harvey opened the door of the ladies' and saw the three of them huddled inside. He threw in the clothes. 'Dress yourselves in those!' he hissed, like some stage villain, before retreating at the entrance of two alarmed elderly ladies.

Eventually the strange trio emerged. To Harvey's eyes they looked horribly unconvincing.

'We can't possibly check in together,' he told them. 'You and Kate must queue at different desks and I'll take Edward. They won't be expecting to see him with a man.'

His mother did her best to reassure the frightened boy that it was all right to go with Harvey. Even so, the kid held back from him as they crossed the floor and refused to hold his hand. Harvey was conscious of Roberto and Gina staring at the queues from across the floor and his heart was in his mouth, but fortunately they were shielded by a family of four as they waited to check in. Once they had their tickets Harvey took the boy over to the departure lounge where he would go through the barrier on his mother's passport.

Gayle soon joined them, and all three waited in suspense until Kate was safely through the check-in procedure. Once through passport control she beamed with relief and hugged her son, but Harvey urged caution. 'They could still get the police to stop the flight. Don't count your chickens!'

Only when they were all installed in their seats and the plane was taxiing down the runway did Harvey permit himself a long sigh of relief. They'd done it! Whatever trials lay ahead for poor Kate and her son, at least he had played his part and rescued the boy from his unscrupulous father. He and Gayle, of course. A wave of gratitude washed over him as he thought of how she'd seen him through this difficult week. She was some woman! The old itch returned as he looked round and saw her sitting in her aisle seat, the T-shirt that she'd changed into making her breasts look round and full. God, he'd like to take that woman to a top class hotel and make love to her non-stop for a week!

Hotel? That was a thought! Harvey suddenly realised that it would be after midnight by the time they arrived in London and they had nowhere to stay. Maybe his dream could become reality after all!

In the event, Kate insisted on putting them up at her place for the night. Harvey hadn't seen her house before, and when the taxi drew up in front of the impressive three-storey mansion in Chelsea he drew in his breath. Of course the Tuscan villa and Maserati had hinted at money – Mafia money, probably – but somehow he'd imagined Kate living in straitened circumstances. All part of the image he'd built up of her, he supposed.

Now the boy's delight at being home again was evident. Despite his fatigue, he rushed excitedly from room to room, making sure it was all just as he remembered it. When Molly Page, the housekeeper, appeared with a smoky Persian kitten in her arms, Edward almost smothered the poor thing to death with his enthusiastic 'cuddles'.

'Let's open some champagne!' Kate laughed. 'There's a magnum in the fridge, Molly. The glasses are in that cupboard, Harvey. I'm just going to put Ed to bed.'

'Ed to bed, Ed to bed!' the boy repeated sleepily. He waved goodnight then disappeared in the arms of his mother.

Harvey went up to Gayle and gave her a hug. 'This makes it all worthwhile, doesn't it?'

'Oh yes!' she beamed, her eyes glowing. He kissed her mouth, softly, and a tide of pure lust surged through him. For a moment he felt her respond, her lips yielding, inviting him in, but then Molly entered with the champagne and they drew apart. Soon Kate also returned, announcing that her son had fallen asleep almost at once, clutching his favourite bear and still wearing his Batman outfit which he'd refused to take off.

'I don't know how to begin to thank you,' she smiled, giving each of them a hug. 'I feel as if I've just woken up from a long nightmare.'

'Only doing our job!' Harvey grinned. 'Here, let me open that.'

Once the champagne was flowing they began to laugh about their experiences. 'I wish I'd managed to get a photo of the three of you in disguise!' Harvey chuckled.

'Well, it worked!' Gayle pointed out. 'Hey, I've just had a thought. Do you suppose Roberto and Gina are still lurking at Pisa airport, waiting for us to turn up?'

They collapsed in giggles while Kate attempted to explain to Molly their master plan. When they'd finished all the champagne, however, she turned her attention to her guests.

'The two guest rooms are on the top floor, either side of the bathroom. Molly has put clean towels in the rooms. You can choose whichever you want.' Then her eyes twinkled. 'Unless you'd prefer to go on posing as man and wife, that is.'

Had she detected the spark of sexual chemistry between them? Harvey didn't know how to reply. Nothing could give him more pleasure right then than a night in the same bed with Gayle. It would set the seal on their success, providing them both with a delightful bonus. But he shrank from suggesting it openly.

'I think I'll go straight up, then,' Gayle announced, avoiding the issue. 'Coming, Harvey?'

They both took their leave and walked up the two flights of stairs together. The first door they opened showed a pleasant room with Laura Ashley décor and a double bed. 'This will do for me,' Gayle said, then hesitated. Her eyes surveyed him doubtfully, but in their depths he saw a flicker of hope.

It was all the encouragement he needed. Closing the door behind him, Harvey resumed the kiss they had begun downstairs, this time allowing his tongue to pass between her open lips and into the welcoming embrace of her mouth. He could feel his cock rearing insistently and knew he desired her with an appetite that it would take all night to sate.

As they kissed he unfastened her bra beneath her T-shirt and unzipped her jeans. While she ran her fingers through his hair, he found the taut globes of her breasts and caressed them gently, making her moan with delight. Soon she was tearing off her own clothes and starting on his. When they were both naked she led him to the bed and they arranged themselves in the 'sixty-nine' position. Harvey gasped as her lips delicately brushed his tumid glans and his own mouth nuzzled her bush, watering as he scented the musky juice secreted just below. His tongue slipped in between her labia and tasted the first sweetness, eliciting a long sigh of pleasure.

Now Gayle had taken the whole of his erection into her mouth and was sliding up and down it, sending him into shivers of ecstasy. Harvey deepened his exploration of her pussy, probing with the tip of his tongue until he found her wet entrance, then pushing in until she was wriggling and squeezing, thrusting her bulging clitoris against his lips. He took the hint and began to apply gentle friction to her slippery mound with his fingertip. In less than a minute she was coming in a welter of liquid bliss, moaning loudly as she continued to suck him.

It took only a few more thrusts of his dick to propel Harvey into a climax of his own that swept through him like a flash-flood. Over and over he spasmed, groaning as he was engulfed by a wave of ecstatic release that left him utterly satisfied. He righted himself and lay with Gayle in his arms, drinking in the spicy after-sex smell of her, loving the feel of her soft body cuddling up to him.

'God, I needed that!' she murmured.

'Me too. It's been hard keeping my hands off you this past week. Did you know that?'

She turned her face up with a grin. 'I suspected as much.'

'You're quite some woman, Gayle. I admire your guts. As for the rest of your body . . .'

He swept a hand down over her breasts and stomach, coming to rest on the hairy mound of her delta. She pressed her mouth to his and soon they were kissing deeply, rousing the fires within once again. Harvey pinched her nipple gently, tweaking it back to its former ripeness, and then his hand slipped lower to the warm haven between her thighs. She sighed and let them part, giving him full access to her still-moist pussy where her labia felt soft and smooth as silk. Imagining how it would feel to slide inside her, Harvey noted with pride that his prick was hardening again. Gayle noticed too. She encircled the base of his erection with her finger and thumb, pressing to make him harden, then began to slide the ring up and down until he was well-lubricated.

'Come inside me,' she whispered.

He needed no second invitation. 'Get up on all fours,' he murmured, nibbling briefly at her ear. 'I want to take you from behind.'

She obeyed instantly, presenting her gorgeously rotund buttocks for his inspection. He got onto his knees behind her and, after rolling on a condom, nudged his way into her front passage while he massaged her breasts. Gayle arched her back and threw back her head in sensual abandon as he thrust into her, biting softly at the nape of her neck. She shuddered and ground her round bum against his stomach, gripping him with her inner walls at the same time. Harvey let the full weight of her breasts fall into his hands, squeezing them and pulling the long nipples through his fingers, making her squeal with joy.

After a few minutes of enthusiastic banging away Harvey slowed the pace and their lovemaking grew more subtle, more delicate. He touched her breasts with featherlight strokes and moved in and out of her slowly, pausing at the end of the upward stroke so that her clitoris got the full benefit of his glans pushing against it. For a while he came right out of her, licking her pussy from behind until she begged him to enter her again. This time he rode her hard, feeling the gathering energy moving swiftly towards its peak, knowing that she was feeling it too. When the first electric fire spurted from him she was already billowing around him like an ocean wave, undulating along the length of his shaft as he gave himself up to the mind-blowing intensity of the discharge.

At last Gayle collapsed, face down, with Harvey on top of her. He slid down her back until his head made a pillow of her round, soft buttocks and there he lay, dozing, until his heartbeat returned to normal and he wanted her in his arms again. She snuggled up happily, her body curled cosily into his, and Harvey thought, 'I could get used to this!' He wriggled down until his mouth could reach her nipples and lay there suckling while she stroked his hair. It was incredibly relaxing. His hands explored the enticing curves of her, breasts and stomach, hips and thighs, and soon he felt another burgeoning erection take form. It was amazing – he hadn't been so randy since he'd first discovered masturbation!

This time Gayle wanted to do it sideways. She put her thigh over his and soon he was gilding in and out of her while he nuzzled her cushioning breasts, feeling her juices ooze and slurp around his turgid organ. She was incredibly wet, so much so that he was afraid he would slip right out of her, but somehow they kept it together and gradually quickened the pace until he was bouncing around inside her with total confidence. He felt her come, gasping and clasping in a series of fierce spasms that told him this was the most powerful of her climaxes yet. But this time it didn't trigger him. Slowing right down again, he continued to ease himself in and out of her slack vagina while she lay back in lazy delight.

'Oh Harvey, that was wonderful!' she whispered. 'Are we going to keep it up all night?'

'As long as *I* can keep it up, we will!' he grinned. 'Is this okay for you? I mean, you don't mind me continuing right now?'

'Do I *mind*?' She giggled, making her cunt convulse around his prick. He took the softened nipples between his fingers and soon firmed them up again, evoking little moans of pleasure from her, and knew that soon she would be raring to go again. This time he wanted to be on top of her. Carefully he swung his leg over until he could kneel above her. In the light of the bedside lamp she looked incredibly beautiful: the blonde hair dishevelled and darkened with sweat, her eyes a deep navy blue in which small points of reflected light swam; her generous pink lips open and slightly pouting, like the exotic petals of some nectar-yielding flower. There was a special glow to her skin, a patina of essential oils mingled with the ruddy glow of satisfaction. He wanted to lick her all over, as if she were a delectable sweetmeat.

His lips lowered to where her nipples reared up to meet him and he took each of the hard buttons into his mouth by turns, making them slick with his saliva. Then he kissed her mouth, loving the way those plump lips felt against his own, and the way she curled her tongue around his. His hands roved down her sides, feeling the narrow indentation of her waist and the sensuous curve of her hips, then reaching round to grasp her fleshy bottom. She was such a feast, such a special treat! Was it just because she was so physically attractive to him that he wanted to make love to her over and over again, or was there a more deeply-felt rapport between them?

The question burned in his brain as Harvey lunged into her more strongly, feeling the soft thud of his glans against her cervix as he plumbed the hothouse depths of her quim. She shuddered and came in a series of tiny ripples, stimulating the velvety skin of his penis so delightfully that he couldn't help but come with her, letting himself drift into a gentle release of all his tension. He sank into her gratefully, feeling the energy flow out of him in one smooth flood, giving himself up to the infinite bliss of the experience until it slowly faded.

They lay side by side in what Harvey thought would be just another respite from their sweet exertions, but it wasn't long before he was asleep. He awoke while it was still dark outside, but the bedside lamp was still on and the alarm clock told him it was half-past four. Gayle was sleeping peacefully, one arm flung over her head so that her breasts were uplifted, the pink nipples slack and a couple of inches in diameter. Harvey quashed the urge to make love to her while she dozed. It didn't seem fair to rouse her from such a relaxed slumber.

But he found he couldn't get back to sleep himself. Eventually Harvey rose, careful not to waken her, and went into the bathroom. He took a leak then ran himself a bath, wallowing in the pine scent of the bubbles. He felt strangely disorientated, a bit like jet-lag, but knew it had nothing to do with his recent travelling. No, it was Gayle who was making him feel like this. The emotions that their love-making had stirred up in him were ones he hadn't felt for years. An urge to both master and protect the woman, to have and to hold her. Jesus, what was he thinking? Harvey recoiled in horror from the idea that he might want more than just sex from her, that he might be – heaven help him! – in love with the woman. That was a catastrophe that he'd promised himself would never happen again.

Chapter Eleven

Harvey had said he would ring her, but instead a bunch of red roses arrived for Gayle. The note thanked her for 'everything' and said he would be out of town for a week on a job but would phone her when he got back.

Red roses. Was he aware of the symbolism? Gayle tried not to read too much into the gesture, but it was obvious that he cared about her. Equally obvious was the way she felt. Ever since their last incredible love-making session she had been feeling horny as hell, and now she had to wait a week before she had a chance of repeating the experience.

Yet something in her urged caution. It was only sex, after all. More important, perhaps, was their relationship as fellow sleuths. The more she thought about it, the less possible it seemed to combine the two. What did she want him to be, a lover or a colleague? If he offered her another job, maybe she'd better turn it down. But then she risked losing him as a lover too. Oh, why did things have to be so complicated!

Soon, however, a new assignment came in that promised to occupy her fully over the next few days. She was asked to call on Patsy Martin, chief executive of Martin Enterprises, for a confidential interview. The impressive penthouse office, in a converted warehouse, was all deep-pile carpet and potted plants. Sitting informally in soft leather chairs, Gayle formed her impressions of her prospective client.

She'd done her homework and discovered that Patsy Martin was a self-made woman who had taken over her late father's declining clothing business and turned it into a going concern. Specialising in fetish wear and sports gear, she had gained a reputation as the 'Vinyl Queen'. Today, though, Patsy was dressed in a conventional lime-green suit with a navy silk blouse that set off the striking auburn curls that tumbled, in controlled profusion, to her shoulders. Her manner was quiet and friendly, but Gayle sensed the iron will that lay behind those steel-grey eyes.

'Gayle, thanks so much for coming to see me. You were recommended by a friend of mine, Donna Lewis.'

'Oh, yes.'

'She was very happy – if that's the right word – with the investigation you undertook for her. I know it ended badly and she's now filing for divorce, but I share her view that it's better to know for certain than be tormented by doubts. In my case, I prefer to find out the truth about my man before I commit, rather than after.'

'I see. You want me to run a check on your fiancé?'

She nodded. 'A woman in my position has to be extra careful. I'm worth a lot of money, and my business is my life. When I met Mitchell, six months ago, I wasn't looking for a relationship, but I suppose you could say I fell in love. Quite a feat for a woman whose head has always ruled her heart.'

'It happens to the best of us,' Gayle smiled wryly. 'Tell me more about Mitchell.'

'He runs a used-car business. We met on holiday in the Bahamas, strangely enough. Perhaps our holiday romance would have remained just that if he hadn't happened to live in Manchester but, somehow, the magic stayed with us. He wants to marry me, but I have to be sure that there are no skeletons in his closet. I want to know about everything: education, business, money, sex. He tells me his parents are dead and he has no siblings, so I want you to check on that too. But I won't try to teach you your job. I'm sure you know what's involved.'

'I'll do my best. I can't guarantee a hundred-per-cent coverage, of course. No one can do that. How about if I spend three days on it, for an agreed fee, and give you a report after that?'

'Fine. Whatever your usual fee, you can double it. This is of vital importance to me, and I want to make sure I get the very best out of you.' Her look hardened. 'I can tell you this, Gayle. Sex with Mitchell is the best I've ever had. But if I find out that he's been deceiving me he'll be out of my life faster than a turd from a poop-chute.'

The crudity startled Gayle. Clearly there was far more to this woman than met the eye. As she left the building, Patsy Martin's predicament struck her as being not dissimilar to her own. With Harvey, too, she'd had the best sex she had ever known, but she knew little about him. Not that there was any question of them being about to tie the knot. Still, it gave her food for thought. If she ever did become that serious about a man, would she check out his background the same way she was about to do for this client? She liked to think she would trust him enough not to feel the need, but maybe old habits would die hard.

Checking on people's backgrounds was not Gayle's favourite occupation, neither was she particularly experienced at it, but she had one great advantage. Mac the Hack. Josh MacDonald made a living out of providing information which he hacked out of confidential computer files. Few aspects of an individual's life were inaccessible to Mac. However, he came expensive. The first thing Gayle did when she got home was make two lists, one of the information she could easily obtain herself from public records or her own contacts, and another of the hard-to-get details that only Mac could provide. Then she gave him a call.

Deciding to start her own enquiries with Mitchell's business, Gayle rang the Trading Standards office, then the AA and RAC to see if he was on any car dealers' blacklist. It seemed not. She checked out his licence to trade, and scanned the court records of bankruptcy hearings and fraud. As far as she could ascertain he was about as honest as any other second-hand car dealer in the business.

To check out his school record, she phoned posing as a potential employer and gathered that he had only two exam passes: in Maths, and Craft, Design and Technology. Not the brightest of guys. Or else he was the type that couldn't be bothered, preferring to leave school at the earliest opportunity and make his own way in the world. She suspected the latter.

Gayle phoned her contact on the *Evening News*, Jim Noakes, to see if Reeves' name had featured in any news items over the past five years. The only information he came back with was that Mitchell had organised several charity events and was a founder-member of the Northern branch of the Jensen Owners' Club.

All Gayle's enquiries seemed to come to the same conclusion: Mitchell Reeves was squeaky clean. Even Mac's results pointed in the same direction. The man's GP file was computer-linked to the hospital records, both of which gave him a relatively clean bill of health. The only health information that Mac couldn't obtain was from the STD clinic where a first-names-only policy prevailed. Financially, too, he was in excellent health with an impeccable credit record and a solid portfolio of investments, insurances and assets.

The only blot on his copybook concerned his family background. Apparently he did have a half-brother, who was currently serving a ten-year jail sentence for drug dealing. It was understandable that Mitchell would want to distance himself from such a character.

When Gayle returned to Patsy's office late on Thursday afternoon, she thought she had the case sewn up. If there was any dirt to be dished on Mitchell Reeves it could only be obtained from mixing with the criminal fraternity, and that was beyond Gayle's scope. She took enough risks as it was and had no desire to end up at the bottom of a canal. If Patsy wanted that kind of research carried out, she could always recommend Harvey.

But it seemed Patsy had something far more up Gayle's street in mind.

'You've covered everything except his sexual history,' she remarked, after perusing the four-page report. 'I already know quite a bit about that. I have the names and addresses of nine former girlfriends, and I could ask you to interview them all, but that would take a lot more time and I want this settled soon.'

'I don't think that line of approach would be productive, in any case. It's his behaviour now that should concern you, not his past. If he's cheating on you—'

'There's no significant other woman in his life, I'm sure of that,' she broke in. 'I have the key to his flat and I've surprised him enough times. I've also seen his phone bills and I've had him followed, on several occasions. But I suspect that he sometimes gives in to temptation with call girls, or picks up a girl for the night when he's away from home. That's my main worry. You have to be so careful nowadays, and if he's exposing himself to disease that shows a disregard for my safety that I couldn't tolerate.'

Gayle wondered how she could be so cool about it all. But she'd already guessed what Patsy was going to say next and pre-empted her. 'You want me to test his fidelity, is that it?'

'That's what you did for Donna, wasn't it? To devastating effect, I understand. Well, I'm prepared to be devastated if that's what it takes to ensure my own safety. I'll pay you to try and seduce him, and if you succeed I want hard evidence in the form of tapes and photos. If you don't . . . I'll invite you to the wedding!'

Patsy had found out that Mitchell was travelling to Blackpool on business the following day and spending the night there. If he was prepared to be unfaithful, she believed that the 'Kiss-Me-Quick' seaside resort would be just the sort of place to tempt him.

'He's staying at the Marina Hotel. He asked me to go with him, as a matter of fact, but I told him I had too much on. I can give you his schedule that I copied from his diary, so you'll know where and when to find him.'

'Have you got a photograph?'

'Of course.' She went to her desk drawer and pulled out a photo of a tall, well-built man with glossy dark hair, greying a little at the temples, hawk-like eyes and a thin-lipped smile. Gayle could tell, even from the photograph, that he was a man to be reckoned with.

She went home to prepare for the trip, packing sexy underwear and a seductive dress into a small travel-bag. Mitchell's last appointment of the day was at a garage on the way to Fleetwood. Gayle decided to make sure he checked in at the Marina, and then catch up with him at the end of his business to see where he decided to spend the evening. With luck he would visit a bar where she could approach him, or else she would have to rely on catching him when he returned to the hotel at night. Remembering how useful disguises had proved in Italy, she packed a brown wig and sunglasses, then decided to give Harvey a ring.

Hearing his answerphone, Gayle hung up. He was probably not back yet and she didn't want to leave a message. She was disappointed. It would have been nice to chat before she set out on her assignment. For some reason she was feeling unusually nervous about this particular job. She took out the photo of Mitchell and studied it again. There was something chilling about the man, despite that apparently relaxed smile, and she found herself hoping that he would rebuff her advances straight away.

In the morning, Gayle drove to Blackpool and arrived there just after ten. By that time, she reasoned, Mitchell should have made his reservation at the Marina and be at Oldfields Garage on the edge of town. She went straight to the hotel, but when she enquired at the desk she was told that no Mitchell Reeves had booked there.

Gayle cursed silently. She could think of several possibilities: he'd checked in at the Marina under an assumed name; he'd reserved a room somewhere else; he'd decided to return to Manchester that night; he was planning to spend the night with a mistress. Any of those options made her job more difficult, since now she would have to tail him most of the day. Getting back into her car, she drove to Oldfields Garage.

Through the plate-glass window of the showroom she could see an inner office where Mitchell was engaged in conversation with two other men. From her vantage point in the parked car, Gayle saw the three men come out to the used-car lot and inspect the vehicles. At last the wheeling and dealing was done. Mitchell got into his own BMW and zoomed off towards his next appointment.

It was a tedious day, but Mitchell stuck more or less to

schedule. At the next stop he parked in the road and Gayle managed to fix a tracer bug to his vehicle, which made it easier to keep tabs on him. Around seven o'clock he dropped into a fast-food restaurant and came out munching a burger. Gayle was curious as to what his next move would be. From now on she would have to rely on the trace if she lost him on the road, but if that failed her she'd have no way of catching up with him.

To her surprise, Mitchell took the motorway back to Manchester. When he stopped at a garage in Salford for a chat to the owner, Gayle rang Patsy on her mobile phone to see if he had reported any change of plan.

'No, I don't know what the hell he's up to!' the woman retorted. 'He told me he was staying in Blackpool tonight and returning tomorrow.'

'Well, something might have cropped up during the day. Anyway, I'll soon find out where he's going. Will you be in for the rest of the evening, in case I need to phone you again?'

'Yes. Do phone if you can.'

She sounded anxious. Gayle let Reeves pull into the stream of traffic, then followed several vehicles behind. Eventually he parked near the Chinese quarter and left his car. Gayle gave him a few seconds then took her travel bag and began to track him on foot. She saw him enter a bar called Smiley's and followed him in, going straight to the ladies' cloakroom.

There she changed into her slinky pink dress and put on the brunette wig. In front of the mirror Gayle turned her lips sugar pink and her eyelids smudgy grey until, satisfied with her appearance, she went upstairs to where a jukebox was playing old house music. Mitchell was leaning on the bar at the far end, smoking a small cigar with a glass of whisky in front of him, talking to a big black guy in shades and a purple shirt. Trying to look as if she'd arranged to meet someone there, Gayle went up to the bar and ordered herself a Coke.

It didn't take her long to make eye contact, and she could tell at once that he was interested. The question was, would he be prepared to take it any further? In a few minutes the two people who were positioned between them at the bar moved away, and Gayle sidled up closer. The black guy gave her a warning stare, trying to see her off, but she merely ordered another drink. She shifted on her seat, conscious of Mitchell's eyes burning a hole in her ass the whole time. If only the black guy would disappear she could find out for sure whether he wanted her or not. This was a scene she had enacted a hundred times, yet tonight it felt different – more edgy, more funky. The bar was full of sleazy characters and she was being taken for a whore. So be it. That was what Patsy wanted to find out, wasn't it, whether he picked up girls in bars?

She turned and gave him a deliberate smile. He took the bait, moving to a closer stool. There was an aura around the man that made her feel tense, but she overcame her feelings and asked him for a light. Although she didn't normally smoke, it could be a useful ploy on occasions. He leaned over and flicked the flame on a gold Cartier lighter. She dragged in the smoke, trying not to cough. 'Thanks.'

'My pleasure. Are you waiting for someone?'

'I was.'

'I see. Can I buy you a drink?'

It was the same old routine, as predictable as Christmas. Gayle allowed him to get her a Bacardi and Coke. He was sitting next to her now and she could smell his expensive aftershave, notes of sandalwood and vetiver. But there was an underlying hint of something else: the scent of danger, perhaps?

'I've not seen you in here before,' Mitchell said, for openers. Gayle was pleased. She had been in that particular bar several times on business. Her disguise must be working.

'It looks like my date's not going to turn up,' she commented, looking at her watch. 'I looked in here earlier but he wasn't around then either.'

'Shame. But maybe I could make it up to you. The name's Mitch, by the way.' He held out his large hand to her and she felt the smooth, cool palm as she shook it.

'And I'm Pamela.'

Well, Pam, it would give me great pleasure to take you out to dinner. I know a very nice restaurant, not far from here.'

Somehow Gayle had not expected this. She'd imagined a more direct approach, but if she was going to get a free meal out of it, who was she to complain?

He took her to a place run by a family Gayle knew to be part of the Manchester 'Triad' scene. Now she was more glad than ever to be working in disguise. As far as she could, Gayle avoided the territory of the notorious Chinese Mafia.

The meal was excellent, and Mitchell was charming throughout, fending off her discreet enquiries with pat answers that suggested he had done this sort of thing before. He told her he had no parents and was unattached, said he had built up his used-car business from selling salvaged vehicles for scrap as a teenager, and that he now had a flat in the same luxury waterfront complex as a member of a famous rock band. All of which she knew to be true.

The subtext to his conversation, however, was a desire to impress. He complimented Gayle on her perfume, which he accurately identified, sent the wine back saying it was not what he'd ordered, and commented that the Peking-style

Duck was nothing like he'd had in Beijing. If he'd wanted to convey the image of himself as a sophisticated man of the world, then he had succeeded. However, Gayle had met too many of his sort to take him at face value.

What makes him tick, she wondered, as she ate her lychee sorbet. Even more interestingly, what was his bedroom style? She had known men like him who regarded women's sexual potential as a challenge, and would not accept that their partner was fully satisfied until she had experienced multiple orgasms induced by a variety of means. Their own satisfaction lay in gratifying the woman's urges, not their own, yet the whole thing was a power trip.

On the other hand, sometimes men like him were indifferent to the woman's pleasure, treating them roughly, even cruelly. Was that how Patsy liked it? If so, she wouldn't be the first powerful woman who enjoyed being over-powered by her lover.

At the end of the meal he invited her back to his flat for coffee. Gayle reflected on the prospect warily. There was a snake-like cunning to the man, something predatory in the way he looked at her, that made her blood curdle.

'Do you mind if I make a phone call first?' she asked him. 'I should tell my flatmate I'll be out late, or she'll be worrying about me.'

He raised his black brows for an instant but then nodded curtly. As she made her way to the pay phone, Gayle was praying that Harvey would be at home. She wanted him to know where she was, just in case. However, all she got was his answerphone. After leaving the details on the tape, she returned to where Mitchell was in a quiet huddle with the restaurant owner. As she approached they broke off their conversation hurriedly.

'Ah, Pamela – ready to leave?' He gave a wintry smile and

helped her on with her jacket, then they went out to his parked BMW. As Gayle sank into the soft upholstery and fastened her seat-belt she felt his hand on her knee, briefly, and a slight shudder went through her, but it was more from fear than sexual excitement.

They whizzed smoothly through the streets until they reached the modernised wharf area, where dancing points of light floated on the canal waters from the windows above. He took her up in the lift to his penthouse flat, where the dazzling opulence of the décor made her gasp. The place was kitted out like a five-star hotel with Chinese silk carpets, gold-tasselled drapes, a top-of-the-range hi-fi and video system and some very select antiques, most of them oriental. A huge semi-circular sofa was arranged around an antique Italian table, inlaid with a mosaic, that looked as if it could have been lifted from a Roman villa. One thing's for sure, Gayle thought, he's not after Patsy's money!

'Make yourself comfortable,' he smiled. 'How do you like your coffee – espresso? Cappuccino? Maybe *corretto*, with a dash of brandy?'

'Just with milk, please. No sugar.'

While she waited, Gayle surveyed the room searching for clues. One thing was certain: Mitchell Reeves was a very rich man indeed. More wealthy than any small-time car dealer had a right to expect. He was up to something, but she was unlikely to get any clues from the man himself. Gayle sighed. If only Harvey had been around this week. She could have done with picking his brains before she got involved in this case. Something told her Reeves would be a hard nut to crack. While he was busy in the small adjacent kitchen, she opened her bag and started her tape recorder.

As they drank their coffee Mitchell came to sit beside her. He moved in close, despite the fact that the vast sofa could seat six comfortably, and she knew he meant business. When his hand strayed to her hair she felt the first expectant buzz tingle its way down her spine, and knew that she must decide just how far she was prepared to let him go. Down to her underwear, perhaps, then she would plead scruples. As he plunged his fingers deeper into her fake hair, she pondered which of her well-worn excuses would work best on him. A recently-broken heart, making her wary of entering too soon into a new commitment? An absentee boyfriend she was unsure about? A divorce pending but not yet finalised? A dose of thrush, or the clap? She'd once told a guy that she was awaiting the results of an Aids test, which had stopped him in his tracks, but somehow she felt it would be harder to bullshit Mitchell. He was obviously a man used to seeing through people, and if he wanted something . . .

Suddenly Gayle felt her head being yanked back as the wig was ripped off and thrown across the room. Strong arms pushed her back against the cushioning sofa and Mitchell's menacing face was thrust close to hers. 'Next time get a wig that *feels* real, too!' he snarled.

His eyes were mean slits, staring darkly into hers. Gayle's stomach gave a sick lurch. 'I just wanted a change—'

'Don't give me that crap!' He snatched the bag from her and turned its contents out onto the sofa. 'Who the fuck are you working for, bitch?'

'No one! I told you, I was waiting for someone else . . .'

He was sorting through her things with brutal indifference. She held her breath as he found the 'cigarette case' that was recording their conversation but, to her immense relief, he tossed it aside. Picking up her purse, he opened it and found her credit card.

'Gayle Webster,' he read. 'Okay, Ms Webster, what's your game?'

She felt herself trembling all over, and her words came out as a faint squeak. 'Nothing, honestly. Pamela's my middle name and I prefer it to Gayle.'

He was twisting her arm behind her now, hurting her. 'Well, Gayle, maybe you like your sex a little rough, know what I mean? Some women do, you know.' Before she realised what was happening, he had pushed the shoulders of her dress down. 'Nice tits,' he snarled, then seized her flimsy lace bra with both hands and ripped the cups apart. 'Pity about the bra!'

He seized her freed breasts, squeezing them aggressively, and gave one of her nipples a sharp nip with his teeth, making her cry out. 'That's just for tasters!' he grinned. 'Now are you going to be a good girl and tell me who you're working for, or do I have to get really tough with you?'

Gayle felt petrified, but knew she had to stick it out for a while or Patsy might take the flak. 'Look, I don't know what you're talking about. I just happened to be in that bar tonight, waiting for a guy called Jimmy. That's all.'

'Jimmy who?'

'Carter.'

It was the first name that popped into her head. Mitchell gave a contemptuous laugh. 'I presume we're not talking about the ex-president of the United States here.'

'No, no! Another Jimmy Carter.'

'Is he an undercover agent too?'

'I don't know what you mean.'

His face came close to hers again, making her shrink from the brutal determination in his cold eyes. 'Oh, I think you do. You've come here to snoop, and I mean to find out who you're working for. Time for a little more pressure, I think.'

Mitchell seized her dress again and pulled it roughly down over her hips. Gayle felt the zip break in the back and soon the lower half of her body was also exposed, showing the scanty white lace triangle that barely covered her pubis. He pinged the frilly garters hard against her thighs, making her wince, and laughed.

'Don't wear much underwear, do we? I suppose you thought you'd turn me on with this outfit. Well I got news for you, babe. It takes more than lace and frills to light my fire. I don't get off on seeing women naked – it's the naked fear in their eyes that gets me going. I like to see a girl squirm. Like now, when you're not sure what my next move will be. That's the best part. Kind of like being a prick-tease, except it's *my* prick that's going to do the teasing!'

She watched as he unzipped his fly and drew out the largest penis she had ever seen. It reared at her like an obscene forearm, the purple head almost as big as her fist, the shaft thicker than her wrist. He laughed at her obvious shock.

'I'm rather well-endowed, wouldn't you say? Trouble is, there aren't many women who can take it.' Uneasily, Gayle thought of Patsy. What kind of a sex-life could this man give her? The thought of trying to accommodate that monster was more alarming than arousing.

Mitchell knelt on the wide sofa and shuffled closer to her on his knees. He pulled her hair back, making her squeal, and the minute her mouth was open he thrust the enormous glans into it. Feeling her lips stretched around it, her mouth crammed full of alien flesh, Gayle thought she would choke and began to panic. But then she reminded herself that if she stayed calm and breathed steadily through her nose she would come to no harm.

'I like a good blow job,' he sneered, starting to thrust against the roof of her mouth, making her gag. 'But if you don't do it the way I want I'll ram this number right down your fuckin' throat. Got the picture?'

Terrified, Gayle nodded. What was she supposed to do? There was a limit to the technique she could employ when her lips and tongue were completely immobilised. But then Mitchell began to move slowly in and out of her, allowing her tongue to slip a short way down his shaft before he thrust in again, stuffing her mouth. She did her best to lick around his sensitive frenum, but he insisted that she should stroke the rest of his shaft and fondle his weighty balls.

'Okay, now let's talk!' he began, his voice low and cajoling, a tone that Gayle found even more intimidating than his overt anger. 'I know you've got me by the balls but, believe me, if you give me the slightest provocation I'll squeeze your nostrils and block your airway until you thrash around like a fish out of water. Do you understand?'

Gayle had no doubt that he meant what he said. Wide-eyed with fear, she nodded. 'Good. As long as we understand each other. Now then, I'm going to run through a list of people you could be working for. We'll stick to initials. If any of these characters hits the spot you can nod, okay? That way no one can accuse you of naming names.'

He gave a sarcastic laugh and began to reel off a list of initials, most of which meant nothing at all to Gayle. After a while he grew impatient and suddenly pushed his prick halfway down her throat with suffocating force. She began to cough and splutter, but he pushed all the more, making her gag while she fought for air. Then, just as suddenly, he pulled right out of her and turned her face down on the sofa, pinning her down with his legs while he reached for something nearby. Soon she felt a thick silky rope binding her wrists and knew that he must have taken the tasselled gold cord from one of the curtains.

'That's better. I like the sight of a woman's arse, and

yours is particularly to my liking.' He stripped off her panties and gave each of her buttocks a slap. 'Nice and firm. Should stand a lot of punishment. A bit pale, perhaps, but we'll soon improve on that.'

Gayle felt him rise from the sofa. She craned her neck and saw him approach a corner cabinet in Chinese green lacquer with red and gold dragons. He opened the cupboard and drew out an antique whip with a scarlet tassel hanging from the ebony handle that was inlaid with ivory. The business end was a bundle of dark plaits.

He walked towards her, fondling the whip in his hand. 'You might think that this was a regular cat-o'-nine-tails,' he told her, smiling. 'But you'd be wrong. It was specially made in the eighteenth century for the brothels of Paris. The hair is all from the original prostitutes.' His grin widened. 'Whores' hair, you might say! And woven into the plaits are some of their teeth which, I understand, give a rather . . . let's say, "stimulating" effect. I only use it on very special occasions. You should feel honoured.'

Gayle shuddered, knowing that he meant to use it on her until she came up with a name. It crossed her mind that she might have to invent someone, to give herself a breather. But if he ever found out that she'd lied to him she knew that she would never feel safe in that city again. The man was a dangerous psychopath. What else he was, she had yet to discover.

Chapter Twelve

When Harvey first heard Gayle's voice on his answerphone his face lit up, but the smile soon faded. At the name of Mitchell Reeves he gave a low whistle. Had the woman gone completely crazy? Evidently she hadn't a clue what kind of animal she was mixing with.

The news that she would be alone with that psychopath filled Harvey with horror. It was a Beauty and the Beast scenario out of his worst nightmares. Although he'd only just that second returned from his trip to Leeds, he went straight back out again and got into his car. After starting the engine he did a time-check: ten-twenty-five. Gayle had rung from the bar at nine-forty. With luck they would only have been in Reeves' flat for half an hour or so.

Harvey drove at once to the waterside apartments. There was heavy security for the luxury flats, so he buzzed his friend Joe and was relieved when the familiar voice answered.

'Hi, Joe, it's Harvey. Can you let me into the building, mate? I'm on a job.'

'Sure.'

There was a click and the door swung open. Just inside the door was a plan of the flats with the tenants' names displayed. Harvey got into the lift and rose swiftly to the top floor where he alighted in a corridor. Outside was a roof garden and just around the corner was Reeves' flat. The question was, how was he going to get in there?

Harvey stepped through the patio doors into the garden area: potted plants around a fountain. Cautiously he skirted the wall of the building until he reached Reeves' huge picture window, offering a bird's eye view of the city. Fortunately he hadn't yet bothered to close the heavy curtains, although one of them had fallen half across. The lights were low inside, but as Harvey peered around the edge of the window, he could see into the spacious sitting-room.

The sight that met his eyes made him gasp in dismay. Although the back of the sofa was hiding most of the action from view, he could see that brute Reeves wielding some kind of whip, although no sound penetrated through the double glazing. Presumably Gayle was lying prostrate on the sofa. Harvey looked around desperately. He knew there was no point in trying to force an entrance through the window, which would certainly be alarmed. With his heart thudding loudly, he made his way back into the building.

There was nothing for it but to try and con himself into the place. Harvey knew the names of several of the man's associates but the only one he'd met personally was a guy called 'Crab' Jones. If he could imitate that gravelly accent he might be able to fool Reeves into opening the door. Before he did so he took the precaution of putting on his dark glasses, the best he could do by way of disguise. He wasn't going to waste time going back down to the car. Gayle needed him now, like she'd never needed him before, and he wasn't going to let her down.

With a shaky finger he pressed the intercom button. There was no reply. He pressed again more insistently and eventually a voice snapped, 'Go away! I'm busy!'

'Mitch, it's me, Crab!'

Harvey managed to get the words out before Reeves became incommunicado. There was a pause, then an angry voice said, 'What the hell do you want? I told you not to come here.'

'It's real urgent, Mitch. Couldn't wait.'

'It fuckin' well better be!'

In the few seconds it took for Reeves to walk to the door Harvey waited like a loaded spring, knowing he would only have a split second of advantage when the door finally opened. If Reeves kept the door on a chain he stood no chance at all. He heard a bolt being drawn, then to his relief the door opened wide enough to give him his chance. He barged forward, head down like a battering ram to buffet Reeves in the solar plexus and wind him. In the dim interior he could see Gayle kneeling terrified on the sofa, hands behind her back and red weals across her buttocks. There was no time to untie her hands, but Harvey was relieved that her feet were free. They made for the door where Reeves was still staggering around trying to catch his breath.

Giving him a kick on the shin for good measure, Harvey pushed past him and raced for the lift. After him came the villain's curses. 'I'll get you, you bastard, whoever you are! Whatever it takes, I'll have you skinned alive. And the girl!'

Despite his urge to flee the area as soon as possible, Harvey stopped off at Joe's apartment halfway down. Gayle needed some clothes, and if they could only lie low for an hour or so their getaway should be easier. Joe welcomed them with raised brows but said nothing, fetching a dressing gown for Gayle then offering them a drink.

'Don't tell me you've been messing with Reeves!' he groaned, before Harvey could say a word. 'You want to get me evicted? That would be the least of my worries.'

'I'm sorry Joe, but what else could I do? Anyway, he'll

assume we're on the road by now. He's probably put his boys on our tail. I reckon we're safe here for a while.'

'I hope you're right.' He turned to Gayle. 'You're lucky, sweetheart, my ex-wife hasn't moved all her clothes out yet. Take whatever you want from the wardrobe through there.'

When the two men were alone Joe asked, 'Do you know what you've got yourself mixed up in?'

Harvey shrugged. 'It's not me, it's Gayle. Someone's put her on the case, but she doesn't know the scene as well as I do. If I'd known what she was taking on I'd have warned her against it, but I was out of town.'

'Is she the girl who does those sex decoy jobs?' Harvey nodded, and Joe shook his fingers with a sharp intake of breath. 'Whew! I've heard a few stories about the whores that man's used and abused. Weird guy. You know he's seeing Patsy Martin? How he manages to keep his image squeaky clean with both her and the Bill I'll never know. If I had his talent for camouflage I might turn to a life of crime myself.'

Gayle reappeared, looking quite fetching in a shapeless blue jersey dress that her curves filled out nicely. She looked better now, more relaxed and with some colour in her cheeks.

'This is really good of you, Joe,' she began as he handed her a coffee laced with brandy.

'I owe Harvey one – or two!' he grinned, stroking his balding scalp. 'Sit down, make yourselves at home. Another whisky, Harv?'

They remained in the flat for around half an hour. The two men caught up on each other's news while Gayle mostly sat just listening, but her mind seemed elsewhere. Once or twice Harvey caught her looking at him thoughtfully, as if she were studying him. He'd not yet got over the sight of her, bound and naked, kneeling at the mercy of that sadist. The emotions that had produced in him were too raw, too complex, to be pondered over yet. All he wanted now was to ensure her safety and, while Joe rattled on about his divorce case, Harvey was wondering how best to guarantee that.

At last Harvey decided it was time to go. 'Gayle, I really don't think it would be a good idea for you to go back to your place tonight.'

'Why not?'

'Because if he does have someone watching the building, they'll follow you. Me too.'

'You could stay here if you like,' Joe offered generously.

'No, I think we've pushed your hospitality far enough, thanks. Is there a back exit from this building?'

'Only through the boiler room in the basement, and that's normally kept locked. But the janitor has an emergency key.'

'Okay. I think we should leave that way, Gayle. We'll cross the yard at the back and get out into Greengate. Then we can book into a hotel for the night. Tomorrow the trail should have gone cold, and we'll be safe to return home.'

'Are you sure?' Gayle's eyes were so big and blue, like a puzzled child's, that he wanted to hug her. 'What about your car?'

'I'll leave it where it is, down a side street. It's doubtful whether Reeves or any of his henchmen will connect it with me. We'll get a cab to the Chorlton Grange. That's near enough to your place to make things easier in the morning.'

Gayle was plainly in no mood to argue, but accepted his suggestion like a dutiful daughter who trusts that Daddy knows best. He found it touching. The girl needed nurturing after her ordeal and, despite his anger and disgust about what that bastard had put her though, he was glad that he was at least on hand to pick up the pieces.

They arrived at the hotel via a quiet back street around midnight and checked into a twin-bedded room. Harvey wanted to make sure he was on hand if the poor girl broke down in the night. As soon as they were alone in the comfortably furnished bedroom, he took her into his arms. 'Gayle, when I heard your phone message I was so afraid for you.'

'Why?' Her eyes looked up into his, large and trusting.

Harvey placed a gentle kiss on her forehead. 'Because I know the reputation of that arsehole. He's Mr Big, or thinks he is. His organisation is behind most of the drug deals on his patch, but that's not the only reason I was worried about you.'

Gayle sank onto the bed, then winced. Evidently her bottom was still sore. Harvey went into the adjoining bathroom and began to run the water for a bath. When he returned she was halfway through undressing.

'As I was saying, the other reason— God, just look at you!' He stared in horror at the pale cheeks of her behind, now displaying great purple weals. That fiend had bruised the skin, drawn blood too. 'He has a reputation for treating women rough,' he went on, tight-lipped. 'I mean, really rough. A couple of prostitutes almost died after he'd had his evil way with them.'

'Oh, Harvey!'

Realising just what danger she'd been in turned Gayle into a shivering wreck. She sat weeping, her hands covering her face. It passed through Harvey's mind that this was the second time he'd had to comfort her after some bastard had abused her. He would make damn sure there wasn't a third.

He sat beside her, putting his arm around her naked shoulders. 'It's okay, you're safe now. I'll run you a nice warm bath, treat your poor behind with antiseptic cream, and you'll feel fine by the morning.'

She snuggled against him, yawning. He chuckled, kissing her again, then went to make sure the water was at the right temperature. When she was in the bath he gently soaped her all over, as if she were a baby. There was an ache around his heart that he identified as guilt that he'd not been there to warn her. But now he would do whatever he could to make amends.

While he patted her dry with a fluffy towel and dusted her down with a complimentary sample of Chanel talc, Harvey asked Gayle about her assignment.

'So it was Patsy Martin who put you on to him. I thought so.' He gave a snort of disgust. 'That woman must like her sex on the wild side.'

'She said it was the best she'd ever had.' Gayle gave a sudden giggle, that filled him with relief. 'And I think I know why.'

'Don't tell me – he's hung like a donkey.'

'Right first time!' Gayle giggled all the more, and Harvey felt irritated with her for the first time that evening.

'They say men with unfeasibly large penises have trouble getting it up,' he said sourly.

'That maybe true of some—'

'You mean you let him fuck you?'

'No, Harvey.' She looked serious now. 'He made me fellate him. I nearly choked on it.'

'And then he beat the shit out of you. Why, because he didn't like your style?'

She looked sheepish. 'No. He saw through my disguise, snatched my wig off. I was afraid he'd find the tape recorder when he turned out my bag— Harvey, I almost forgot! Hand me my bag, would you?'

Gayle took the fake cigarette case out of her handbag and switched on the recorder concealed inside. She rewound the tape and played it. There was the sound of scuffling and some blurred conversation, but it was difficult to make out the words.

'Damn, that was supposed to be my evidence for Patsy! The switch must have got knocked when he threw my stuff on the floor. Shit! I was counting on that. Do you think she'd ever believe me without that kind of proof?'

'I don't know. A woman in love needs some convincing, in my experience.' Harvey picked up the recorder and fiddled with it for a while but clearly the recording was poor, and nothing could be done about that now.

Gayle's voice came, small and bewildered. 'He's leading a complete double life, isn't he, Harvey? How can he get away with it?'

'I don't know. What I do know is that he never gets his fingers dirty and he has an army of guys prepared to cover for him and do his dirty work. He's keeping the drugs business going for his half-brother, Ike, when he comes out of jail.'

'Ah! I ran checks on him and that name came up. But how come the police can't touch them? You were in the Force, can you figure it out?'

Harvey sighed. 'There are several possibilities. The most likely is that they suspect him, but they can't pin anything on him. He never handles the goods, the money is laundered through his legitimate business and his people never get too close. These days it's possible to run a complex drug operation through middlemen without knowing more than a couple of them personally.'

'What else?'

Gayle's expression was dour and he longed to make her

smile. He promised himself that later, as a treat. First he had to answer her questions and allay her fears as best he could.

'Okay, maybe the police are in his pay. It wouldn't be the first time.'

Gayle frowned. 'I think I prefer the number one possibility. At least there's a chance of bringing him to justice then.'

'Or thirdly, of course, he could be innocent. The drugs rumours could be just that, unfounded rumours.'

Gayle gave a sardonic laugh. 'Oh, I don't think so. And neither would you if you'd noticed the contents of his flat. You don't make that kind of money out of a couple of used-car lots, I'm convinced of that.'

Harvey shrugged. 'Maybe he's looking after the flat for Ike, how should I know? But one thing I do know, it's time you got some rest.'

He flicked out the main light and left only one bedside lamp glowing. The soft radiance flattered Gayle's peachy skin, making her look quite delectable. Harvey bent to kiss her goodnight and she put her arms around his neck, wanting to prolong the contact.

'Hey, I said rest!' he chided her playfully, after she'd deep-tongued him.

She looked up at him kittenishly from the pillow. 'Is that what you want to do?'

'It's what I want *you* to do.'

'Oh!' Gayle pouted at him, wriggling seductively in the bed. Harvey felt his prick stir and knew that she was tempting him, but still he resisted. 'I'm going to take a shower now. See you in the morning.'

He strode determinedly from the room and into the bathroom, where the steam still lingered after Gayle's bath. Stripping off his clothes, he turned on the jet of water and stood beneath it, letting the stream cascade down his body. It felt so good after the stresses and strains of the day. Soon he was wallowing in creamy lather, trying not to think about Gayle lying naked in bed in the next room. He knew he wouldn't have to try too hard to seduce her, but she might hate him in the morning, tell him he was no better than that sex maniac Reeves. The poor girl must still be in a state of shock and he should treat her with care.

When he returned she was still awake. Her wide eyes stared up at him from the pillow, clear and defenceless. He felt another surge of anger against Reeves well up inside him.

'Harvey . . .'

'Yes?'

'Do you think we could sleep in the same bed tonight?' He frowned down at her, but she continued, 'This bed is big enough for two, if we cuddle up. The thing is, I'm scared of sleeping alone. I'm afraid I'll have nightmares.'

Harvey went to sit on the edge of the bed. This was not the Gayle Webster he thought he knew. The hard-nosed seductress had given way to the hurt child, and something inside him was responding with infinite tenderness to her plight. He put his arm around her and she nestled into him happily. 'Are you sure that's what you want, Gayle?'

'Mm. We don't have to do anything, just cuddle.'

'All right.'

Harvey drew back the duvet and she moved over. The bed was of generous proportions, more like a small double, and there was indeed plenty of room. Feeling her warm flesh caress his, Harvey uttered a sigh of satisfaction. They embraced face-to-face, breast-to-breast, and he felt every curve and hollow of her body fit perfectly into his. For a long time he lay immobile, listening to the slowing of her breath as she slipped gradually into sleep, and knew that he was providing her with the security she needed to get a good night's rest. That made him feel good.

Some time in the small hours Harvey awoke to find himself with a sturdy erection. Gayle was on her side with her back to him, and his prick was in the crevice between her soft buttocks. His arm was around her waist with his hand on her mat of downy hair.

Suddenly she turned again in her sleep and her breasts were thrust against his chest, making his penis rear with excitement and press into her round belly. Harvey groaned quietly, trying to move away from her. Now that he was fully awake he would have the devil of a job to get back to sleep again with a stonker like that on him. In the dim light from the partially closed curtains he saw the blissful innocence of Gayle's face and chuckled softly. She hadn't the least idea what she was doing to him, the little flirt. Even in her sleep the habit of seducing men died hard!

She began to mumble, meaningless jumble at first that was impossible to distinguish. But then he heard her say, quite clearly, 'I've got to go back, got to make it work.'

Harvey lay quietly, waiting for more, but she just moaned a little then flung her arm over him, almost hitting him in the eye. She was a restless sleeper tonight, that was for sure. He tried to restrain her as she tossed and turned at his side, but her agitation was growing. Suddenly she sat bolt upright, her eyes staring into the darkness, panting heavily.

Harvey sat up too and put his arm around her. 'It's all right, love,' he murmured. 'It was only a dream. I'm here.'

She turned her wild eyes on him. 'Harvey? Oh, Harvey!' Thankfully she fell into his embrace. 'Thank God it's you! I was afraid . . . I was dreaming that he'd broken into my house, that he'd come to get me . . .'

'It's all right.' Harvey kissed her forehead, stroked her hair. She clung to him eagerly, her thigh entwined with his, and he felt his wavering erection take heart again.

Gayle felt the movement against her stomach. She reached down and enclosed his cock in her velvet-smooth hand. 'I much prefer yours, Harvey,' she smiled.

'Look, I don't think this is such a good idea . . .'

'I do. Remember, after that business with Paul Goodman, I wanted you to make love to me, just to heal the wound? Well, I feel the same way now. I need to be reassured.'

'No, Gayle, I . . .'

But she was stroking him in gentle persuasion, pumping his prick up to its full extent, reaching down to caress the taut sac that held his balls, making him want her uncontrollably. Their mouths met on a quest for kissing, deeply satisfying kissing, with lips and tongues drenched in each other's saliva and their taste buds coming to zinging life. Gayle tongued him thoroughly, making him remember how that same organ felt as it brushed over his glans, and his penis ached for the touch of her: lips, tongue, fingers and then the ultimate – sweet, wet pussy. His hand moved down to her slim waist, feeling the full curve of her breast as it went, then on to the sleekness of her thigh. Tentatively he stroked her buttock but she didn't wince. One wound, at least, must be already healed.

'I want you, Harvey,' he heard her lips say to his.

Gayle began wriggling down his body until her mouth was forming a cushioning ring around his glans. He groaned as the nerve-rich skin responded in a sunburst of sensation to her liquid kisses, the hot bliss spreading from his groin to his navel. Her breasts were squashed between his thighs. Lifting one leg he managed to make a footstool of her bum, pressing the spongy flesh and making her wriggle all the more. His hands plunged into the tangled mass of her hair, stroking the scalp beneath.

A hunger was growing in Harvey, making him restless. He pushed the duvet further back and whispered, 'I want to lick you too.' They swung into position and he parted the swollen folds of her sex with his fingers, seeing the moist pinkness within. The tip of his tongue ran down between her labia until he found the source of the liquid, where he lapped contentedly. Gayle sighed and opened her legs wider, inviting him to delve further into her secrets. He found her trust in him heartening after all she'd been through. Carefully he inserted a finger into her slippery quim, feeling the walls tighten around it. He moved it slowly in and out, encouraging her juices to flow even more, lubricating her inside and out.

'I want your prick in me, filling me up just enough,' she sighed.

The veiled reference was to that monstrous organ she'd described, the giant cock that could be used as a weapon against her, battering into her defenceless body, bruising the vulnerable tissues. Harvey knew he could not betray her trust. He must be infinitely tender with her, must give her no cause for alarm. As he reached for the packet of rubbers in his wallet she lay back with a delicious moan, her breasts lifted high and the hard nipples demanding his attention. He took one of them between his lips and gave it a sensual mouthing. Gayle pressed her thighs together and squirmed voluptuously.

Before he entered her Harvey caressed her compliant body all over, from the familiar contours of her face to the padded soles of her small feet. He could feel her flesh glowing beneath his fingers, every inch responding keenly to his touch. Only when he sensed that she was vibrating with desire, like a finely-tuned instrument, did he prepare to enter her.

Harvey took infinite pains to control himself, holding back the urge to plunge straight into that tempting wetness like a diver into a pool. Instead he plugged her with his glans and let her do the work, twitching her muscles to simulate kissing with her tumid lips. It was hard to stay there without moving. Harvey kept his pelvis clenched hard in an effort to maintain his position but it needed immense willpower. His mind tried to seduce him, reminding him of how it felt to slide into that warm, wet chasm, but he forced himself to think instead of Gayle inside Reeves' flat, bound and naked, until his anger threatened to overwhelm him and he focused instead on her lovely face.

There in the half-light, in the full bloom of her passion, Gayle looked incredibly beautiful. At first her eyes were closed in ecstasy, a slight frown between her brows as if she couldn't quite believe in the exquisite feelings that were coursing through her. Her lips were parted slightly, like those below, and the tip of her tongue protruded, pink and glistening. With her head thrown back, the slim column of her neck rose cleanly from her shoulders, with a pulse visibly throbbing in the hollow of her throat.

Harvey found her open vulnerability very moving. His eyes dropped to the swell of her breasts, and he couldn't resist tracing around their curves with delicate fingers, making them expand even more. His nails flicked against the straining nipples, and Gayle groaned out her tortured appreciation as the tension between desire and frustration grew in her. Knowing she wanted more of him, Harvey pressed forward another inch until the whole of his glans was inside her and he could feel her fingers on his shaft, massaging the loose skin and making it more and more difficult for him to remain in control of himself.

When her roving fingers moved to his testicles, Harvey could hold out no longer. He slid easily down the slick shaft of her pussy, holding his breath until he came to rest against the hard knob of her cervix. She sighed out her satisfaction, gripping him tightly with rhythmic squeezes, letting him know how glad she was to have him in there. For a long while he just lay there like a docked vessel, wallowing in the tropical heat of her quim.

At last he slowly pulled back and began the gentle see-sawing, the rhythmic rocking in the cradle of her pelvis that would bring them both closer to ecstasy. The tenderness Harvey felt for that woman right then was overwhelming, stirring up in him emotions that he was sure he'd never felt before. He wanted to hold her safe in his arms forever, to ensure that the smile never faded from those lovely blue eyes, to take her to heaven and back with the most wonderful orgasm she'd ever had.

And now it was beginning; those first tremulous stirrings deep within were turning all her erogenous zones into one great quivering arena of pleasure. Harvey felt the walls of her vagina contract fiercely around his penis as the sensations veered swiftly towards the climax, her inner journey accompanied by rapturous cries of wonder as the cataclysm swept her up.

Afterwards Harvey realised, from the dribble of liquid in his condom, that he had also climaxed, but beside his vicarious enjoyment of Gayle's orgasm it had seemed insignificant. It was with a great sense of fulfilment that he lay back, taking her into his arms, and pressed small kisses to her cheek and neck while she half-swooned in his arms. She had trusted in him, and he had not failed her. Now she was murmuring gratefully in his ear, 'That was so beautiful, Harvey.'

'No, it's *you* who are beautiful,' he replied gallantly, but it was no empty compliment; he really meant it.

They dozed until dawn when, unable to sleep but needing to rest, Harvey slipped carefully from her bed and got into the other one. He was eventually awakened by the sun streaming in through a chink in the curtains. A glance at his watch on the bedside cabinet told him it was almost ten o'clock. Soon the chambermaids would be wanting to clean the room. He glanced at Gayle, still sleeping sound as a babe, and tiptoed into the bathroom so as not to waken her.

When he emerged, however, she was sitting up smiling at him, her luscious breasts just peeping over the top of the duvet with their nipples flaccid and relaxed. There was a lustre to her skin and a brightness to her eye that told him she was thoroughly refreshed after last night.

'You look great!' he grinned, kissing her lightly. 'Shall I call room service and have them deliver some breakfast?'

'Mm! I'm starving!'

While they feasted on coffee and croissants, Gayle talked practically non-stop. She was clearly worried. 'I just don't know how to put it to Patsy. I mean, for all I know she might like the kind of rough treatment he handed out to me. And all that stuff about him being a drugs baron is just hearsay, isn't it? There's no proof. But it's not just Patsy I'm worried about. What if he finds out that I was working for her? I know I was in disguise, but someone in that bar might have recognised me. I'm terrified he'll track me down, Harvey, and then heaven knows what he'll do to me.'

'If he thinks you were checking him out for Patsy, that's one thing. But if he suspects you of working undercover for the police, that's quite another. I think it would be best if you laid low for a couple of days. You can stay in my flat, if you like. I'm pretty sure no one saw me there yesterday.

Except Joe, of course, and we can trust him.'

'Can we?' He kissed her anxiously tense mouth, feeling it soften beneath his lips. 'Oh Harvey, I hope so!'

'I was at school with Joe. He won't let us down.'

'Well, I have to phone Patsy today. Maybe I'd better do it right now, and get it over with.'

She picked up the bedside phone and got an outside line. Harvey heard the crisp voice of the businesswoman answer, her tone becoming circumspect as she heard who the caller was.

'Shall I come to your office later today?' Gayle suggested.

'No . . . let's meet for lunch. The Lace Pagoda does a very good business lunch. I'll see you there at twelve-thirty.'

Harvey saw Gayle blench. She opened her mouth like a fish but nothing came out and soon there was a click as Patsy replaced her receiver.

'What's the matter, love?'

'She wants to meet me in the same restaurant Mitchell took me to.'

'The Lace Pagoda, I heard. Well, that figures. If Reeves is the villain I take him for, you'd expect him to move in those circles. Look, I don't want you going there alone, okay? I'll take lunch there myself, keep an eye on you.'

'Would you?' She looked at him doubtfully. 'I'm sorry to be such a nuisance. If you've got work of your own to be getting on with—'

'That can wait. I tied up a case very nicely in Leeds this week, but as far as I'm concerned until I read my e-mail and listen to my phone messages, I'm free.' He grinned, putting the breakfast tray on the floor and taking her into his arms again. 'Come on, give us a kiss! Then we'd better get out of here.'

The kiss lingered, turned into an embrace and then a

series of caresses, but Harvey called a halt before they got too embroiled in each other again. There would be time enough for more of that later, especially if she were staying in his flat. A warm thrill of satisfaction went through him. Working alone in Leeds, he had missed her companionship as well as her professional help. Now they seemed destined to be working together again. He would have been perfectly happy, if only they'd been dealing with anyone but Mitchell Reeves.

Chapter Thirteen

Gayle looked nervously round the restaurant. A Chinese waiter came up to help, and when she said she was meeting Miss Martin she was taken to a corner table in an alcove and offered an aperitif. While she sipped her grapefruit juice she saw Harvey enter with a nonchalant air and walk to a table on the other side of the room, from where he had a clear view of the corner. Then Patsy appeared, looking cool in a blue-grey suit with a cream silk blouse.

'Hullo, I hope I haven't kept you waiting.' She slid easily into her seat murmuring 'dry sherry' to the hovering waiter. 'Mitch often brings me here,' she smiled. 'The food's excellent.'

It was difficult to believe she could be so naive, but Gayle reflected that if Patsy was occupied with building up her own business, maybe she really didn't have time to find out about Mitchell's. Sitting there with her, Gayle felt exposed. What if Reeves walked in right now and saw them together? She was glad of Harvey's reassuring presence, but if it came to a showdown, what could he do against Reeves and the restaurant staff who, presumably, would be on his side?

Stop being paranoid and face your bridges when you come to them, she told herself sternly. But her heart was fluttering wildly nonetheless as she agreed to the set meal for two.

'So, how did it go?' Patsy asked in a low voice, after the first dishes arrived.

Gayle had already decided what to say. 'He fell for it, I'm afraid. We went to his flat—'

'Describe it!' She did her best until the other woman gave a satisfied nod. 'Okay, I believe you were there. Then what?'

'He made a pass at me. When I tried to put him off, he took down a curtain cord and tied my hands behind my back so that he could take me by force. I'm sorry, Patsy, but it's the truth.'

She looked scornful. 'Are you sure he didn't tie you up because you were causing trouble? I've never known him be anything but gentle with me.'

'Why would I lie? Look, I know this is hard for you to take but that man behaved quite violently towards me. He had this antique whip, made of plaited hair, and he lashed me with it. I think he's some kind of sadist.'

Patsy gave a laugh so explosive that it had to be genuine. '*Sadist*? You must be joking.'

Gayle felt herself growing angry. Angry both with Reeves, for apparently living so complete a lie that his fiancée had no idea about his true sexual tastes, and angry with Patsy, for not believing her. The woman was regarding her with a hostile stare and Gayle felt like walking out. Why should she bother to convince this idiot? She might be a brilliant businesswoman, but when it came to her love life she needed her head examined.

'Why did you bother to hire me if you won't believe what I say?'

'I told you, I need concrete proof, not hearsay. Do you have any?'

'I tried to make a tape recording but it's too blurred. Mitchell turned out my bag and it dropped on the floor. I think he suspected I might be working for someone.'

'Not very good at your job then, are you?'

Gayle leaned across the table and spoke in a venomous whisper. 'Now look here, I risked a great deal going to that bastard's flat on your behalf. Not only did he horsewhip my butt, he also forced me to suck his oversized dick until I nearly choked on it. God knows what more he might have done to me if I hadn't managed to get out of there in time.'

The stern look on Patsy's face faltered a little, but she refused to abandon her stance. 'If you'd said that he seduced you, made love to you, I would have believed you. What I can't believe is that he would be rough with you.'

'It's the truth. And I have reason to believe that he's up to no good in other ways, too. He's not to be trusted, honestly. You asked me to help because you weren't sure about him, and I'm telling you your suspicions were well-justified. If I were you, I'd have nothing more to do with him. I'd also be very careful how you end the relationship. He's the type to take revenge.'

For a while Patsy was quiet, chewing on her food. Then she said, 'Okay, get me proof of some kind and I'll believe you.'

'I can't. He already suspects me. I can't possibly go back to him. It's too dangerous.'

The scornful look returned to Patsy's face. 'Can't you do anything? Spy on him, bug his apartment or something? Surely you must have some idea how to catch him out, or you're no good at your job.'

Gayle sighed. She wanted to wash her hands of the case, but two things niggled at her. One was the thought that Patsy would not be safe if she continued to see the man. The other was a burning desire to see that rogue put behind bars where he belonged.

'I'll think about it,' she said at last. Maybe she and Harvey could figure out a way of achieving both objectives. By working in tandem they'd pulled off that kidnapping case triumphantly. What a coup this one would be!

Patsy left the restaurant first, after Gayle had promised to phone her at home that evening. Harvey was waiting outside in his car by the time Gayle left. In the boot was a suitcase full of her things and they drove straight to his flat. On the way she told him about Patsy's reaction.

'Stupid bitch!' he said. 'What does she want – blood?'

'I feel bad about the whole thing, Harvey. It seems like unfinished business. I'm going to have to charge her for my time and expenses, naturally, but if she doesn't believe me—'

'She's a fool! Really, Gayle, you have to learn to quit while you're on top. Or, in this case, still alive. And I'm not joking.'

'But it doesn't seem right that he's allowed to get away with it. Can't we do something? I thought maybe if we got some tapes, photos of him—'

'Are you mad? The guy's got his personal security sewn up. You saw that place. It's like a fortress. The only way I managed to get in was by pretending to be someone else.'

'But *I* could maybe get in again. If I managed to convince him that I'd been getting off on our last encounter, and you'd spoiled my fun.'

Harvey glared at her. 'Are you totally crazy? I just don't believe I'm hearing this!'

'Look, I think I know a way to do it, Harvey, only I need your help. Please hear me out before you make up your mind.'

Gayle outlined her ideas briefly. There hadn't been much

time to plan in detail, but it seemed to her that there was at least the core of a workable strategy there. Harvey sat with his eyes on the road, saying nothing, but she could tell he was giving it some credence.

At last he drew up outside the large Edwardian house where his flat was. He switched off the engine and paused, thinking hard. Then he turned to her with a reluctant grin.

'You've really thought it through, haven't you? And you think this chap Clive will come up with the goods?'

She nodded. 'Yes. He's helped me out a couple of times before.'

'Okay, if you're sure you want to go for it . . .'

'Harvey, you're an angel!'

She threw her arms around his neck and kissed him, feeling his unshaven jowls graze her lips. After all the apprehension of the morning his assent came like a cheering wave, lifting her spirits. She followed him from the car into the house, curious to see what kind of place he was living in. 'It's not very clean and tidy, I'm afraid,' he warned her as he unlocked the door.

It was a typical bachelor's dwelling, functional and lacking the personal touch. Gayle glanced quickly around the bare walls and gave the motley assortment of furniture the once-over. The place had been assembled haphazardly, without regard for either style or comfort. Only the hi-fi system and bookcase stuffed with paperbacks were evidence of any cultural leanings on Harvey's part.

'Not much of a home, but it's all mine,' he grinned. 'I bought it outright with a legacy from an uncle. Kitchen's through here. I'll put the kettle on.'

The kitchen was surprisingly modern and clean. Harvey admitted to having spent some money on it. When he had the time, he said, he liked to cook. Gayle could picture him there in his loneliness, music blaring as a substitute for company, making a culinary treat for himself before settling down in front of the television. She mentally juxtaposed an image of the pair of them having breakfast in bed together, laughing and cuddling, wallowing in togetherness. In inviting her to stay with him for a few days, had he been hoping to bring some of that warmth home with him?

Maybe I've got it all wrong, she thought wryly as she followed him into the bedroom. He could have wild parties here most weekends, rock'n'roll till the early hours, women queuing at his door . . .

Somehow she didn't think so.

Harvey said he was prepared to give up his bed and sleep on the sofa in the lounge. Gayle felt disappointed. Although she hadn't gone so far as to presume that they would sleep together, a large part of her had hoped they might. As she stowed her clothes in the wardrobe space he'd cleared for her, she wondered if he was already regretting the fact that they'd made love a couple of times.

He might be, but she would never forget how good he had made her feel. Twice he had rescued her from self-pity and self-disgust, but the last time his tender loving had been exquisite, making her think that perhaps there could be more to their relationship than either of them was prepared to admit. Yet she knew that if she became emotionally involved with him, it would be a distraction from the dangerous work they were about to do together. For the time being, at least, she must keep her personal feelings on hold.

A phone call to Clive Moore later that afternoon told her what she needed to know. His help was crucial: without it the whole operation was a non-starter. She rang him at his lab at UMIST and he assured her that he could give her what she wanted by the following morning. That meant that she could try to locate Reeves tomorrow evening. She would go to the same bar she'd met him in before, and if he didn't show, someone there might know where he was. Aware of the danger involved in asking after such a notorious character, she nevertheless knew it had to be done. For Gayle was determined that she would have one last try at nailing Reeves. With Harvey's help she might just succeed.

They spent the whole evening planning it, going over and over every detail and covering as many contingencies as they could imagine. When Gayle's eyelids began to droop, Harvey cradled her in his arms for a few seconds, and the tender feelings that had flooded through her the previous night resurrected themselves, making her long for him keenly. But all he did was kiss her lightly on the lips, then let her go.

'You'd better go to bed now, love, and get a good night's rest. You'll need all your strength tomorrow.'

His smile seemed tinged with regret as he turned his attention to his camera and other essential equipment.

Gayle slept only fitfully, uncomfortably aware that Harvey was just a few yards away on the other side of the wall. Her body craved him like never before, and before she could sleep she had to put her hand between her thighs and rub away the hungry itch that was plaguing her. She imagined that he was inside her, his cock rousing her with long, smooth strokes while he kissed her mouth and fondled her breasts, and as the first sharp spasms hit her she couldn't resist calling out his name. Afterwards she was worried that he might have heard, but if he had he chose to ignore it.

Next morning Gayle drove to Clive's lab and picked up the chemical cocktail he'd prepared for her. His cheeky grin told her that he was especially proud of his recipe this time.

'It should take a maximum of ten minutes to take effect,' he told her. 'After that you've got a minimum of thirty minutes, maybe forty if you're lucky.'

'And you're quite sure it's safe?' she asked, anxiously.

'Let's put it this way – it works fine on elephants!'

'Oh Clive, you're incorrigible!'

'I do my best. Now scram, before my supervisor checks in and I get into a whole lotta trouble for chatting up pretty girls when I should be working.'

Gayle left the lab in good spirits. Clive always had that effect on her. As she got into her car, she reflected that if she hadn't known that he had a wife and baby she might have wanted him. Hell, what was she thinking of? Having one irresistible man in her life was more than enough to cope with.

For the rest of the day Gayle caught up on the business she'd let slide while she was working for Patsy, and Harvey did likewise. They'd arranged to meet back at his place at six, where he'd promised her a home-cooked curry. When it was put in front of her however, delicious though it looked, Gayle found she'd suddenly lost her appetite.

'God, Harvey, I'm so scared!' she admitted. 'What if Clive's stuff doesn't work?'

'Then it's Operation Scarper, like we planned, remember? Don't worry, Gayle, whatever happens I'll be around. And I intend to tell Joe what's going on too, so we'll have a bolthole in the building if things get too hot. Relax, sweetie, and try my Rogan Josh. It was once the talk of Oldham, you know.'

Gayle managed to eat half the food, which was very good, but then she went into the bedroom to change into what she thought of as her working gear: a clinging dress in pink satin with spaghetti straps and a ruched bodice. There seemed little point in going to the bar in disguise now that Reeves knew what she looked like, but she did her best to lay the paint on thick and make herself look attractive in a tarty, obvious way. When she emerged, Harvey surveyed her thoughtfully.

'You know how I like you best? First thing in the morning, when you've no make-up on, your hair's a mess and your face and body are totally relaxed. Then you look fantastic!'

Gayle smiled, feeling suddenly shy of him. He knew how to say things that touched her deeply, and yet he delivered them in such a matter-of-fact tone that they didn't seem at all romantic. Whatever Harvey felt for her he was keeping to himself, and his occasional compliments only served to confuse the issue.

But now was not the time to speculate on Harvey's secret feelings. All she needed to know was that he would be there for her when the time came. And she'd never needed any man in her life more than she did right then.

Smiley's Bar was half empty at eight when Gayle walked in, feeling horribly conspicuous. The barman nodded at her in recognition. She ordered a Coke, nothing more. Tonight of all nights she needed to keep a clear head.

'Waiting for someone?' the barman asked ironically, as he handed her the glass.

'Yes. Mitchell Reeves. Have you seen him?'

'If I had, I wouldn't tell you in case he didn't want you to know.'

'Sorry, I only asked!'

She noticed the black guy who had been talking to Reeves last time. He was giving her a suspicious look. At last he came up to the bar and leaned over it, right beside her. 'You asking after Mitch?'

'Yes.'

'Well, don't! That's my advice!'

He walked out of the bar, and Gayle wondered what on earth was going on. Her pulse was racing, and as she put out her hand to clutch the glass she could feel her fingers trembling. Maybe it was time to drink up and get out of there. She'd had two explicit warnings, and that should be enough. Downing her Coke she rose from her stool, only to feel a heavy hand on her shoulder. 'Well, if it isn't Little Miss Make-Believe!'

She knew who it was without turning round. Not just from his voice, either. There was something about the very air around him that chilled her bones. She turned, forcing a smile. 'Mitchell! I was hoping I might bump into you here. How are you?'

It was absurd, this play-acting, and both of them knew it. But she also knew he was curious. Why had she come back into the lion's den after he'd given her a good mauling?

'Surviving. And you're looking lovely as ever, my dear. How is your clever friend, the actor? Surviving too, I trust?'

For a few seconds fear clutched at Gayle's heart. Had Reeves noticed Harvey sitting in his car outside? Unlikely. She forced herself to concentrate on the script she had prepared for herself. 'I wouldn't know. I'm not seeing him any more. The thing is, Mitchell, I discovered something about myself last time we were together.'

'Oh?' His eyes glinted at her like black flashlights. 'What do you mean?'

Gayle gave a little giggle. 'Oh, you know, what we did. I found out I liked it, a lot.'

'You did?' He reached up and pinched her cheek. 'And all along I thought I was punishing you for being a naughty girl. Now ain't that a funny thing!'

'Of course, I knew that some women liked it rough. I mean, I'd read about it and stuff. But it never occurred to me that I might be one of them. Well, you wouldn't know till you tried, would you?'

228

'I suppose not. Except I've always known what I like, but then I'm different.'

'You certainly are! But my boyfriend wasn't like that, and I found ordinary sex quite boring. When that idiot barged in and spoilt our fun I was only just starting to get off on it.'

'Shame we were interrupted.'

'Mm.'

She gave him a coy, simpering look and hoped he would get the message. He finished his whisky and then leaned close, whispering in her ear, 'in that case, I think maybe we should go back and carry on where we left off. Is that what you want me to say?'

Gayle flashed him a conspiratorial smile. 'Only if you have the time, Mitchell.'

'If you have the inclination, I have the time. Come on, babe!'

The BMW was parked right outside the door. As she slid into it, Gayle glanced down the street to where Harvey was sitting behind his windscreen, his face covered by a copy of the *News*. Praying that he'd noticed them, she fastened her seatbelt and braced herself as Reeves raced the engine savagely then glided off into the night.

As she walked into the penthouse apartment, Gayle gave an involuntary shudder. She couldn't forget what had happened there last time, and now she was asking for more of the same – was she mad? But then she remembered why she was there, and thought of Harvey. She had seen his car nose round the corner when they'd pulled up at the private car park and hoped that soon he would be out on the balcony with his telephoto lens. Now all that was needed was for Mitchell to take a drink.

'What would you like to drink?' he asked, echoing her thoughts.

'Whatever you're having yourself.'

'Whisky, then.'

Gayle watched him pour two generous tumblers. Opening her bag, she took out a tissue. Secreted within it was the tiny phial Clive had given her. She pretended to blow her nose then kept hold of the tissue and its contents as he handed her the glass.

'Cheers!' She took a mouthful then broke the seal of the phial with her thumb and, while Reeves wasn't looking, tipped the contents into her glass then replaced tissue and empty phial in her handbag. Smiling seductively she asked him whether he had any heavy metal music.

'I think there might be some Metallica around somewhere.' He turned towards the collection on the wall, searching with his finger. 'It's not my bag, but whatever turns you on.'

Gayle knew she only had a few seconds. She reached towards the side table where he had placed his tumbler and switched them. He turned round just as she was raising his glass to her lips and murmuring, 'I just love a man who is masterful, powerful, dangerous. And you are all of those things, Mitch. You really do it to me.'

Reeves gave a sly smile as the heavy beat started to blare from the CD player, and from his pocket he produced a flick knife. Before Gayle realised his intention, he had sliced through the thin straps of her dress and the bodice was hanging loose over her bare breasts. She felt her heart plunge like a lift down a shaft. 'Take a drink, you swine, for God's sake!' she prayed.

There was a mean look in his eye as he moved in again, holding the knife in front of him, and Gayle felt her knees buckle under her. She sank onto the sofa, putting her glass on the floor, and he carefully pulled down what remained of her dress until she was naked from the waist up. Then he sat down beside her on the sofa, still holding the knife. He placed the flat of the blade over her nipple and began to tease it, rolling it lightly back and forth across her breast. Gayle shivered at the touch of the cold steel and felt her nipple slowly pucker into prominence. Then he repeated the performance with her other breast.

'That's better,' he smiled, snapping the knife shut and placing it on the table. 'I like to see a woman's tits fully aroused. Makes me think she wants me.'

'Oh, I do!' Gayle murmured. She held her breath, waiting for him to notice the half-full glass on the table beside the knife, but he ignored it. Instead he went to a drawer and took out a thin cord, but when he held her hands behind her back she cried, 'Wait a minute, Mitch. I want to finish my drink first.'

Gayle picked up her whisky from the floor by the sofa, hoping he would take the hint. To her great relief, he raised his own glass to his lips and downed the lot in one go. Now it was just a question of stalling until the drug took effect. Meekly she let him bind her wrists, then knelt down on the sofa at his command. She felt him pull the remains of her dress down over her hips, exposing her bottom clad in black nylon.

She saw him move to the table and there was that sinister click again, the sound of the knife-blade kicking into active life. Gayle was trembling all over. How anyone can find this sort of thing erotic, I don't know, she thought, as a host of doubts assailed her. What if he'd found out about her and was about to take revenge in some unspeakably horrible way?

Mitchell's hands were smoothing the transparent cloth over her buttocks, stretching it tight. She could hear him breathing heavily and wanted to say something, anything, to break the tension, but her tongue was stuck to the roof of her mouth. Then she felt a tiny prick between her buttocks and the faint sound of tearing material as he began to trace down her arse-crack with the knife point, ripping the nylon as he went. Gayle's whole body went rigid, feeling the cold blade insinuating its way between her bum cheeks as her panties fell away.

'That's better,' she heard him croon, his voice heavy with menace. 'Lovely plump buns you have, my dear.' His hands were all over them now, stroking, pinching. 'So deliciously smooth and meaty. Almost good enough to eat!'

'Ow!' Gayle gasped, as his teeth sank into her left buttock.

He laughed. 'Gotcha! The surprise element is half the fun, don't you find?'

She felt his weight lift off the sofa and sensed that he'd got to his feet. Craning round, she saw him slip out of his trousers, grinning at her. The front of his pants could not contain his erection, and the swollen purple glans was rearing over the top like a creature trying to escape. Laughing, Reeves pulled off his underwear and stood there in his shirt with the giant prong rearing up, reminding Gayle of pictures she'd seen of the Greek god Priapus, famous for his gargantuan organ. She began to pray that Clive's potion would work on the bastard before he tried to enter her with that obscene thing.

'When Mother Nature gave me this little present, she gave me the best thing a man can have: self-confidence!' He smiled, stroking his grotesque shaft as affectionately as one might pet a kitten. It responded by expanding even more. 'I never had to wonder if another man's willy was bigger than mine. I never had to work at impressing the girls. Men are envious of me, and women worship me. You can't ask for more than that now, can you?'

He disappeared into the bathroom and came out with a tube of something. Gayle's doubts redoubled. Supposing Clive had let her down this time, and his stuff didn't work? What if it were the wrong dosage? Reeves was a big man and had probably developed a tolerance for most drugs. She peered through the large window to see if there was any sign of Harvey, but could see nothing except the night sky glowing a dirty orange from the street lights.

Reeves knelt down on the sofa again, directly behind her, and something cold was squirted between her buttocks. As his fingers worked the cream into her crack she realised, with sickening horror, what he was planning to do. God, that was going to hurt! She had a virgin arse, and it would be stretched to buggery by that outsize cock. Gayle stayed very still, frozen with fear, and when he pulled her cheeks apart and she felt his bunched fingers probe the greased orifice, she thought she was going to faint.

He went only part of the way in, but it was still horribly painful, making her cry out. Then his hand was replaced by the hot ball of his glans and Gayle felt her terror redouble. She tried her best to relax, knowing that if she resisted it would be worse for her, but still she could not imagine accommodating that enormous dick. Reeves began to push against the delicate tissues of her anus that were already hurting, stretched wider than ever before. She began to feel as if she would split right in two. She prayed to the nameless drug that was supposed to be acting on Reeves' body right now: work, damn it! Soon it would be too late for her and the hideous deed would be done, leaving her a shattered wreck, both physically and emotionally.

'Shit!'

Gayle heard the curse, and at the same moment felt the pressure against her arse reduce. She realised that the huge erection was beginning to shrink and grow feeble, and remembered that Clive had told her that would be the first sign that the drug was taking effect. Her heart lightened but then, to her dismay, she saw Reeves walk over to the cabinet where he kept his paraphernalia. This time he pulled out not a whip but a large dildo, almost as big as his prick.

'Temporary hitch,' he grinned, looking down at the shrunken flesh hanging between his legs. 'Don't worry, we'll get it back in shape soon. Meanwhile, this will keep you nice and open. It thrusts just like a real cock and vibrates as well. You're going to love it.'

He flicked the switch and the vibrator hummed into life. But as he came towards the sofa, Gayle saw his eyes glaze a little and he staggered, knocking over his empty glass as he held onto the small table for support. He righted himself with a grin, but then made a sudden nose dive against the sofa and fell in a heap on the carpet. The dildo rolled away, still buzzing loudly.

Quickly Gayle staggered to her feet. Although her hands were tied she could walk, at least. She kicked her way out of the hobbling dress. Thank God he hadn't tried to shackle her ankles. But of course he wouldn't, would he? The bastard couldn't have done what he did to her if he had. Putting her anger on hold, she hurried over to the window and looked out, pressing her cheek to the glass. There was Harvey, skulking behind a drainpipe, camera in hand. He gave her a thumbs-up and went back through the door to the landing inside.

With her hands still tied, Gayle walked back past Reeves' prone body to the door. Outside she could hear Harvey's stage whisper, 'Open up, Gayle, quickly!'

'Easier said than done, with no hands,' she grunted to herself.

There were buttons set into a plaque on the wall next to the door. One was for the intercom downstairs, another for the light in the corridor. One of the others must be to release the security system. She pressed the bottom one experimentally with her nose. The shutter slid back over the spy hole. Outside she could see Harvey waiting impatiently.

'I'm sorry, my hands are tied. I'm doing my best!' she called.

She pressed another button and there was the click of a bolt sliding back inside the door. But how to open it? She couldn't turn the handle, could she? In desperation she put her mouth round the brass knob and tried to turn it with her teeth. It budged a little. All the while she was conscious of seconds ticking away, wasting valuable time. She realised that she hadn't taken note of the time when the knockout drops had first taken effect, so she had no idea how much longer they had. With a desperate effort she clenched her teeth round the doorknob once more and this time managed to get it all the way round, clicking the latch open. Hurriedly she jumped back, not wanting to get hit in the mouth as Harvey made his entrance.

'Good girl!' Swiftly he went behind her to fumble with the knots that secured her wrists.

At last she felt the cord loosen and she shook it off her hands. 'Oh, Harvey, I thought that stuff would never work on him. He tried to bugger me, and—'

'I saw, and got some clear shots,' Harvey said tersely. 'We don't have long. Let's start searching. I'll do in here, you take the bedroom. Be quick, but be thorough.'

Forgetting her sore arse, Gayle hurried into the large bedroom, curious as to what she would find. His king-size bed was draped with black satin and there were disturbingly erotic paintings on the walls showing scenes of phallic worship, bisexual orgies and bestiality. Gayle shuddered and looked away, wondering where she might find evidence to incriminate him. But as far as she knew there was no law against possessing pornographic art, only selling it.

There was an alcove leading off the bedroom, perhaps originally designed as a walk-in wardrobe, that Reeves used as a computer work-station. Gayle walked over to it and switched the machine on. After all the gobbledygook as it loaded, she tried to access some of his files, but every time she was asked for the password.

'Damn!' she muttered. Picking up a disk she inserted it and tried again. It was still protected. She took the disk out and was about to replace it in the plastic storage case when a thought struck her. If Reeves had anything to hide it would be right there, in her hand. She looked around for some spare disks and found a half-empty box of blanks. Hurrying back into the lounge she told Harvey and the pair of them returned to the bedroom.

'Can you copy these?' she asked him.

He nodded, slotting in the disk again and putting his hands on the keyboard. In a few minutes he had made copies of three disks. Gayle fervently hoped their efforts would bear fruit. They'd had to select the three more or less at random, gambling on what they might contain, but it was the best they could do. Switching off the machine, they tried to put things back as they had been to allay suspicion. Now they had to get out of there before the chemical cocktail in Reeves' system had run its course.

'Okay, time to go!' Harvey told her. 'Get yourself dressed.'

'I can't. He cut my straps.'

'Well wrap it around you as best you can. We've no time to spare now. He could wake up any second.'

Gayle did as she was told, holding up the front of her dress as they made for the door. They went down in the lift and out into the night air. She shivered as a chill wind made goose flesh of her, and Harvey put his jacket around her shoulders as they made for his car.

Quickly they sped along the deserted street in the direction of the centre. Gayle lay back in her seat, exhausted, suffering from the after-effects of shock. Her butt was so sore she could hardly bear the feel of the seat under her. Helplessly she felt the tears stream down her face.

'Don't cry, sweetheart, please don't cry,' Harvey begged her. 'It's okay. You're safe now.'

'But for how long?' she moaned. 'And what if there's not enough evidence on those disks to convict him, what then?'

'We'll face that if and when the time comes. My immediate worry is how do we get the things decoded? I don't have enough computing expertise for that.'

'Neither do I. But I know a man who does!'

Gayle grinned through her tears and he smiled back. 'That's my girl! Who is he?'

'A chap called Mack. He's a computer hacker. He did some background checks on Reeves for me.'

'Excellent. Where does he live? We could leave the disks with him right now. They'll be safer with him.'

Gayle felt chilled again. What was he saying, that Reeves might send his men to search Harvey's flat and her own? Her relief at escaping from the penthouse began to fade as she realised that she would not feel completely safe again until that villain was caught, sentenced and imprisoned. But that all took time and meanwhile he was still around, still able to use his network of intelligence to track her down.

She gave Harvey Mack's address and they began to head in that direction. He switched on the car radio, probably trying to restore an air of normality to their life. But the song that was playing right then was inappropriate. Gayle winced as the singer belted out the words, 'You can run, but you can't hide!'

It sounded like an ill omen.

Chapter Fourteen

Harvey stared incredulously at the scrap of paper in his hand. He couldn't believe the message Gayle had scrawled on it. Why had she gone, the little fool? More to the point, where had she gone? She'd left no clues at all as to her destination.

If only she'd discussed it with him they could have worked something out together, but now it was too late. Miserably he reread the brief message in case he'd missed anything: 'I'm sorry, Harvey, but I'm too scared to stay in Manchester. You'll be safer, too, with me out of the way. Good luck. Gayle.'

He tore the note into shreds and flung it into his waste bin. If only she'd waited a few more hours! Reeves and his gang of hoodlums had been rounded up on the basis of the evidence contained in those disks, and bail had been refused. Gayle would have been safe after all. On the way back from Patsy Martin's office, where he'd managed to convince her that she was better off without that sadist, he had bought some champagne, intending to drink it with Gayle by way of celebration. Now the bottle stood there mocking him.

Harvey realised how little he knew about the woman who had invaded his life like a plague and left him still suffering the symptoms. In the fraught days since they'd snatched the vital evidence he'd tried to take care of her, to give her the comfort and reassurance she needed, but he must have failed. And now his flat seemed like a metaphor for his life: horribly empty without her.

For three days he tried to get back into work again, taking on a few non-demanding jobs and declining anything that was not to his liking. But everything seemed to remind him of Gayle. He walked past Smiley's, and remembered waiting outside for her to appear with Reeves. He had a postcard from Kate on holiday with Edward, and it was addressed to both of them. He saw a woman in a similar jacket looking vaguely like her, and for a few seconds his heart swung into its aerobics routine only to fall flat when she turned around. Then he went home and had to face the chair where she'd sat, the mug she'd used and, worst of all, the bed where they'd made love.

And oh, the ache in his balls that would never cease! Harvey knew he could have relieved the physical itch with any number of women, but only one could ease the ache in his heart as well. And she was God knew where.

Then, just as he was giving up hope of ever hearing from her again, a postcard arrived from Preston. The message was brief once again, but this time it gave him hope. 'Don't worry about me, Harvey. I'm much happier now I'm out of Manchester. But I'm quitting the business, making a new start. Love, Gayle.'

Preston – so she hadn't gone far. If she was still there, of course, and hadn't just sent him the card as she was passing through. Well, it was all he had to go on. Although it was a Saturday, Harvey had to cancel a couple of appointments. He did so without a qualm then went straight out to his car.

As he tore down the motorway Harvey made his plans, just as if a client had asked him to trace a missing person.

His head was filled with possibilities, short on probabilities. If she was really as scared as she'd made out, Gayle might have changed her appearance and identity. He had no photo in any case. That would make it trickier. But Preston wasn't that big a place, not like Manchester. With luck someone might have noticed a new face in town.

It was noon when he arrived so Harvey popped into a pub for a pint and a sandwich. There was a table in the bar with tourist information, leaflets about places of interest and a hotel guide. He flicked through the list of local hotels and B & B addresses. The girl had to be staying somewhere and she wouldn't have had time to move into a place of her own just yet. A methodical search of hotels and guest houses seemed his best bet.

Armed with the guide and a town plan, Harvey began to cruise through the streets. Confused by the one-way system he found himself going round in circles, so he parked in a multi-storey near the shopping centre and proceeded on foot. He went into every likely establishment he came across, but after he'd checked the registers of a dozen or so the hopelessness of the task began to depress him. If she had changed her name there was little point in him bothering. Maybe he'd be better off calling on the employment agencies. After all, she'd said on the card that she was changing career and she couldn't survive for long without a job of some sort.

The agency staff were harder nuts to crack than the hotel receptionists, however. Even his PI accreditation card cut no ice with some of them. 'I've never seen one of them before. For all I know you could have forged it,' a frizzy-haired clerk informed him and, he had to admit, she was quite justified in being suspicious.

By five-thirty he was no nearer his goal, and the agencies

were closing. Realising he needed a refuelling stop, he went into a pizza restaurant and ordered a Four Seasons. Then, as he was strolling back down Fishergate towards the car park, he came across a hotel that bore the 'Routiers' sign. Although he'd had more than enough of checking registers he decided to give it a try.

When he entered the small hallway the reception desk was unmanned. Harvey had already given up on the place and was making for the door when a familiar voice called, 'Can I help you, Sir?'

He turned, unwilling to believe he could be that lucky, but the face looking towards him from behind the fake-antique counter was hers all right. When their eyes met, Gayle gave an embarrassed smile and made a strange choking sound, halfway between a laugh and a sob.

Harvey covered the space between them with a couple of paces. 'Gayle! Thank God I've found you. It was pure luck. I've been searching everywhere—'

'Oh, Harvey, you shouldn't have come.'

'Why not? I had to see you. I had to tell you—' He broke off as a middle-aged couple entered and Gayle had to be about her business. When they disappeared upstairs he asked when she came off duty.

'I've only just come on, for the evening shift. I won't be through until eleven, when the night-porter takes over.'

'What the hell are you doing working here anyway?'

'It was all I could get at short notice. Look, I've got to fill out this form. Please don't hang around here, Harvey, or you'll get me the sack.'

'Where are you staying?'

'Here.'

'Fine. Have you got a spare room?'

'Yes, but—'

'Okay, book me in. I'll see you at eleven. We can go for a meal, if you like.'

Gayle looked doubtful, but she gave him the key to a room on the floor above. For a while Harvey lay on the single bed with his hands behind his head and his eyes closed, basking in his success. He was convinced that Fate had intervened to hook him up with her again. He sighed. In all his career he'd never before felt so pleased to trace someone.

But was Gayle just 'someone' or was she *the* one, the one he'd been hoping might come along and transform his life into something wonderful? Over the past few days he had missed her so badly and longed to hold her in his arms again but now, faced with the reality of her presence, his confidence was fading. If she'd felt the same way about him, would she have gone off like that? Reason told him that she wouldn't. Yet he hadn't told her how he felt – would that have made a difference? It might be the quickest way to lose her. After all, they'd only known each other a couple of months.

Harvey spent the evening in a daze. He didn't feel like going out, so he switched on the television but paid it scant attention. Once or twice he sauntered down to the bar, hoping to snatch a few minutes with Gayle, but they were always interrupted and he found it frustrating. In the bar a travelling salesman tried to engage him in conversation, but he was in no mood for small talk and soon returned to his room.

Promptly at eleven he went down to reception, but had to wait another ten minutes until Gayle could finally leave her post. 'Where shall we go?' he asked her, happily. 'Fancy a bite to eat?'

'Not really, Harvey. I ate before I came on duty.'

He felt deflated. She wasn't making this any easier. The

pubs would be closing, so what one earth were they going to do, walk the streets? Gayle wouldn't thank him for that. She looked absolutely exhausted.

In the end he just bought her a drink in the hotel bar. Harvey wanted to tell her about the outcome of the Reeves job, but she didn't seem very interested.

'Look, I tried to leave all that behind me when I left Manchester,' she told him dully.

'I just wanted you to know there's a very good chance that bastard will end up with a good long sentence, that's all. Patsy Martin says she wished she'd never set eyes on him.'

'How did she take it?'

'Badly at first. When she heard about the drug trafficking she went white. I think she might have known about his half-brother, Ike. I reckon she suspected he was involved in something like that all along but she wanted proof.'

'Mack had no trouble deciphering those disks, then?'

'No. He told me they were encrypted in PGP and he had the keys to all versions of that. He said it was a doddle. And the evidence on them was enough to incriminate not only Reeves but most of his dealers.'

'What was the police reaction?'

'Cautious optimism that this time they'd get a conviction. They'd suspected him for months, but didn't have enough on him to even get a search warrant. They tried to set him up with an undercover agent but it didn't work.'

Gayle gave a grim laugh. 'That was why he was so suspicious of me! I was an idiot, wasn't I? A fool rushing in, and all that. I suppose it only goes to show that I wasn't cut out for the job. I should have developed a better nose for trouble and turned down a case like that.'

'How can you say that? You succeeded where even the police had failed!'

She shrugged. 'I was lucky. But I got my fingers badly burned, Harvey, not to mention my butt! No way would I consider going back into that line of work again.'

'So what are you going to do, be a hotel receptionist for the rest of your life?'

'No, this is only to tide me over. I thought I might retrain. Maybe take a word-processing course. I did one years ago, when I wanted to get into journalism, but they told me at the Job Centre that I need to be familiar with Windows 95.'

'So are you planning on staying here? Why Preston?'

Gayle turned to him with a look of helplessness in her eyes. He wanted to hug her, to kiss her, but something about her manner was inhibiting him. 'It was the first place I came to that wasn't Manchester.'

'Is that a good reason for choosing to stay?'

'I don't know.' She frowned, putting down her empty glass. 'Look, Harvey, I didn't ask you to come here and right now I'm too tired to answer all these questions. I'm going to bed.'

He walked up the stairs with her, but outside her room she bade him a firm goodnight and turned her back on him. Harvey was about to walk away, but before her door closed he called, 'Can I see you tomorrow?'

'It's Sunday, my day off,' she told him, wearily.

He took that as a good sign. 'I'll see you at breakfast, eight-thirty,' he said, blowing a kiss.

When he returned to his room, however, depression settled on him like a damp cloud. So Gayle wasn't coming back to Manchester. That meant he probably wouldn't see her again. He almost wished that he hadn't met up with her, that she'd vanished from his life completely by now. That might have made it easier to bear. To have her all but tell him to his face that she didn't care enough about him to stick around was incredibly painful.

But she had agreed to see him tomorrow, he reminded himself. That would probably be his last chance to tell her how he felt, try to change her mind. At any rate he would do his damnedest to get her to spend the day with him. He would make it a day they would both remember for the rest of their life. Smiling at the prospect, his spirits began to lift as he imagined taking her on a trip to Blackpool.

In the morning he felt less confident as he sat in the hotel breakfast room, waiting for Gayle to appear. When she did his heart leapt to see her, still sleepy-eyed but wearing a bright floral mini-dress that made her look about sixteen. She threw him a weak smile and joined him at his table.

'Give me black coffee!' she moaned. 'I'm not used to working split shifts. I have to do five till eight in the morning, then six to eleven at night. It's thrown my biological clock right out.'

He waited until she had consumed three cups of the beverage before springing his surprise on her. 'How about a trip to Blackpool?'

'God, Harvey, you must be joking!'

'I'm not, actually. Why?'

'Well, the last time I was there it was to tail that rattlesnake Reeves. Bad memories.'

'All the more reason to replace them with good ones. Honestly, Gayle, we could have a great time. I'm sure we both need cheering up.'

A smile crept round the corners of her mouth. 'I've not been there for years. Not just to enjoy myself, I mean. My gran used to take me when I was a kid.'

'So you'll come?'

'Well . . .'

'We could ride on a tram, go on the pier and up the Tower. Visit the Pleasure Beach . . . whatever you like.'

For a moment her face lit up like a little girl's. Harvey squeezed her hand and said cajolingly, 'Go on! Let me spoil you for once. It'll be fun!'

'Oh, all right.'

Harvey felt overjoyed. If she'd refused he would have driven back to Manchester in a black mood, but now he had a whole wonderful day to spend with her. And to cap it all, the sun had just come out.

Gayle brightened visibly once they were on the road in Harvey's car with the sunroof open, her blonde hair fluttering in the breeze. It was early September, so they would have to stay until dusk at least to see the illuminations. Harvey kept stealing sidelong glances at her as they belted along. He couldn't help himself, despite the bitter-sweet thoughts that the sight of her provoked. Although he longed to drive the car off the road into some quiet lay-by and take her in his arms, covering her tanned throat with kisses and feeling the softness of her breasts without their bra, he knew he had to keep his distance from her. This day had to be perfect, and he wouldn't risk spoiling it for the world.

When they arrived Blackpool was full of holidaymakers and the atmosphere was very lively. Harvey took Gayle by the hand and they walked the Golden Mile, taking a look at whatever she fancied along the way. They went on all three piers, visited the sharks in the Sea Life centre and had a donkey ride, all before lunch. Fish and chips in Harry Ramsden's was followed by a tram ride all along the sea front to Fleetwood and back again.

'Oh Harvey, I'm having such a lovely time!' Gayle told him, just before they got off the rickety vehicle. She kissed him on the cheek, but he turned her mouth to his and gave her a long, luscious kiss instead. Her blue eyes surveyed him thoughtfully, but she said nothing. Harvey knew that at some point in the day he would have to bare his soul to her, but not too early in case she reacted badly. Even so, he felt burdened by his feelings.

'What shall we do now?' he asked her, as they indulged themselves with a cream tea.

'Let's go up the Tower.'

She clung to him as they peered through the gold-painted iron girders at the view and his longing for her became unbearable. In the distance they could see the skeletal tracks of the giant roller coaster rearing up to the sky at the Pleasure Beach. He decided that would be their next destination. He'd always loved funfairs but, like Gayle, he'd not been to one for years.

They wandered amongst the attractions, looking at everything before they decided what to go on. They were spoilt for choice with so many different rides. They passed by an old-fashioned wooden roller coaster, a monorail, ghost train, water chute and a pirate swing boat that swung to dizzy heights. But over and above everything loomed the red, white and blue track of the tallest ride in the world.

Gayle was excited by the old-fashioned carousel, and begged him for a go. Harvey was pleased to oblige, especially as he could hop up behind her and put his arms around her waist. Sitting astride, Gayle's thighs were on view beneath her short skirt and she was drawing quite a few glances from the bystanders. The gaudy fairground organ struck up a Sousa march and round they went, gathering speed, their horse seeming to overtake the one next door only to be overtaken in turn by the horse on the other side. Harvey pressed close to Gayle, feeling the lower slopes of her breasts swelling above his hands, his erection growing as the rollicking motion of the horse thrust him repeatedly against the firm cushion of her buttocks. To make matters worse she insisted on wriggling her hips, massaging his crotch as they spun round. A couple of blokes in the crowd noticed her doing it and began pointing and laughing.

'Stop it, you little minx!' Harvey complained in her ear, but she just giggled. Helplessly he began imagining how it would feel to be thrusting into her wet pussy from the rear, finding the warm welcome he hoped for, and his cock yearned for her like never before. 'Do you have to be such a prick-tease?' he whispered angrily, but the ride was already slowing and she just gave him a cheeky smile over her shoulder.

Maybe that hadn't been such a good idea after all, Harvey reflected, as he staggered down from the platform. Gayle seemed none too steady on her pins either. Her face was flushed and her hair awry, making her more desirable than ever.

'Now it's my turn to choose,' he told her. 'Come on!'

Harvey pulled her through the crowd with grim determination, half-angry with her for getting him so worked up. If she wanted thrills and spills, he knew how to give them to her.

'Oh no!' Gayle protested as he led her towards the queue for the giant roller coaster. 'I'm not going on that. No way!'

Harvey held her firmly by the wrist and pulled her into line at the end of the queue. 'Oh yes you are! You had your choice, now I'm having mine.'

'No really, Harvey, I've been watching it. I couldn't possibly!'

'Of course you can. You can't come here and not have a ride on The Big One.'

Gayle gave him a mock-reproachful grin. 'Harvey, did you have to remind me of Reeves?'

She can joke about it, he thought. That's a good sign.

They shuffled forward in the queue as another thirty punters got on. Someone called, 'Last couple of rides before closing now!' At last it was their turn. While Harvey paid, Gayle took a nervous glance at the poster warning heart patients and pregnant women not to even think about it, and soon they were clambering into their seats. They were right at the front of the second car from the rear. Behind them four lads got on together, evidently well tanked-up to give them Dutch courage.

'I can't believe I'm sitting here,' Gayle murmured, as the train began to gather speed.

Slowly, almost painfully, the five linked cars began the interminable climb to the terrifying summit. As they were cranked up higher and higher the whole of Blackpool and the countryside beyond was visible below. Harvey felt a sick dread as he realised there was no way out. They were going to have to make that insane descent now, no matter what.

Looking down the track during the few seconds pause at the top gave him a shock. It seemed a practically vertical drop. He looked at Gayle and she had her eyes closed, holding onto the rail in front of her for dear life, her hair drifting around in the wind. Harvey was about to lean over and kiss her when the train gave a sudden plunge and twisted to one side. There were screams of fright. Somehow it was no consolation that they were securely held in, since the whole car seemed about to go. Despite having already seen the ride in operation, Harvey became instantly convinced that they were going to plummet through space and would fall to their doom. Some daredevil in the car in front threw both arms up into the air and shouted, 'Look Mum, no hands!'

They raced down the track at an incredible, stomach-churning speed, their hysterical screams borne away by the wind. At last the thing swooped up the other side and there was a few seconds' respite as it began to climb again, much faster than before. Harvey looked at Gayle and this time her eyes were open and gleaming intensely blue. Her cheeks were bright pink and her mouth was half-open, with a film of sweat on her upper lip, making her look as if she'd just had an earth-shattering climax. Maybe she had.

Harvey risked taking his hand off the rail and gave her a quick hug, but once the car began its second drop he clung on again. This time he knew what to expect and the swoop, not being from such a high point, was not so bad. He began to relax and enjoy it as the car whizzed around the bends, but it was over all too soon. They slid smoothly to a halt and were helped out at once, ready for the next eager customers.

Photos had been taken of them in the car and Harvey offered to buy one for Gayle, but she shook her head. 'No thanks, I'd rather just remember it. Wasn't it amazing? I've never been so scared and so thrilled at the same time in all my life.'

'You enjoyed it, then?'

She turned her glowing face towards him and gave him a kiss on the cheek. Her lips were hot and moist, rousing him further. Then he heard her whisper, 'Fantastic! But can we go somewhere dark and private now?'

Harvey laughed. Putting his arm around her slender shoulders, he steered her back towards the ghost train. As he approached, the little train stood empty and a man was putting up a 'closed' sign.

'Hey, excuse me!' Harvey called. The man looked round, a fag in his mouth. 'Couldn't you let us on? Just one more ride?'

'Nah!' He drew in the smoke, staring at them through half-closed eyes.

Harvey left Gayle standing there and went up close. He adopted a matey tone. 'My girlfiend's been looking forward to this all afternoon. We saved the best till last. Go on – I'll make it worth your while.'

'Let you on for a tenner then,' the man grinned.

Quickly, before he changed his mind, Harvey grabbed Gayle's hand and pulled her into one of the cars. She giggled, her skirt riding up to show her knickers as she clambered in. The man got into his booth and started up the ride, giving them a wink as they glided past.

'We've got it all to ourselves, Harvey. How exciting!'

'Yes, isn't it,' he grinned smugly, drawing her into the crook of his arm.

They went slowly into the black, artificial world of disembodied heads and clammy fingers, screams and moans, looming phantoms and dangling bats. But very soon they were entering a far more pleasurable zone. Their own private world consisted of warm wet tongues, eagerly roving hands and restless, interlocked thighs. Beneath the minuscule dress and tiny knickers, Harvey could feel Gayle's swollen breasts and clitoris and knew she wanted him. His cock was rearing and the minute he unzipped his fly she was in there, holding his shaft lightly while she wriggled on the hard seat to give his fingers access to her streaming cunny.

'God, Harvey, do we have time to do it?' she murmured. 'I'm so hot for you right now!'

'I can feel. That ride got you going a treat, didn't it? Quick, slip your panties off.'

As they fell to the floor of the car something dangly caught in Gayle's hair. She screamed and giggled. Harvey pulled down his pants and prepared to enter her, not knowing exactly how long he had to complete the act. His adrenalin was flowing fast now and he felt almost as elated, and as terrified, as he had at the pinnacle of The Big One. What if, just as they were getting their rocks off, the train suddenly came through the final doors and exposed them to the curious gaze of the crowd? It didn't bear thinking about.

Undeterred, and fuelled by his unremitting desire for her, Harvey knelt astride her on the wooden seat, holding on to the sides of the car. It was painful for his knees, so he softened the impact with her panties under one knee and her cardigan under the other. The train was swaying from side to side but he managed, after a bit of ungainly fumbling, to locate her vagina and plunge straight in.

The surge of bliss that filled his body was worth all the waiting. Feeling her yield to him so utterly, her thighs up around his waist so that he could penetrate deep into the plush warmth, almost brought tears to his eyes.

'This is so good!' she murmured, moving her lithe hips so she could grind her mons hard against him. 'I was so excited by that ride. I wanted you so badly, Harvey.'

A split-second of doubt threatened to spoil Harvey's joy, making him wonder if she'd be that horny if they hadn't ridden on The Big One. But he ignored it, reminding himself that he too had found the experience arousing, and focusing instead on his growing exhilaration. The feelings were similar to those the roller-coaster induced, but they came in different proportions: uninhibited pleasure spiced a little with fear, instead of the other way around.

Harvey increased the pace, while around them mayhem seemed to break out. From the volume of noise, and the frequency with which they were assaulted by various dangling things, he guessed they were nearing the climax of the ride. Despite the distracting apparitions, he could not take his eyes from Gayle's face. In the weird phosphorescent light she appeared fey and witch-like, but he still found her beautiful.

Throwing back her head, Gayle reached the point of no return. With a loud moan, she surrendered to the series of spasms as they pulsed out their measured dose of ecstasy. Harvey watched her face distort, saw the intense feeling in her glazed eyes and felt his own rush begin. He lunged forward, pushing her against the back of the seat as the ejaculation shot from him and the sensual excitement spread through his veins like bubbles through champagne.

'We did it!' As Harvey recovered from his mindless rapture the sudden realisation dawned, adding icing to the cake. 'We made love in the ghost train!'

And they'd finished just in time. The bright lights of the amusement park were just seeping through the rubber flaps at the exit as they struggled back into normality. The train trundled through into the evening air and Harvey gave Gayle a quick kiss on the cheek as it drew to a clanking halt.

The man was awaiting them, impatient to get home for his tea. 'Okay?'

'Yes, great. Thanks a lot.'

Harvey saw Gayle blush as she hopped out of the car, trying ineffectually to hold down her skirt. She giggled like a schoolgirl, taking his arm as they skipped through the last of the crowds making for the exit. 'Oh Harvey, aren't we naughty!'

'It's all your fault, coming on to me like that. And wearing that wicked dress, too.'

'Now what?' she asked, as they came back out on the road again. 'Oh look, the illuminations!'

The whole of the sea-front parade was filled with brilliant dancing lights, row upon row as far as the eye could see. They walked back towards the car park with Gayle exclaiming at each new design of birds or flowers or abstract patterns. She clung to his arm, awe-struck, until they reached the Tower which was still open.

'Let's pop in here for a drink,' Harvey suggested.

They sat at little round tables in the baroque splendour of the Tower Ballroom, watching assorted couples, some in full evening dress and others in more casual clothes, moving sedately around the dance floor. After they'd finished their drinks Gayle pulled Harvey to his feet. 'Come on, let's trip the light fantastic!'

Harvey was horrified. 'I've never done ballroom dancing in my life!'

'It's a waltz, dead easy. I'll teach you.'

'No, Gayle. I'll only make a fool of myself, and you too.'

'No excuses! You wouldn't let me off going on the Big One, would you?'

Very reluctantly, cheered only by the thought that it would give him another chance to hold her in his arms, Harvey let her pull him onto the polished floor. He was surprised at how quickly he mastered the basics, and was soon propelling her around with ease. His arm felt snug around her waist, and the scent of her hair in his nostrils was sweet.

But then the music changed to a rumba, which Gayle admitted was far too complicated for them to tackle. After watching for a while longer they left the genteel entertainment of the ballroom and went back down into the street. A sudden chill, that had little to do with the external temperature, struck Harvey. It was getting late and he had to be up early tomorrow morning to interview a prospective client.

As she so often did, Gayle echoed his thoughts. 'I'd love to stay here longer, Harvey. It's been a wonderful day. But I've got to get up at five tomorrow and I'll get the sack if I fall asleep on the job.'

He kissed her pale, cool forehead. 'Thanks for coming with me, Gayle. You've made it all worthwhile.'

They returned to the car in silence, each lost in their own thoughts. Harvey was calculating whether he could afford to spend the night at the hotel in Preston. He was reluctant to leave her now, while the spell of happiness that he'd been able to cast over them both, and which had lasted all day, was just starting to fade. Somehow he had to find the right words to tell her how he felt about her. Veering onto the motorway he ran through a few openings in his mind, but they all sounded false and unconvincing, so he reached for the radio and put that on instead. Maybe someone else's words could help him find the key to her heart.

By the time they reached Preston, Gayle's head was lolling on the headrest, and when Harvey drew up outside her hotel she came to with a jerk.

'I was spark out!' she yawned, unbuckling her seat belt.

Harvey took her in his arms. 'Gayle, I can't bear to think that I won't see you again. Today has been so wonderful.'

'Yes, hasn't it? A real holiday. But I have to think about my future now, get myself a proper job instead of temping. And I have to do that here, Harvey.'

She got out of the car and he joined her on the pavement, clutching at both her arms to make her stay a moment longer. 'Gayle, when can I see you again?'

'I don't know. Perhaps it would be better if we parted now, after such a lovely day. Good memories, you know?'

Her eyes were misty with fatigue, scarcely registering his anguished face as he pleaded with her. 'Don't say that, Gayle, please! I have to see you again. There are things we must talk about. I know now isn't the time, but—'

'You're dead right. I can't think about anything but bed. And before you give me some wisecrack, I'll say goodnight.

Goodnight, Harv, and thanks for a brilliant day!'

He stood and watched her go, loving and hating her at once. Oh, why did it have to be so complicated? Why couldn't he just tell her he loved her and take the consequences? Because it was the truth, wasn't it? He had evaded it for long enough. Hardly remarkable, though, when you thought about it. Maybe Gayle had guessed and was trying to save him embarrassment. She didn't feel the same, obviously, and didn't want to hurt him.

As he sped back towards Manchester, radio blaring, Harvey thought of how she'd seduced him into making love, not just that day but on many other days, and felt a sick hatred well up in him. He'd been just like one of her clients, caught in her honey trap, but he didn't mean a thing to her, the bitch! She'd cleared off and left him to pick up the pieces, not just of the Reeves case but also of his own shattered heart. Even after a wonderful day like today, she felt nothing for him. She could let him go off into the night without a qualm, like a whore and her john. Yes, that was all she was really, no more than a prostitute who used her body to trick men into wanting her.

Savagely Harvey turned off the motorway and headed for home, telling himself he was better off without Gayle Webster.

Chapter Fifteen

The damp chill that September brought in ever-increasing doses was getting Gayle down, she reflected, as she whizzed round the shops during her Friday lunch-hour. Then she realised she wasn't being honest with herself. The way she felt had little to do with the weather, and a lot more to do with the fact that she was living alone in a strange town and doing work she didn't much care for. That it might also have to do with the absence of a certain rugged private investigator was a further possibility, but she steadfastly refused to consider that one.

The bitter-sweet memory of their day in Blackpool was now just that, a memory. It could be locked away forever if she so chose, or brought out at some far future date when there was no pain attached to it. Yet she couldn't dismiss so easily the nagging voice which told her she had thrown away the best chance of happiness to come along in years.

Back at the office, Gayle took up her position at the computer. She was lucky to get this job so quickly, she told herself, especially as they'd agreed to train her. Yet it was so hard to get used to working inside the same four walls each day. The people were friendly enough, and she'd made quite a mate of Jenny, a single woman in her mid-twenties, who promised to introduce her to whatever Preston could muster by way of a social scene.

'Still on for tonight?' she asked towards the end of the afternoon. Gayle nodded. 'I'll see you in the Rufford Arms at eight, then.'

It didn't take long for Gayle to work out that the Rufford was a gay pub. When Jenny appeared, dressed in dungarees and looking totally different from how she did in the office, the penny dropped.

Jenny saw her surprise and grinned. 'I thought you knew. Oh well, you do now. Come on, let me buy you a drink.'

Gayle was soon introduced to a small crowd of Jenny's lesbian friends. It seemed that she had already been talked about, and was something of a celebrity due to her previous unorthodox occupation. She began to wish that she hadn't confided in Jenny quite so readily.

'You must have a pretty sour view of men, after all you've been through,' one of them commented, with smug assurance.

'Not all men, no. You have to remember I only got to deal with the cheating ones.'

'Surely any man would cheat on his woman given the chance? It's only fear of being found out that stops them.'

'Yeah!' another girl laughed, 'They're afraid of losing their number one security blanket!'

Some of the group were interested in her job from other angles, and listened enthralled when she told them about the child-kidnapping case she'd taken on with Harvey.

'You must have felt you'd done a really great job there,' Jenny smiled.

'Yes, I did.'

The comparison between her work then and now was disturbing, and Gayle tried to dismiss it from her mind. But another girl turned the knife in her wound. 'It must be a bit of a come-down, working in an office. Why did you quit detective work?'

'I got involved in something that frightened me. I mean, really frightened, major league crime. I didn't feel I'd handled it very well, so I got out while the going was good.'

Mercifully they decided it was time to move on to the disco at that point. It was being held in an upstairs room and already the insistent beat could be heard in the bar, pounding away above the ceiling. Gayle was looking forward to the chance to let off steam. She felt she needed it.

The atmosphere in the disco was hot and sweaty. Most of the dancers were wearing the bare minimum and Gayle felt conspicuous in her jeans and cropped T-shirt. Jenny had nothing on beneath her dungarees, and when she danced her small breasts bobbed away behind the square of denim. Despite herself, Gayle found the spectacle of so much erotically-charged female flesh arousing. She felt her own inhibitions loosening, and as Jenny pranced and swayed in front of her with increasing enthusiasm, they exchanged flirty smiles and glances.

This is ridiculous, Gayle thought, but in that environment it felt perfectly natural. Jenny, small and dark with intense brown eyes and a ready smile, was becoming more and more attractive to her. Combined with the attraction was a strong curiosity: just what was it like to be lesbian? Although Gayle had sometimes fantasised about making love with a woman, she had never done it in reality.

The DJ put on a slow number, the lights dimmed and all around the room couples were dancing close, embracing each other without embarrassment, even kissing and caressing. Gayle felt the soft touch of Jenny's fingers on her bare arm. Soon they had their arms around each other's waist and Gayle could feel herself being drawn into the other woman's spell. As the music progressed Jenny put her dark head on Gayle's shoulder. It felt so comfortable, cosy almost.

Gayle relaxed and hugged her close, forgetting everything but the welcome glow that was filling her inside, blotting out thoughts of everything else.

When the music ended Jenny lifted up her head and gave Gayle a brief kiss on the neck, making her skin tingle. 'Thanks!' she smiled.

Then, to Gayle's surprise, she was suddenly abandoned. Jenny went over to greet a couple of friends, leaving her at a loose end. But within a few seconds Trish, one of the women she'd been talking to downstairs, approached, offering to buy her a drink.

Gayle accepted gratefully, glad to be rescued from her sudden isolation. They took their drinks back to a free table in the corner, and Trish began giving out erotic signals almost immediately. She was a striking woman with cropped auburn hair and startlingly green eyes, but Gayle found her a bit intimidating.

The talk became more and more explicitly sexual. Fixing her with a mesmeric gaze, Trish asked Gayle point-blank if she'd ever had an affair with another girl.

'Well, no,' she admitted.

'But don't tell me you haven't thought about it,' Trish grinned. Gayle gave a half-smile. 'Been attracted to someone?'

'Not really, I—'

'But you like being here now, right?'

'Yes, it's a good atmosphere. Great music.'

'And you feel at ease? You can be so much more relaxed when there are no men around, don't you find?'

'Mm . . .'

Trish moved close, her green eyes two dancing points of light in the semi-gloom. 'That's what making love with a woman is all about, too. Total relaxation, no hurry, no pressure.'

But Gayle was feeling far from relaxed right then. Trish had taken her hand and was stroking her fingers with gentle insistence. Although half of her wanted to leave this woman's presence, an equal part of her was fascinated, wanted more. She could sense the desire welling up in her, and it was strange to know that another woman was the cause. Yet it made her feel good, too. Powerful, but in a different way from how she'd felt about the men she'd seduced.

'Shall we dance?' Trish was asking her as the beat picked up.

Somehow Gayle thought she would feel safer on the dance floor with other women around. She nodded, rising from her chair. Trish led her by the hand into the centre of the gyrating couples and at once began making sensual movements that showed off her statuesque figure. Her head was tilted back as she wiggled her shoulders and hips, regarding Gayle from between half-closed lids and adding to the erotic effect.

Trish was wearing a low-necked purple top and leather shorts, showing off her firm, unsupported breasts and long legs. Gayle tried not to look too obviously at the stiff protruding nipples as they pointed provocatively in her direction. Much to her relief the other woman kept her distance, content, at least for the time being, to show off her magnificent figure and tantalise her partner from a distance.

As she looked around the crowd it came as a shock to Gayle that some of the women were dancing topless. Trish noticed too and began to pull up her T-shirt slowly, staring at her partner all the while. Although Gayle felt embarrassed and wanted to look away, she found she couldn't help staring as the rotund breasts with their large and shamelessly erect nipples came into view. She blushed to see Trish smiling at her. 'Why don't you take yours off?' she suggested. 'Don't be shy.'

Gayle felt her cheeks flush even more as she shook her head. It was all getting a bit much for her. The tug-o'-war going on inside her was hotting up and she was uncertain which was stronger, the urge to go or stay. If she stayed, what would happen to her? She was disturbed to find that her crotch was throbbing with arousal despite her misgivings. Did she fancy Trish after all?

Then she felt a hand on her shoulder and turned to see Jenny standing there with a smile. Gayle was relieved to see that the bib of her dungarees was still in place. 'Okay?' she smiled.

'Mm. I could do with a drink.'

'Come on, then. Excuse us, Trish. See ya!'

As they pushed through the crowd, Jenny murmured, 'Was Trish hassling you? She can be a bit over the top at times.'

'I'm okay,' Gayle smiled. 'I'm just not used to this kind of thing, that's all.'

'Have you had enough? We could go downstairs if you like, have a chat.'

'That would be nice.'

The bar downstairs was nearly empty and Gayle was glad of the quiet. She asked Jenny whether anyone at work knew she was gay.

'Let's put it this way, I haven't made an issue of it. I share a flat with Tony, he's gay too, and a lot of people think we're a couple. We don't try to deceive anybody, but if they find out the truth it doesn't bother me.'

'How long have you known you were lesbian?'

'Since I was around thirteen. I used to get turned on by pictures of models, female pop stars. When you walked into my friends' bedrooms their walls were full of male pin-ups but I had Sigourney Weaver and Kate Bush on mine.'

'Did you have your first affair when you were still at school?'

'Yes. I had a crush on a student teacher. She was doing her teaching practice at our school. I used to show her love poems I'd written and ask her opinion of them. I never said they were inspired by her, of course, but it was fairly obvious. I knew from the way she responded that she fancied me too, but she was too scared to do anything about it. So we waited until the summer holidays . . .'

Gayle found the story very intriguing, not to say arousing. She could recall having crushes on older girls at school too. But when she asked for more details, Jenny said she didn't want to talk about it in public. 'Tell you what, let's go back to my place. It's just around the corner. We can talk more privately there.'

'Well, I don't know. It's getting late . . .'

Jenny gave a grin. 'Come on, Gayle. You don't have to worry about work tomorrow.'

Although she suspected she might be getting into deeper waters than she could cope with, Gayle finally agreed. They walked round to the two-bedroomed flat in a small modern block. Tony was out when they arrived. After putting the kettle on, Trish sat cross-legged on her bed while Gayle sat in the armchair opposite looking at the pin-ups on the wall. The blatant sexuality of the photos was startling at first, but after a while she got used to it and began to find the pictures quite aesthetically pleasing.

'You wanted to know about me and Vicky.' Jenny picked up the thread of her story as they sipped their hot chocolate laced with rum. 'I knew where she lived and I knew she'd just finished with her boyfriend, because she told me so.

Whether her feelings for me had anything to do with it, I never knew.'

'So she wasn't lesbian herself, then?'

'Not when I met her, no. She came out after we broke up. Anyway, I used to hang around her house hoping for a glimpse of her. It was quite painful really. I was too shy to just knock on her door. I found out she used to go to the open-air baths, so I started going too. Seeing her in her bikini just knocked me out. She had a fantastic figure. Not unlike yours, actually.'

Gayle began to feel self-conscious again. She crossed her legs tightly, squeezing her thighs together, and a rush of energy filled her groin. 'So which of you made the first move?'

'She did. Said she had a book of poetry at home I might like, and suggested I should pick it up after we'd been for a swim. Once I got inside her flat she offered me a coffee and we started to chat. We just went on and on talking, mostly about education and literature and stuff. She cooked me a meal and we had some wine, and then we lay down on the floor listening to music, but still she didn't make a move. I had the hots for her so badly I could hardly bear it!'

'Did you say anything?'

'No. I was still in awe of her. After all, she had been my teacher. But then she started telling me how pretty I was. She stroked my hair, said she'd always wished hers was darker. And then she said she liked my mouth. "Lovely kissable lips," she told me, and that was it. Before I knew it we were kissing passionately and I was halfway to coming.'

'And it felt right, did it, kissing a woman?'

'Better than my wildest fantasies! I'd rehearsed it so often in my imagination but when it actually happened I realised that I'd had no idea. Even at sixteen I was totally inexperienced. I'd never been interested in boys, and although I knew about masturbation because the other girls talked about it I hadn't tried it myself. Didn't know what an orgasm felt like, can you believe that?'

'I think I had my first one in my sleep.'

'Lucky you! Looking back on it, though, I realise Vicky hadn't much of a clue either, although she did her best. After we'd kissed for a bit, she undressed me and played with my breasts. I can remember being astonished that I enjoyed it so much. It seems incredible now.'

'Did she undress too?'

'Yes, eventually we were both stark naked, rolling around on the floor. Her boobs were much bigger than mine and I found touching them really exciting. In a way I was more adventurous than her, more prepared to experiment. Once we'd broken the ice I seemed to be the first to do everything.'

Gayle's voice grew hoarse as she asked, 'And did you do . . . everything?'

Jenny gave a self-satisfied smile, stretching languidly on the bed. 'Oh, yes! It didn't take me long to realise that I preferred to be the dominant one. I loved to eat pussy. Couldn't get enough of it. And Vicky liked to just lie back and let me do it to her, for hours on end. Once I counted the number of times she came in one session: fourteen!'

'You must have had a fantastic summer together!'

'It was paradise! But like all good things it had to come to an end. She got a teaching job in London. We were apart for three months, although we wrote to each other. Then I went down to visit her at Christmas, but by then she'd got in with a gay crowd. It was my first experience of the scene and I hated it. Her friends made me feel young and gauche and provincial, and I was madly jealous of them. We had a blazing row and I came back home. After that we lost touch.'

'But by then you knew for sure you were gay?'

Jenny nodded. 'I had an affair with another girl in the sixth form. Swept her off her feet and managed to get her to chuck her boyfriend, which I counted a victory. I knew what I was doing sexually, you see, and he didn't. She'd never climaxed with him, but she did with me. It didn't last, though. She was just flirting with lesbianism and after a couple of months she fell for this older guy.'

'Were you upset?'

Jenny nodded. 'I tried desperately to keep hold of her. I even asked her why she preferred him to me. She told me she loved sucking cock! I knew I couldn't compete with that. It was then I decided I would only go for girls I knew were gay. Straights were too much trouble.' She gave a wicked grin. 'Mind you, I've broken that rule a couple of times since!'

'Have you ever lived with a woman?' Gayle wanted to know.

Jenny shook her head. 'Never. It's not my way. I suppose I'm too promiscuous. The fact is, I love the challenge of a new woman. And I like discovering new bodies, too. It's amazing how different pussies can be. You wouldn't think there could be so many variations on the same basic theme.'

Riveting as she found Jenny's confessions, Gayle realised that soon she would have to face up to her own feelings. It seemed as if a lesbian experience was on offer, but she didn't know whether she was ready to take such a step.

Jenny must have sensed her confusion because she said, rising from the bed, 'It's been good to talk to you, Gayle. Helps put things into perspective sometimes, especially if it's with someone who isn't on the scene. But if you want to go home now, it's okay, I don't mind.'

She was close now, sitting on the floor at her feet with a

catlike smile. Gayle felt helpless, unsure of what she wanted, caught in the grip of feelings she couldn't analyse. Wordlessly Jenny knelt up and pulled her close until their lips touched. She withdrew a few inches, her eyes questioning, and Gayle felt the urge within grow strong and insistent. She pulled Jenny back again and sought her lips, this time with resolve, wanting a taste of the exciting new sensuality that was on offer.

Before she knew it they were kissing passionately and Jenny's fingers were deftly undoing her bra. Gayle felt the other woman's hands grasp her breasts with firm insistence, kneading them until they swelled and hardened. The eager tongue was invading her mouth, working expertly to rouse her and making her feel weak and desirous, ready for whatever Jenny chose to do with her. She let her take off her T-shirt and bra, then the rapacious lips moved down to her breasts where they suckled fiercely, covering both nipples with saliva until they were slick and throbbing.

'Oh, this is amazing!' she moaned, overcome by the sudden realisation that this was a woman making her feel so good. Leaning back in the chair, she let the practised fingers free her from her jeans, lifting her bum to let Jenny pull them off, then giving a groan as those same nimble fingers found the soggy centre of her vulva through the clinging pants. While her female lover continued to alternately kiss her lips and nipples, Gayle remembered what she'd said about loving to eat pussy and her clitoris became hard and prominent. Sensing this, Jenny began to press at her mound through the sodden nylon of her knickers, making her squirm.

Soon Gayle longed to be free of the obstructing pants. She pushed them down and Jenny helped to get them off her until her damp, fuzzy bush was exposed.

'Put your legs over the arms of the chair,' Jenny

murmured, and Gayle obeyed. Now her vulva was stretched open. Jenny was gazing at it with smouldering eyes, parting the swollen outer labia to get a good look at the pink inner lips and the protruding bud at the apex. Gayle's hunger grew.

'Sweet!' Jenny smiled, dipping her finger briefly into the open entrance and making Gayle gasp. She stroked her clitoris gently a few times, then bent her dark head between the widespread thighs.

Gayle gave herself up completely to the delicious sensations as the probing tongue moved tantalisingly around her vulva, licking and tasting. All the while hands were stroking her thighs, her stomach, reaching up from time to time to caress her breasts, making the whole of her body tingle and yearn. The wicked little tongue continued to skirt around her clitoris without actually touching it, so that soon her pussy was on fire with frustrated longing. Now it was entering her with a series of fierce probes; now she felt the whole of her pussy being sucked of its copious juices; but still her clitoris was clamouring for more direct stimulation, making her wriggle and moan in a futile attempt to make contact.

Suddenly her vagina was invaded by eager fingers, taking Gayle into a new realm of sensual appetite. Jenny was giving her a thorough internal massage, stroking the soft wet walls of her cunny and plunging deep in towards her womb. In and out went the pleasuring hand, over and over, stimulating the flow of her secretions until Gayle felt awash with lubrication. Yet still she remained on the verge of coming, waiting for that final surge of lust to tip her over the edge.

While the knowing fingers continued to work their magic in her quim, soft lips came to caress her nipples, hardening them again. Gayle felt a tingling radiate out from her breasts to cover her whole body. Jenny's warm mouth passed from breast to breast and back again, sucking in as much of the firm flesh around the nipple as she could, while down below her hand was stirring, stirring, making a wet mush of everything that lay between her thighs.

Then, at last, came the longed-for friction on her aching clitoris. Deft fingers first found the right spot and then Jenny's tongue took over, flicking back and forth over the enlarging nub until it felt huge and solid, throbbing with active life. Gayle gave a long sigh and relaxed into the escalating sensation, confident that soon she would reach her destination. Despite the ease with which she gave herself up to it, this same-sex encounter was still strange to her. With her eyes closed it could be anyone making love to her, she reflected. Black or white, old or young, woman or man. It could be Harvey . . .

Harvey! The image of his face came sharply to mind, catching her unawares. How easy it would be right now to imagine that he was down there, taking her on a short cut to paradise. Her womb leapt at the thought of him and triggered a climax that racked through her with an almost agonising force. Although her vagina was suddenly filled with Jenny's fingers, prodding her rapidly in a bid to increase her satisfaction, Gayle felt empty and detached from what was happening to her body. The shuddering reflexes felt as if they had little to do with her, as if she were watching it all happen from afar instead of being intimately involved.

Afterwards she lolled in the chair, dazed and disappointed, while Jenny covered her stomach and thighs with slow kisses. All she wanted now was to be alone. But she had to be tactful. It wasn't the other woman's fault, she reminded herself. She had done her lesbian best to make sure that Gayle had a good time. But although Jenny would have been aware of what was happening physically, she couldn't possibly have known what was going on inside Gayle emotionally, and there was no point in mentioning it.

Gayle had enough sense to realise that if she told Jenny that the experience had only made her miss her last male lover all the more, the other woman would be deeply hurt, and she couldn't risk that. Wearily she remembered that they had to face each other again on Monday morning. Already the prospect was distasteful to her.

'Gayle?' She opened her eyes to see the bright brown gaze of her lover seeking approval. 'Come on, love, lie down on the bed and cuddle for a bit.'

Although she did so, Gayle still felt uncomfortable. Her instinct was to flee, but she submitted to Jenny's continued embraces until she felt too tired to move.

'Do you want to stay?' came the crooning voice in her ear. 'I'd like you to.'

'Mm,' Gayle murmured, rolling over to sleep.

Several times in the night she was woken by Jenny's attempts to make love to her. The woman seemed voracious, and Gayle was surprised. Her previous notions about lesbian love had been vague but she had pictured it in soft focus, all tender kisses and gentle strokes, not this fierce consuming passion that seemed insatiable. As the night wore on, Gayle could feel her body becoming totally eroticised. She drifted from titillating dream into voluptuous action and back again, her nipples and clitoris in a state of continual arousal, her flesh hot and vibrating all over.

When she finally awoke, Gayle's instinct was to get out of there as soon as possible. She rose carefully, without waking Jenny who was sleeping soundly after the labours of the night, and dressed quickly before going through into the hall. There she scrawled a note on the back of an envelope she found in her bag, saying simply 'Thanks for a great night'. Although her mixed feelings made her feel a mite hypocritical, she felt it would be unfair to blame Jenny for how she felt.

As she drove home from the pub where they'd met last night, Gayle's misgivings grew stronger. How would she feel when she had to face Jenny again on Monday morning? Would she be under subtle pressure to repeat the experience? Just what had she got herself into? She began to regret her spur-of-the-moment curiosity. Yet she knew it had been more than that. Since splitting with Harvey she had felt lonely and in need of comfort. Jenny had offered her warmth and affection and that, more than the sex, had been what tempted her.

Now she must face the consequences. As Gayle drove past the office where she now worked, a dull depression took hold at the thought of carrying on there, pounding a keyboard day after day just to earn a living. She knew she craved the freedom and excitement of being a freelance investigator. Okay, it was dangerous, but only when her adrenalin was flowing did she feel fully alive, turned-on. Maybe she'd overreacted to the Reeves case, cut and run before thinking it through.

So what was to prevent her setting up in business again in another town? Wearily Gayle acknowledged that she just didn't have the guts to start from scratch once more. It had taken her several years of hard graft to build up her contacts and reputation, and she didn't fancy going back to taking on any job that came her way just to pay the rent. No, she sighed as she drew up outside her house, it looked like she'd burnt her boats and would be stuck in this dead-end job, or something like it, for the foreseeable future.

'I'm sorry, Mrs King, but I really don't think I could take this case on without a partner.'

Harvey saw the pretty blue-grey eyes of Marcia King fill with tears. He knew how desperate she was, but he'd meant what he said. If he took on another child-kidnap case by himself, his chances of success were slim.

'But what about the woman who helped you get Edward back?' she said pleadingly. 'Couldn't you ask her to help you just once more? Kate spoke so highly of you both.'

'Miss Webster has left the profession. She's moved away from Manchester and has another job now. I'm afraid it's impossible.'

'And there's no one else you could use?'

Harvey shook his head. The look of hopelessness on the grieving mother's face was unbearable. His mind began to work overtime, searching for some way he could help. She'd said her little girl would almost certainly be on the road with the Travellers by now. That might make her easier to trace. But he knew from experience that he needed a female accomplice to divert suspicion and help allay the child's fears. Maybe there was some way round it. If Gayle would consent to helping him out on a couple of weekends . . .

'Look, leave it with me, Mrs King, and I'll see what I can do. But I can't make any promises. I'll get back to you later this evening.'

'Oh, thank you!'

Marcia King's gratitude seemed pathetic as she clutched at the straw of hope he'd just given her. For a moment Harvey felt guilty. His own hope of persuading Gayle to work with him one more time was minimal. Still, he just had to try.

As soon as the woman had gone Harvey picked up the phone. When he rang the hotel in Preston where he'd last seen Gayle, they told him she had left the place a couple of weeks ago, leaving no forwarding address.

'Blast!' Harvey replaced the receiver with a curse. Now what the hell was he going to do? He hadn't the time to go to Preston on a wild goose chase after Gayle. Then he remembered that she'd got her hotel post through the Job Centre. Perhaps she'd gone back there again and they had her home address. It was worth a try.

Harvey rang pretending to be the manager of the hotel, saying that he wanted to forward some extra pay that was owing to her. The clerk gave him Gayle's new address without a murmur, and he decided to go straight there. It was five o'clock: if she finished work at half-past she might get home by six. He couldn't afford to hang about.

The house where Gayle was living was in a dingy street of largeish houses turned into flats. He drew up outside and waited for her car to appear. Half-six came round, then seven, and still there was no sign of her. Harvey felt his resolve diminishing fast. It had been hard enough to pluck up the courage to come and see her, but the longer she unwittingly kept him waiting, the crazier the whole idea seemed. She'd made it pretty clear that she wanted nothing more to do with him. Now she would think that he had an ulterior motive in asking her to help him on this job. Well, maybe he had.

Deep in thought, Harvey missed the moment when Gayle's car rounded the corner and stopped further up the road at the end of a long line of parked cars. It was only when he saw her in his rear-view mirror, coming along the pavement on foot, that he knew she'd returned. With his heart thudding painfully in his chest, he got out of the car as she approached, took a deep breath and confronted her.

'Gayle, hullo!' he began, uncertainly. His tone brightened, but sounded false to his ears. 'I was hoping I'd catch you.'

'Harvey?' When she turned those clear blue eyes on him

he went to jelly inside. 'What are you doing here?'

She seemed far more composed than he was, and deep within he was disappointed. In his fantasy she would have thrown her arms around him in delight, welcomed him back into her life. This puzzled frown was far more disconcerting.

'It's . . . er . . . business,' he told her. 'Do you mind if we talk inside? I mean, if you're not in too much of a hurry or anything.'

'No, I'm in no hurry. Okay, come on up. I live on the first floor.'

'I noticed your house in Chorlton was on the market.'

She shrugged, but said nothing. Following her trim form, Harvey scarcely registered the details of the large barely-furnished room she showed him into. At once she went through to the adjacent kitchen and put on the kettle. 'Tea or coffee?'

'Coffee, thanks. Look, I'm sorry to turn up without warning like this, but something urgent's cropped up.'

'Work, you said? Is it to do with Reeves?'

'No. As far as I know, they're still preparing the case against him. We won't hear anything for at least another month. It's not that I've come about.'

'What then?'

She wasn't making it any easier for him. Harvey stood at the door of the kitchen while she poured boiling water into two mugs. He found the sight of her distracting. Little details of her appearance kept drawing his attention. He'd forgotten how freckled her nose was, for example, and how the corners of her mouth were slightly dimpled. That soft wool blouse was making her look particularly shapely, too, as it draped the solid curves of her breasts in flattering folds.

'Harvey?' She was handing him his coffee now, looking at him with a slightly quizzical expression. 'Shall we sit down?'

They sat opposite each other, Harvey on a folding chair with an uncompromisingly hard seat. It crossed his mind that he wasn't supposed to get too comfortable. 'Gayle, I know you've started a new life here, with a new job and . . . what is your new job, by the way?'

She wrinkled her nose. 'Office work. Nothing special, but I am honing my word-processing skills.'

'Good. I . . . er . . . don't suppose you miss the other, then?'

'I wouldn't say that. But I can't go back now. If that's what you've come about—'

'Not exactly.' He made an effort to come clean. 'It's just that I had a woman come to see me today who is really desperate to get her daughter back. She'd been in contact with Kate Merridew and we'd been recommended. Of course, I had to tell her that you were no longer available to do that kind of work.'

'I'm sorry, Harvey.'

'But the poor woman was distraught. She has no one else to turn to. There's another daughter at home, and she misses her sister too. It's a very sad case, but at least there's no question of the child having been taken abroad. She's in this country somewhere, and Marcia has a strong suspicion that she's been taken on the road, with some New Age Travellers.'

'Really?'

Heartened by the flicker of interest in Gayle's eye, Harvey went on to explain the ins and outs of the case. He'd decided it would have to be an undercover job. If he took it on he would have to pose as a traveller himself, gain the confidence of the others, try to find out whatever he could. With winter approaching it would be easier, since they would be pulling into whatever sites they could find up and down the country.

'Bit of a risk of confrontation with the law, too, don't you think?' Gayle commented.

'Yes, but I'd be prepared for that. I could work solo for a while until I'd located the girl, then I'd need help from a female partner. You're the only person I could attempt it with, Gayle. That's why I had to try.'

She looked thoughtful, cradling her mug in her hands. 'I can't just throw in my job.'

'I wouldn't ask you to. Like I said, I'd do all the preliminary work myself and only call you in towards the end, on a weekend. Once you'd won the child's confidence we could rescue her and take her back where she belongs. Remember how it was with young Edward?'

She smiled, giving him new heart. 'I'll never forget.'

'Well, then.'

Harvey fell silent. There was no more he could do. He finished his coffee and stood up. 'I said I'd let Mrs King know this evening, so I'd better ring her and tell her it's no go.'

'No, wait.' Gayle put her hand on his arm. His heart ached cruelly. Having to just stand there without being able to embrace her was torture to him. 'Look, I don't like to think of another child being taken like that. Who does? But I'd made up my mind that I wasn't going to work with you again.'

'Okay, I know.'

'Except . . .' Her face was contorted with indecision. Harvey waited, not daring to hope. 'It's not just the work, you see. It's you. I couldn't go on like we were, trying to work with someone I'd got involved with. It was just asking for trouble.'

'I see.' He turned to go, stumbling towards the door. 'I'm sorry I bothered you, then.'

Desperate hands pulled at his shoulders, trying to make him stay. He turned round and Gayle was somehow swept into his arms. She clung to him joyously, her breasts pressed against his chest and her face uplifted, silently begging for a kiss. As he bent to oblige, a surge of pure relief went through him as he sensed everything would soon be resolved.

'Heck, I always fancied a life on the open road,' she grinned when the long kiss finally ended and they settled together on her sofa again. 'Why don't I just throw in my boring old office job and we can get a beat-up old bus and I'll braid my hair and you can grow dreads and we'll get a couple of lurcher dogs and we'll rescue the little girl and then, who knows? Maybe we won't ever get back to normal life again!'

Harvey smiled indulgently at her. 'With you, my love, life could never be normal.'

She snuggled up to him, gently teasing. 'What makes you think you're going to get a life with me, then?'

'I don't know. But I'll tell you one thing: it's not much of a life without you, Gayle.'

He knew then, from her Queen Bee smile, that she felt the same way as him. His lips sought hers, and at once it was as if they had never been apart. Their bodies had proved wiser than their foolish, complicated minds, knowing all along that they were meant for each other. As their kiss deepened, Harvey felt his doubts dissolve in bliss. Maybe this isn't a bad way to go after all, he thought, drowning in the sweetness of the honey trap.

A Message from the Publisher

Headline Liaison is a new concept in erotic fiction: a list of books designed for the reading pleasure of both men and women, to be read alone – or together with your lover. As such, we would be most interested to hear from our readers.

Did you read the book with your partner? Did it fire your imagination? Did it turn you on – or off? Did you like the story, the characters, the setting? What did you think of the cover presentation? In short, what's your opinion? If you care to offer it, please write to:

> The Editor
> Headline Liaison
> 338 Euston Road
> London NW1 3BH

Or maybe you think you could do better if you wrote an erotic novel yourself. We are always on the look-out for new authors. If you'd like to try your hand at writing a book for possible inclusion in the Liaison list, here are our basic guidelines: We are looking for novels of approximately 80,000 words in which the erotic content should aim to please both men and women and should not describe illegal sexual activity (pedophilia, for example). The novel should contain sympathetic and interesting characters, pace, atmosphere and an intriguing plotline.

If you'd like to have a go, please submit to the Editor a sample of at least 10,000 words, clearly typed on one side of the paper only, together with a short resumé of the storyline. Should you wish your material returned to you please include a stamped addressed envelope. If we like it sufficiently, we will offer you a contract for publication.

Dangerous Desires

J. J. DUKE

In response to his command, Nadine began to undress. She was wearing her working clothes, a black skirt and a white silk blouse. As she unzipped the skirt she tried to keep her mind in neutral. She didn't do this kind of thing. As far as she could remember, she had never gone to bed with a man only hours after she'd met him . . .

There's something about painter John Sewell that Nadine Davies can't resist. Though she's bowled over by his looks and his talent, she knows he's arrogant and unfaithful. It can't be love and it's nothing like friendship. He makes her feel emotions she's never felt before.

And there's another man, too. A man like Sewell who makes her do things she'd never dreamed of – and she adores it. She's under their spell, in thrall to their dangerous desires . . .

0 7472 5093 6

Adult Fiction for Lovers from Headline LIAISON